'Gripping and blackly humorous' *Observer*

'The power of this book, though, lies in the warm personalities and dark humour of the Skelfs, and by the end readers will be just as interested in their relationships with each other as the mysteries they are trying to solve' *Scotsman*

'Wonderful characters: flawed, funny and brave' *Sunday Times*

'This enjoyable mystery is also a touching and often funny portrayal of grief' *Guardian*

'This is their third outing and the stories get better each time ... Told with a wry humour and affection, the novel underlines just how accomplished Johnstone has become' *Daily Mail*

'A tense ride with strong, believable characters' Kerry Hudson, *Big Issue*

'Exceptional ... a must for those seeking strong, authentic, intelligent female protagonists' *Publishers Weekly*

'Keeps you hungry from page to page. A crime reader can't ask anything more' *Sun*

'If you read one life-affirming book this year, make sure it's this one' Nina Pottell

'A powerful and epic multi-layered story. Doug Johnstone is a true literary master' Michael Wood

'A noir heavyweight and a master of gritty realism' Willy Vlautin

'Compelling and compassionate characters, with a dash of physics and philosophy thrown in' Ambrose Parry

'The perfect free-range writer, respectful of conventions but never bound by them' James Sallis

'Bloody brilliant' Martyn Waites

'Dynamic and poignant ... Johnstone balances the cosmos, music, death and life, and wraps it all in a compelling mystery' Marni Graff

'Pacy, harrowing and occasionally brutal ... it had me in tears'
Paddy Magrane

'A poignant reflection on grief and the potential for healing that lies within us all. A proper treat' Mary Paulson-Ellis

'A total delight ... Johnstone never fails to entertain whilst packing a serious emotional punch. Brilliant!' Gytha Lodge

'The Skelfs are the stars of this series, without a shadow of a doubt, but Doug Johnstone creates such memorable situations and supporting characters that they remain etched in your consciousness long after you close the book'
Jen Med's Book Reviews

'I love this series, and cannot praise it highly enough. My name is Raven and I am a #Skelfaholic, and very proud to be one too'
Raven Crime Reads

'This series keeps getting better and this is a very special read indeed' Hair Past a Freckle

'Another stonker of a read from Doug Johnstone. His writing captures wonderfully the crackle of a frayed temper, the atmosphere that surrounds death, the pain of grief and, of course, the city of Edinburgh. The Skelfs are a brilliant concept'
Swirl and Thread

'It's always a delight to meet up with the Skelfs once more, they are so relevant and have to deal with so many issues that are often only experienced by females, making life that little bit harder and more difficult than if they were male'
Random Things through My Letterbox

'I can't really name another thriller that has ghosts, stalkers and fake deaths all alongside the day-to-day business of a funeral director. If you haven't read any of this original and addictive series, I highly recommend it to you!' On the Shelf Reviews

'Just when you thought you couldn't love the Skelfs more, Doug Johnstone finds a way to turn up the heat' Live & Deadly

'A unique combination of mystery, thrills, drama, science ... An amazing series' From Belgium with Book Love

Other titles by Doug Johnstone, available from Orenda Books

ABOUT THE AUTHOR

Doug Johnstone is the author of eighteen novels, many of which have been bestsellers. *The Space Between Us* was chosen for BBC Two's *Between the Covers*, while *Black Hearts* was shortlisted for the Theakston Crime Novel of the Year, and *The Big Chill* was long-listed for the same prize. Three of his books – *A Dark Matter*, *Breakers* and *The Jump* – have been shortlisted for the McIlvanney Prize for Scottish Crime Novel of the Year. Doug has taught creative writing or been writer in residence at universities, schools, writing retreats, festivals, prisons and a funeral directors. He's also been an arts journalist for twenty-five years. He is a songwriter and musician with six albums and three EPs released, and he plays drums for the Fun Lovin' Crime Writers, a band of crime writers. He's also co-founder of the Scotland Writers Football Club. Follow Doug on X/Twitter @doug_johnstone and Instagram @writer-dougj, and visit his website: dougjohnstone.com.

Living is a Problem

Doug Johnstone

**ORENDA
BOOKS**

Orenda Books
16 Carson Road
West Dulwich
London SE21 8HU
www.orendabooks.co.uk

First published in the United Kingdom by Orenda Books, 2024
Copyright © Doug Johnstone, 2024

A catalogue record for this book is available from the British Library.

ISBN 978-1-916788-26-8
eISBN 978-1-916788-27-5

Typeset in Garamond by typesetter.org.uk

Printed and bound by Clays Ltd, Elcograf S.p.A

For sales and distribution, please contact info@orendabooks.co.uk or visit
www.orendabooks.co.uk.

This book is dedicated to everyone I've ever been in a band with.
Maybe we didn't realise it at the time,
but we were doing something worthwhile.

LIVING IS A PROBLEM

1

JENNY

She loved Saughton Cemetery because it was ordinary. The ancient graveyards in the centre of Edinburgh were full of famous people, ostentatious monuments, statues of long-dead blokes – and they were always blokes – who built the city or led the enlightenment or colonised the world. Those cemeteries had plenty of tourists snapping pics for their socials, but none of them would know Saughton even existed. This place was for real dead people. Jenny's kind of people.

They were burying Fraser Fulton, who died in his sleep from a suspected heart attack. He'd had a post mortem, though, because any death in Saughton Prison is suspect. The fact that you could see the high walls and razor wire of the prison from here added a little poignancy to proceedings – he was being buried within sight of the place he spent his last days, banged up for attempted murder in some gang-related thing Jenny had read about in the *Daily Record*.

She looked around. Fraser was popular, two hundred mourners, his coffin to the side of the grave on wooden planks.

Leading the funeral party were Fraser's widow, Ellen, and her grown boys, Harvey and Warren. The men were big and hard, squeezed into suits, pinched faces, shaved heads. Ellen wore a classy black suit with trainers, like she might need to make a quick getaway. Her dyed-blonde hair was elegant and her nails and lipstick a demure purple. A large spread of white chrysanthemums spelled out *DAD* on top of the bamboo coffin.

The Fultons had seemed like a traditional family, so Jenny was surprised they'd gone along with the biodegradable coffin and the

Skelfs' no-embalming rule. Her daughter Hannah had suggested that rule and they all agreed to putting no more poison in the ground.

Jenny threw Archie next to her a look. He'd been there for her when she needed it, through the mill with an abusive and murderous ex-husband. She'd lost herself for a while, but thanks to Archie and her family, she was much more together now. And she was happy doing funerals. She'd resisted the family businesses for so long, both the funeral directors and the private investigators, but she'd come to realise that this – a sense of peace and quiet at a stranger's funeral – was what she needed. Other people's grief was so much easier to handle than her own.

She took the netsuke from her pocket, Archie smiling at her. He'd made it for her a couple of years ago, a carved wooden fox in the Japanese style. She kept it on her like a talisman. Since she'd been carrying it, her life had got better. She wasn't the kind of person to believe in superstitions, but it felt good nonetheless.

The Church of Scotland minister was a large man with slicked-back hair like a Teddy Boy. Harvey Fulton stepped forward as the minister spoke and draped a Hearts scarf over the coffin. Made sense, Tynecastle was just a walk up the road.

From this corner of the graveyard, Jenny could hear the Water of Leith burbling behind them. The river wrapped round the cemetery and the nearby allotments on three sides. There were often allotments next to cemeteries, and Jenny wondered if there was something in that. Maybe the corpses in the ground had fertilisation power, good for your courgettes.

This wasn't the scenic part of the Water of Leith that fed into the sea, or the section that trickled through woodland near the Gallery of Modern Art. Here it ran between industrial estates and gyms, car dealerships and supermarkets. Across a fence were rows of sixties terraces, pebble dash and orange brick, the kind of house that was everywhere in Edinburgh outside of the centre. The city that tourists never saw. Another reason why Jenny loved it here.

She turned to Archie, took him in. Shaved head, neat beard, some grey in it now. Solid body, muscle not fat. She kept her voice low. 'Do you think he really died of a heart attack?'

'Coroner said so.'

'Seems suss, in prison and all.'

'You saw his body, he clearly liked to eat and drink.'

Jenny liked spending time with Archie, they'd developed a deep and solid friendship. They were the same age, but Jenny always used to think of him as older. Probably because he seemed more mature than she ever felt. He'd accumulated skills and knowledge over time, whereas she felt like she'd spent decades struggling to keep her head above water. She had never felt in control, until now. She liked it, and she liked him.

She became aware of a noise above the minister's eulogy and the faint traffic rumble from Longstone Road. The minster heard it too, stopped speaking. A few mourners glanced at each other.

'Look.' Archie nudged her and pointed at the sky.

She saw a drone coming in fast, high above the allotments then swooping down and arcing over the mourners before hovering above the grave. Some arsehole was buzzing a funeral, what the hell?

The drone had come from the west, where the prison was. Jenny had heard stories about drones being used to smuggle phones and drugs *into* prison, but she'd never heard of anything like this. And besides, the drone was just sitting there, twenty feet off the ground, filling the air with noise.

The mourners shook their heads, outraged.

'Ever seen this before?' Jenny said to Archie, as they both stepped forward.

'No.'

Jenny noticed a canister strapped to the drone's underbelly as it turned left and right, checking everyone out. She looked around the graveyard, but of course the pilot could be miles away, watching through the camera mounted on the front.

'Wait,' Archie said, stepping closer. 'Are those nozzles?'

As he spoke, the six jets on the feet of the drone burst into life, spraying everyone with liquid.

'What the fuck?' Jenny said.

Pepper spray. Some motherfucker was attacking their funeral with pepper spray.

The mourners panicked as the drone dropped a few feet, screams and cries as the Fulton boys ushered their mum to shelter under a willow tree.

Tears streamed down Jenny's cheeks as she tried to find something to cover her face. She blinked, stinging pain in her eyes as she ran for shelter. Mourners were running down the path, covering their mouths and noses, gasping for breath.

Jenny could only catch glimpses through her own stinging eyes. The drone turned left and right spraying in every direction, then swung down to target the Fultons. Warren waved an arm to bat it away but he was nowhere near. Ellen was crying on Harvey's shoulder, both of them eyes tight shut. The drone seemed to angle to get as much pepper spray as possible on the funeral party, the noise of its rotors like lawnmowers.

Then Jenny saw Archie bend down under a tree that spread over from the allotments, pick an apple from the ground, take aim through tear-stained eyes, and launch it. The apple sailed through the air and hit the drone, taking out two of the rotors. The noise cut out as the drone swayed like a drunk before plummeting, bouncing off Fraser Fulton's coffin, the remaining rotors tangling up in the Hearts scarf, before it fell into the open grave.

2

DOROTHY

The noise in the room made her feel alive. A dozen people making music together, causing the air to vibrate in ways that could move listeners to tears. She wished everyone could experience this sense of togetherness. Being in a band – good or bad, folk duo to orchestra – was a direct link to the earliest humans, beating drums and dancing around a campfire, finding something spiritual in the communal act of creation.

Dorothy looked around the studio loft, the rehearsal space two floors up from the undertakers and private investigators. The sun flickered through the window, dappled by the trees outside. There was sweat in the air from all the members of The Multiverse, a ramshackle bunch of musicians and singers thrown together by chance.

They were playing 'I Saw' by Young Fathers, two of the younger members of the refugee choir were big fans. Dorothy loved it, primal and powerful tom beats. She was accompanied by Gillian, the multi-instrumentalist who could play anything, now pummelling away on two floor toms, the pair of them holding the song together. Dorothy's vintage Gretsch kit wasn't built for this kind of workout, but she hammered her floor and rack toms regardless, watching for the breaks to play simple, effective fills, occasional cymbal crashes. This song would have enormous power in front of a crowd, it felt like it'd been dug from the earth.

The choir were hollering the words while Zack sat in the pocket on bass, his girlfriend Maria splashing synth swathes over the top, guitarist Will chugging along with a simple riff. His wife, Katy, was in charge of the choir, refugees and asylum seekers brought together through her church on Morningside. For many of them, this was the only contact they had with their local communities.

Dorothy shouldn't really be here just now, she should be dealing with the funeral business, but this nourished her soul. Besides, Jenny and Hannah had stepped up recently, alongside the rest of them. Archie was a stalwart, Brodie had taken on more responsibility, and Hannah's wife Indy was another rock, stepping into the undertaker role with ease.

Then there was her boyfriend, Thomas, if you could call a retired cop in his late fifties your boyfriend. Dorothy's mood darkened. He hadn't coped well after the trauma of last year, being beaten and almost killed by a rogue police officer. She shook her head and turned her attention back to the song, which built to a crescendo of vocals and drums, overlapping between the gaps until they burst into a final flourish. It was one of those songs you never wanted to end.

The kitchen downstairs from the studio was heaving with band members. They never went straight home after rehearsal, the singers especially lingering, catching up, swapping rumours about Immigration Enforcement. They were protected a little by living in Edinburgh, where the local communities supported their cases to stay. But that didn't stop UK officials trying to extract people.

Dorothy set down pots of tea and coffee on the large, scuffed table, other people clinking mugs, someone getting milk from the fridge. Katy had brought traybakes, millionaire's shortbread and tablet, Dorothy's favourite. Insanely sugary, but who cares when you're in your seventies?

The kitchen doubled as a control room for the funeral and PI businesses. The far wall was covered in two giant whiteboards, a list of deceased and funeral details on one, the other for cases they were investigating. The funeral business was booming, recent moves towards eco-friendly undertaking had boosted their numbers. A lot of people were interested in the most environmentally friendly way to dispose of themselves. Dorothy was pleased.

She turned to the massive map of Edinburgh on the adjacent wall. Her home for more than five decades, it had felt like an alien planet when she first arrived here from the golden sunshine of California in 1970. Nowadays, the Skelfs' funerals and investigations reached every nook and cranny of this intertwined city. The roads and paths were like capillaries and veins, carrying life from Wester Hailes to Leith, Silverknowes to Niddrie.

'Dorothy?'

She turned to see Faiza and Ladan, heads slightly bowed, hands together. Faiza was Syrian, Ladan from Somalia. Dorothy couldn't imagine what they'd been through to get here. Faiza had a bright smile, big eyes and wore a headscarf. Ladan had a nose stud, hoop earrings, her hair in short braids.

'What is it, ladies?'

Faiza threw a look at Ladan and got an encouraging smile in return.

'Is it true you investigate things?'

Dorothy loved this moment, the start of something.

'Is it Yana?' she said. She'd noticed their choirmate had missed a few rehearsals. People dropped in and out, but it wasn't like Yana to skip practice.

Faiza looked at Dorothy. 'No one has heard from her for many days. Ladan and I met her often for tea. She has not returned our messages. She has young children. We're worried.'

Yana was Ukrainian. Her husband had stayed and fought the Russians, but died in combat a few months ago. Dorothy could get her address from Katy. She touched Faiza's hands and smiled.

'I'll look into it.'

3

HANNAH

She stood in the courtyard and looked at the Victorian clock tower, blue sky beyond. She read the inscription over the door, *Patet Omnibus*. She'd looked it up, it meant 'open to all'. Seemed appropriate for the Edinburgh Futures Institute, although the words were from when the building was the old Royal Infirmary. These days, it had all been developed into Quartermile – luxury flats, cafés and shops, and this big chunk that the university had turned into a state-of-the-art, interdisciplinary body that was all 'challenge-led' and 'co-creative'. Hannah loved the idea of an institute for the future, but their website was written in the kind of vague language that made it impossible to understand what they actually did.

But she enjoyed attending random classes here. Her former supervisor in the astrophysics department had a friend at the EFI, and Hannah had been given the all-clear to attend whatever she wanted. Hannah was decompressing after finishing her PhD on exoplanets. She wanted to do something useful, but also wanted to keep learning new stuff. Which was why she was here. She went inside and downstairs to the lecture theatre, beautiful views over the square at the back, a mix of renovated old brick and new glass. Today's talk was on something called Integrated Information Theory by Rachel Tanaka, visiting professor from UBC in Vancouver and practising Buddhist priest.

Tanaka had short grey hair and an infectious smile, wore a large turquoise pendant on a long chain over a dark turtleneck, black jeans and chunky trainers. IIT was a dull acronym for something pretty insane, the idea that consciousness was a measurable, physical entity that emerged in different systems. The maths and philosophy were beyond Hannah's understanding, but it implied that consciousness was inherent in everything.

Tanaka began talking about panpsychism within her Buddhist faith, the idea that the universe is conscious, therefore every element of the universe is conscious. Hannah struggled to get her head around it, but maybe it was a cool way of looking at the world, if it made you act with more respect and consideration.

Tanaka moved on to talking about animism within indigenous cultures, where everything from rocks to weather systems were alive and contained an essential spirit. It had many names, from kami and prana in the east to manitou and orenda in North America. She spoke about the Hearing Voices movement, where Western mental-health experts took seriously the idea that people with so-called auditory hallucinations were experiencing something that had to be taken into account, in the same way other cultures had done for millennia. The movement fought the stigma and stereotypes, the accusations of mental illness, that plagued this subject matter in the West.

Tanaka doubled back to talk about the maths of IIT, in its infancy but already mind-bogglingly complex. That always seemed the way – Western science took supercomputers to work out a fraction of what ancient cultures knew all along, that we are part of an animated universe, that we aren't alone.

The lecture finished to warm applause from the students. For Hannah, the chance to soak this up was a blessing. She didn't have number-crunching data analysis to do, didn't have a thesis to write up. She could just listen and learn.

Tanaka packed her notes and laptop away into a Vancouver Writers Fest tote and walked to the exit. Hannah was ahead of her and decided to loiter at the door, but then felt awkward. Tanaka threw her a big smile.

'Professor Tanaka?' Hannah said.

'Rachel, please.'

'That was fascinating, thank you.' She felt like a dumb under-grad again, unsure what to say to someone so much smarter.

'I'm glad you enjoyed it.'

'Do you *really* think everything is alive?'

Rachel smiled. 'It can be a hard idea to get hold of, if you're not brought up in that culture.'

'And do you think IIT is the answer?'

'There isn't one answer, that's not how knowledge works,' Rachel said. She touched Hannah's arm and they moved to the side of the entrance as the last of the audience filed out. 'Let me ask you something. Do you believe humans are conscious?'

'Of course.'

'Dogs and cats?'

'I guess so.'

'Trees?'

Hannah made a face. 'Maybe?'

'So where do you draw the line. And why?'

Hannah thought about it. 'I don't know.'

Rachel smiled again. 'With all these ideas – IIT, panpsychism, animism – we don't have to draw a line. There is no line. The line is a fabrication of Western dualist thinking.'

'I suppose so.'

Rachel took Hannah in. 'Are you one of my students here?'

Hannah shook her head. 'I just got my PhD in astrophysics. I'm trying to work out what to do next. Your work is really interesting.'

Rachel went into her bag and took out a card, handed it over. It was classy and minimal, Rachel's name and email address, an outline of a tree, branches above the ground, roots below.

'If you want to talk more about it.' Rachel pressed her hands together to leave. 'I'm always looking for smart students.'

Hannah's phone vibrated in her pocket, which made her fumble her goodbyes. She watched Rachel leave then took her phone out.

It was Brodie, who worked for the Skelfs, arranging their communal funerals for people who had no one to mourn them.

'Hey Brodie, what's up?'

He was outdoors, wind blowing, trees rustling.

'I'm at Craigmillar Cemetery. At Jack's grave.'

Hannah swallowed. Jack was Brodie's son, who'd died as a newborn eighteen months ago. Craigmillar had a whole section for baby graves.

'Are you all right?' Hannah said, looking around the empty lecture theatre. The light seemed too bright suddenly, the air too heavy.

'Someone's been messing with his grave.'

'Messing?'

'Maybe it's best if you come and see it.'

4

JENNY

The vibe outside Diggers was one of simmering outrage. The Fultons had booked the pub for the wake and a crowd of people were standing outside now, pouring water from pint glasses into their bloodshot eyes, rinsing out the pepper spray. Inside, the place was rammed with mourners who'd escaped the worst of the attack.

Jenny looked up at the pub sign. It read *Athletic Arms, established 1897* but everyone in Edinburgh called it Diggers. It was on a sharp corner of Angle Park Terrace and sat between two old cemeteries, Dalry and North Merchiston. The story was that the pub was frequented by gravediggers back in the day, who would prop their shovels against the bar after a hard day's graft. Appropriate for a wake, then, even if both those graveyards were full these days.

The Skelfs didn't always hang around at a wake, but it felt like they should be here. Jenny and Archie were sniffing and blinking as they drank pints of eighty shilling, while the Fulton boys wound each other up.

Jenny looked at Ellen. 'I think you should go to the police.'

They'd discussed this in the aftermath of the drone attack, but the family of a man who'd died in prison didn't have a huge amount of faith in the police force. Jenny didn't blame them. She was ambivalent about cops too, since a few experiences with them as a young woman. That had been reinforced by the Skelfs' case a year ago, where two cops were discovered to be blackmailing and coercing vulnerable young women, raping them and eventually killing them. That still wasn't resolved. Don Webster and Benny

Low were out on bail awaiting trial. The one good cop Jenny knew was Dorothy's man, Thomas, but he'd retired on health grounds, the shock of last year taking its toll.

'No cops,' Harvey said. He was twenty, built like a brick shithouse and livid at this affront to his dad.

'If only so that it's on record,' Jenny said.

Harvey's brother Warren shook his head, finished his lager and grabbed another from the window ledge outside the pub. 'We don't want this on the record.'

It was clear the Fultons would deal with this themselves. Which meant a bunch of violence and more guys ending up in jail. Jenny felt duty bound to offer an alternative.

'Who do you think would've done this?'

Warren and Harvey gave each other a look which didn't include Ellen, and Jenny wondered about that. Ellen seemed like the kind of wife who knew full well what her husband was like. When she'd come to the Skelf house to arrange the funeral, she was under no illusions about why Fraser was in prison. It wasn't a miscarriage of justice, he really *had* tried to murder someone and had been taking his sentence on the chin.

'He had his faults,' Ellen said now. 'But my Fraser was a good man who always provided for his family.'

'I just thought,' Jenny said, leaning in to Ellen and lowering her voice, 'before anyone does anything they might regret, I could look into it for you.'

The funeral stuff had been great for getting Jenny on an even keel, but it had become routine. And the Skelfs were private investigators, right?

'Jenny.' This was Archie, a note of warning in his voice. But he knew she was headstrong, and nothing he said would change her mind.

'You?' Warren said with a snort. 'What could you do?'

'I'm a private investigator.' Jenny took a business card from her pocket and handed it to Ellen, the one she needed to convince.

Warren drank more lager and scoffed. 'What have you investigated recently?'

Jenny stuck her chin out. 'I discovered that my ex-husband murdered one of my daughter's friends. I found him when he escaped from prison. I killed him on a beach in Fife. When his washed-up body was stolen by his sister, I found them both hiding at an illegal camp.'

Warren swallowed and Jenny enjoyed the silence. Hearing it all made Jenny queasy, and she looked at Archie for reassurance. He touched her wrist and sipped his beer.

Ellen turned Jenny's card in her fingers, gulped from an enormous gin and tonic.

'Ellen,' Jenny said. 'I'm sure you don't want to see any more of your family behind bars. If your boys do something stupid in retaliation, you'll never forgive yourself.'

Ellen shook her head and stared at her sons.

'We can handle this,' Harvey said, puffing out his chest.

'I'm sure you can,' Jenny said, then to Ellen. 'But someone not personally invested might get better results.'

Archie cleared his throat. 'Jenny, are you sure...'

She wasn't sure, but she was following her gut. Dorothy did that all the time, and she was trying to be more like her mum. She gave Archie a kind look, and he raised his eyebrows in submission.

Ellen finished her gin and gave a big sigh. 'OK. You can start by talking to the Conways. I'll email you details.'

Warren shook his head and Harvey clenched his fists, but the look Ellen gave them made them both take big drinks and shut up.

Jenny had a case.

5

HANNAH

She jumped off the bus at Old Dalkeith Road and walked to the cemetery entrance. Craigmillar Castle Park Cemetery was the city's newest graveyard, fresh stone wall and iron gates. It was weird seeing a cemetery with only a fraction of its five thousand spaces used up. The driveway down the middle split the grass, modern waiting room on the left, Muslim burial section to the right.

Hannah passed the Catholic area, the spread of newer graves up the hill, the still-empty land on her left. She reached the small section reserved for burying babies, a collection of miniature gravestones huddled together as if they found strength in numbers.

She couldn't see Brodie to begin with, looked to the back of the cemetery where the woods spread up the slope towards the ruined castle. Over the other side of the fence were the Bridgend allotments, then the university's playing fields at Peffermill. So much green space in such a small city.

Brodie walked slowly towards her from the bottom of the cemetery. He was tall and gangly, all arms and legs. His suit fitted well but he still looked uncomfortable in it. His wavy hair was cut short, worry in his grey eyes as he reached Hannah.

'Thanks for coming,' he said. 'I didn't want to bother Dorothy with this.'

He stood awkwardly, rubbing his sleeve.

'You thought you'd bother me instead.' Hannah meant it as a joke, but Brodie's face fell. 'Mate, I'm joking.'

He tried to smile. 'Sure.'

Hannah looked around. A handful of rabbits were munching on grass in the distance.

Brodie glanced at the baby graves then looked away.

'So, want to tell me what's happened?' Hannah said.

Brodie tugged his sleeve. Dorothy had bought him the suit when he started working for the Skelfs last year. Hannah and Indy were the first to meet Brodie, at a stranger's funeral at Mortonhall Crem. Indy twigged that he was turning up to a lot of services. Funeral crashers were rare but it did happen. Brodie had lost his son in childbirth, then split up with his girlfriend Phoebe, as they both struggled to cope. Dorothy had seen that Brodie needed a purpose and employed him in the undertaking business, focusing on the new communal funerals they were conducting.

He pointed up the slope. 'I was just checking the plot was ready for the Fitzgerald funeral. Spoke to William, the grounds-keeper.'

'I thought Indy was running the Fitzgerald burial?'

'I'm helping out. Plus it gave me a chance to come and see Jack.' His eyes flitted in the other direction. 'Two birds, one stone, and all that.'

He swallowed and Hannah avoided filling the silence. Something she'd learned from Gran, to let people talk.

The wind rustled the trees by the allotments, and Hannah thought of IIT, Rachel Tanaka saying that everything was conscious. The leaves on the trees, the grass under her feet, the tomatoes and cucumbers in the allotments, the headstones around her, the rabbits disappearing over the hill.

'Come and see,' Brodie said.

He walked towards the tiny graves and Hannah followed, gazing at the teddy bears on the graves, plastic fire trucks or action figures, heart-breaking pictures of smiling babies, snap-shots of potential lives unlived. A few ultrasound scan pictures, one laminated and taped to the tombstone.

They reached the last grave on the row, the small headstone read *Jack Sweet*. Brodie's surname was Willis, Sweet was his ex-girlfriend's last name. Hannah wondered how that conversation went. The crushing weight of everyday grief.

'Look.'

The grass had been disturbed below the headstone, scratch marks in the muddy earth, dirt scattered around the disturbance. It reminded Hannah of a million horror movies. But the digging was superficial, only a few inches. Nevertheless, she couldn't imagine what it felt like for Brodie.

She looked around the cemetery.

'It must just be an animal,' she said. 'You saw the rabbits over there. Or a fox.'

Brodie shook his head. 'Why would it only dig here?' He waved along the row. 'None of the other graves are disturbed.'

'Who knows what scents are left by other animals,' Hannah said. 'I'm sure it's nothing to worry about.'

She touched Brodie's elbow, and he flinched, kept his gaze on the disturbed earth.

'It wasn't a wild animal,' Brodie said. 'I showed it to William. He's been working here since they opened the place. He knows when a fox or a badger has been digging. Look.' He crouched down and touched his finger against the edge of the small hole, pushed against the earth like he wanted to start digging himself. 'This was made by a sharp edge. William reckoned a trowel or shovel.'

Hannah crouched down too, shaking her head. She stared at the turned earth. Saw a worm wriggling in the muck and smelled the mulch in the air.

'Who would do something like that?' she said eventually.

Brodie stood and rubbed dirt between his fingers. 'Phoebe.'

'Your ex? Why?'

Brodie closed his eyes for too long, opened them again. 'I swear to God, this is her. You need to speak to her. Please.'

He didn't look at Hannah, just turned and walked away. Hannah saw his shoulders shake and knew he was crying.

6

DOROTHY

Dorothy stood with Indy in the front garden watching the two workmen take down the old sign. They placed it on its side against the hedge and Dorothy angled her head to read it: *Skelf Funeral Directors* in sharp blue lettering from the nineties. These days they felt like a completely different company with a new ethos. She wondered what Jim would've made of them now and the direction they were taking.

Indy rubbed Dorothy's arm as the workmen hoisted the new sign into place: *The Skelfs: Natural Undertakers and Private Investigators*. Clean lines, sans serif font. Less formal and stuffy.

'Looks great,' Indy said.

Indy was a big part of how the business was changing. She'd come to them with facts and figures, environmental-impact reports on traditional embalmed burial and cremation. Had a bunch of new ideas. They were no longer embalming the dead. This was initially a blow to Archie, who'd spent years perfecting his techniques, but he understood. Dorothy had put him in charge of managing their new Seafield Memorial Woods, although so far it wasn't much more than a big field with a handful of graves. But they had plans to plant thousands of trees, rewild the entire area and make it the most eco-friendly burial site in the country.

They were also offering resomation at the house, had bought a second machine to double capacity. This was water cremation, where the deceased was dissolved in an alkaline bath, leaving remains similar to cremation, with a fraction of the environmental cost. If the bereaved gave permission, the Skelfs stored the liquid run-off, which contained no DNA or remnants of the deceased, and used it as fertiliser at the Seafield site. It was all beautifully interlinked. And they had plans for human composting, mushroom-suit burial, and any other eco-friendly tech that developed over the coming years. They were making things a little bit better for a future Dorothy wouldn't see.

'Natural undertakers is a lovely phrase,' Indy said.

Dorothy looked at her. Her hair was a mix of dyed purple and pink, recently cut short in a bob and fringe, which she pulled off because she was so beautiful. Big eyes and cheekbones, winning smile.

Dorothy had decided she much preferred 'undertaker' to 'funeral director'. It implied that what they did was an undertaking, a vocation, that they were at the service of the bereaved. 'Funeral director' suggested that the Skelfs were in charge when, really, those grieving should always be the ones in control.

The workmen had fixed the sign to the posts and were packing away their stepladders. Dorothy thanked them both, then they were gone.

Schrödinger stepped from behind the hedge and sniffed where the workmen had been. The adopted street cat walked as if the garden was his dominion. Dorothy admired his confidence.

He walked to Indy, tail up and purring, and wrapped himself around her legs until she picked him up.

She showed him the sign. 'Look, we're undertakers now.'

The cat sensed something in the bushes and squirmed free.

Dorothy looked at the white phone box in the corner of the garden, the wind phone they'd been gifted by an elderly Japanese client. It held an unconnected old rotary phone, and the Skelfs let grieving friends and family use it to speak to their dead loved ones. It created permission, a private space to commune with the dead. Dorothy loved it.

Indy had said that wind phones were springing up all over the world, part of a death-positive movement the Skelfs were part of.

Talking about death in an open and positive way was the best way to deal with grief. Their Communal Funeral project was a part of that too. Dorothy had struck a deal with the council for the Skelfs to conduct the funerals of those who didn't have anyone to mourn them. Old people who died alone, unknown bodies washed up on one of the city's beaches, suicide victims with no note, homeless folk who didn't make it through the night, refugees or asylum seekers living off the radar. Dorothy felt privileged to hold these funerals, to let them know even beyond the grave that their time on Earth meant something.

The crunch of footsteps made Dorothy and Indy turn.

Thomas walked up the path with the aid of a stick, wearing a small backpack. Dorothy's stomach lurched. He smiled when he saw her but his eyes were dull.

Indy hugged him then went to get on with work inside.

Dorothy looked at him, a lot of white in his short hair and beard now, bags under his eyes, a scar on his cheek and a droopy eye from his injures last year. There was much more damage that was less visible. Stab wounds had meant several rounds of surgery on various organs, the stick was needed because one of his knees hadn't recovered. Then there were the mental scars.

The violence they'd both been subjected to had somehow created distance between them. Thomas blamed himself because the perpetrators were two police officers from his station.

'It looks great,' Thomas said, nodding at the sign. A hint of his Swedish accent underneath the Scottish. 'Very *you*.'

'I hope so.' She looked at him leaning on his stick. 'Come inside.'

'Can't,' he said, tapping the backpack. 'I'm on my way to the charity shop.'

This had become his thing, obsessively clearing out his flat. He'd started with big stuff like furniture and paintings. Now he was on to smaller items. It was so obviously a form of PTSD. Dorothy had suggested therapy, but he'd shut down that conversation immediately. She didn't know how else to help, except just to be there for him.

'Please,' she said, rubbing his arm. 'Come in for a minute.'

He smiled at her but looked at his watch. 'It closes soon.'

'I'll come with you.'

'I can go on my own.'

'I know you can, I—'

'Dorothy.' He looked at her. 'It's OK.'

'Thomas, I feel like...' She didn't even know how to finish that sentence.

'I know. I *know*.'

She looked around the garden, at the sign in front of the house. Thought about how she was stepping into the future, how he was stuck.

She sighed and tried to feel the blood moving in her veins.

'OK,' she said. 'Pop in on the way back.'

'I'll try.'

She kissed him on the lips, placed her fingers on his cheek, careful not to brush the scar.

She watched him walk away and felt sick.

7

JENNY

Jenny's main strength as a private investigator was that she didn't give a fuck. That was really her superpower in life too, it made her kind of impregnable. But as she stood outside the Conway house on Barnton Avenue, she had a niggling worry that she might've gone soft over the last year. She'd had no one trying to strangle or shoot her, no one setting her on fire or abusing her. Nothing to fight against.

She needed this, a case to solve involving two-bit rival gangs in western Edinburgh. Barnton Avenue contained some whopping millionaires' pads, but the Conway place was more modest. However, the signs of affluence were still there, three flashy sports cars in the driveway, a glimpse of a hot tub round the side that looked over the wooded garden. This was moving up in the world for a gangster family, and Jenny wondered what the doctors and lawyers living in the street thought.

She walked up the path and heard dogs barking, then saw three Dobermans slobbering at the side gate. Dobermans had been superseded by nastier breeds as the gangland pooch of choice, giving these dogs a retro charm.

Jenny rang the doorbell and waited. Stepped back and looked at the windows. Turned and looked back down the drive. There was a lot of tree cover in this street, mature gardens. Lots of shelter if you wanted to get up to stuff.

The door opened and a skinny young guy in a dark-blue Adidas tracksuit and trainers frowned at her.

'Yeah?'

Jenny was taken aback. Jez Conway was more handsome than

the mugshots she'd seen in the newspapers. He was also young enough to be her son.

'I'm looking for Marina Conway?'

'And who are you?'

The dogs were still barking round the side of the house. Jez stepped forward and shouted at them, and they disappeared.

Jenny flipped a business card out and waved it at him. 'I'm Jenny Skelf, private investigator.'

He sucked his teeth, didn't take the card. 'You don't look like a PI.'

'And you don't look like a "property entrepreneur", Jez.'

He smiled. 'You've done your homework.'

She shrugged.

He took the card, looked her up and down. She was in her late forties now, usually invisible to guys like Jez, but he saw her and she felt a shiver of power in that. She really loved not giving a fuck.

'What's this about?' Jez said, still holding her card.

'I was given this address by Ellen Fulton.'

That made him pay attention. 'What the fuck did that old cow want?'

'She wants to stop a bloodbath.'

'Then she needs to tell her stupid laddies to calm the fuck down.'

Jenny angled her head. 'Maybe you shouldn't have attacked Fraser Fulton's funeral.'

'What?'

Jenny liked to think she could judge when someone was lying, though maybe that was delusional. But Jez's reaction seemed genuine. Maybe this wasn't a dumb tit-for-tat.

'Can I talk to your mum?'

Jez stuck out his lower lip. His manner was exaggerated, like he was always putting on a show. A young man in a position of power, maybe that was his life.

'Come in.'

He walked her through to the back of the house, slid the patio doors open onto a quality wooden deck looking over the garden, woodpigeons in the pines at the bottom. He walked round to an extension on the left, another raised deck, Marina Conway in the hot tub Jenny had spotted before.

Her dyed hair was up in a ponytail, sweat on her upper lip as she sipped bubbly from a flute. Her maroon nails matched her hair, both the colour of Hearts FC.

She frowned as they approached, checked out Jenny. 'This better be good.'

'Private investigator,' Jez said, nodding at Jenny. 'Sent by the Fultons.'

'I wasn't sent by them,' Jenny said. 'Not exactly.'

Marina sighed. 'I'm not getting out.'

'I wouldn't expect you to,' Jenny said.

'Want to join me?'

Jenny laughed, glanced at Jez to see if his mum was joking. Clearly she wasn't. 'I don't have anything to wear.'

Marina shrugged. 'Neither do I.'

Jenny raised her eyebrows and couldn't help glancing at the bubbly surface, trying to see underneath.

Jez rolled his eyes. 'I'll leave you to it.'

He placed Jenny's card on the side of the hot tub and kissed his mum on the cheek, then went back inside.

'What the fuck is this about?' Marina said.

She glanced towards the bottom of the garden. Jenny did the same and saw a fox there in broad daylight. It stared at them then disappeared into the trees.

'The attack on Fraser Fulton's funeral.'

'What attack?'

'A drone buzzed the funeral and sprayed the mourners with pepper spray.'

Marina choked on her bubbly and laughed. 'Really? Wish I'd seen that.'

'You're saying the Conways had nothing to do with it.'

'I swear. When that old prick died, that was the end of it for us.'

'Even though your families have rival drug-dealing operations in the west of Edinburgh.'

Marina took her in for a long moment. 'You have some fucking nerve.'

'Just what I heard.'

'Don't believe everything you read in the *Daily Record*.'

Jenny liked Marina's no-bullshit attitude, but she also wanted to dunk the cow's head underwater until she was a little less smug.

'And even though the Conways are known to use drones in the delivery of drugs and phones into Saughton Prison.'

'"Known to use". If that was true, I wouldn't be sitting in my hot tub drinking Bollinger, would I?'

Jenny saw the fox saunter back onto the lawn, sniffing after something.

'Look, I'm just trying to help.'

'Us or the Fultons?' Marina said.

'Both.'

'Not possible.'

'The Fulton lads want to escalate this,' Jenny said. 'I'm the peaceful alternative.'

Marina shook her head. 'Let them escalate, bring it on. With Fraser gone, they're a headless fucking corpse.'

'Which is why you rubbed salt in the wound with that bullshit at the funeral.'

Marina leaned forward and Jenny saw her cleavage, a bit of nipple. She looked surprisingly firm for her age, maybe she'd had work done.

'Now listen,' Marina said. 'I have no time for those cunts, but we still have rules. Me and Callum, Ellen and Fraser, we're from the old school, where there's still some respect. I swear to you, I had fuck all to do with that.'

'It's funny how people have all the respect in the world for their enemies once they're dead, but none when they were alive.'

Marina leaned back and finished her champagne.

Jenny watched the fox meander across the grass, then disappear again when it heard the Dobermans bark.

'Was Callum there when Fraser died?'

Marina stared at Jenny but didn't answer.

'In Saughton,' Jenny said. 'Did Callum see it?'

Marina breathed heavily through her nose and Jenny knew she'd got to her. 'My Callum had nothing to do with that. He's many things, but he's not a murderer. The post mortem said heart attack, end of story.'

Jenny nodded. 'Maybe I should speak to Callum.'

Marina shifted her weight, placed her glass on the edge of the hot tub, then stood, bubbles and water streaming down her naked body. She had a great figure and Jenny was glad she hadn't stripped off alongside her earlier.

'Feel free to visit him in Saughton. I'm sure he'll be as helpful as I've been.' She bent for a robe and Jenny stared at her arse crack.

'Now fuck off,' Marina said, stepping out of the hot tub and wrapping the robe around her.

8

HANNAH

She parked the body van and got out. This was the new part of Gilmerton, not far from the bypass, old fields turned into identi-kit yellow-and-white homes. She walked down Innes Crescent, more houses being built over the hill, Taylor Wimpey signs every-where featuring a smiling family playing with their dog. This kind of housing estate didn't have the character of Edinburgh's centre, but it was the reality for the vast majority of the city's natives, a barely affordable family home on the outskirts, a decent neigh-bourhood where the kids could play outside, a bus ride into town.

She found the Sweets' house, rang the doorbell, and it was answered quickly by a middle-aged woman in neat cardigan and trousers, short black hair. Phoebe's mum Amanda, presumably.

'Hi, I'm looking for Phoebe?'

Amanda looked her up and down. 'And you are?'

'My name is Hannah Skelf, I—'

'The Skelfs, I know who you are.'

'Mum, it's OK.' Phoebe reached over Amanda's shoulder to open the door wider. 'Come in.'

Amanda disappeared to the kitchen with a scowl.

Phoebe led Hannah to the living room, everything neat and tidy, demure greys and pastels, like a show home. She was pretty, blonde hair in a pony, upturned nose, gap between her front teeth. But her shoulders were hunched and she looked tired. She waved for Hannah to sit, did likewise, her hands in her lap.

'How does your mum know about the Skelfs?' Hannah said.

Phoebe angled her head. 'You're quite famous.'

Hannah's face flushed. Their past cases and personal lives had made the front pages more than once. She hated that, it was anathema for an undertaker. The whole point was to be anonymous, do your work and not get noticed.

'And I know Brodie is working for you now.'

'You're in touch with him?'

Phoebe shook her head. 'Not for months. But I was worried about him after we ... I wanted to make sure he was OK. He said your grandmother took him in, gave him a job. I wasn't sure at first, a job at a funeral parlour, not after what we went through. But he said it was good for him.'

Hannah looked at the mantelpiece. A picture of Phoebe in a graduation gown holding a scroll. Another of her and her parents on a beach somewhere, Phoebe yet to grow into her looks. Hannah didn't know what she expected – a picture of their dead grandson up there? A memorial to a life that never was? Everything about what they'd gone through was unbearable.

'Yeah, he's doing well.'

Hannah looked at the fresh flowers on a table, the delicate standing lamp. She tried to imagine what this place would've been like if Jack had lived, if Amanda and Raymond Sweet had a first grandchild to dote over. The house strewn with plastic toys and cuddly animals, picture books. A changing mat in the corner, nappies and wipes and Sudocrem, high chair through in the kitchen.

'I haven't been able to work,' Phoebe said. 'Since. I know some folk think I'm stupid. It's been eighteen months.'

She swallowed hard, eyes glassy, hands tight in her lap, thumbs pressed together.

'Phoebe,' Hannah said softly. 'If there's one thing I've learned in a family of undertakers, it's that there's no right or wrong way to grieve. No time limit. You feel how you feel and that's OK.'

Phoebe shook her head. 'But I don't want to feel like this. I want to be normal.'

'There's no normal,' Hannah said. 'My mum had to kill my dad in self-defence. My gran found a severed foot in the park. The most important thing is that we have each other.'

Phoebe looked at the doorway to the kitchen.

'Do you have support here?' Hannah said.

Phoebe nodded, pressed her lips into a line.

'Because, if you ever need to talk.'

Hannah was serious and Phoebe seemed to pick up on that, nodded.

Hannah cleared her throat. 'Can I ask something?'

'Sure.'

'Why did you and Brodie break up?'

Phoebe looked out of the window, her eyes wet. 'It was just too much. Seeing it in his eyes every day. He was part of the life I wanted to escape. He felt the same way, I think.'

'He said your family were very supportive.'

Phoebe sniffed and blinked a few times. 'That's true. My folks have been great.'

Hannah didn't know how to say this. 'But he told me that he had no one to speak to.'

'I don't remember it like that.' Phoebe's face hardened. 'Why are you here?'

Hannah took her phone out. 'Brodie was at Jack's grave this morning.'

She held out a picture of the disturbed earth by Jack's headstone. Phoebe took her phone and stared at it for a long time.

'This was taken today?'

Hannah nodded.

Phoebe kept her eyes on the screen. 'Why would an animal do that? Is Jack not buried deep enough, is that what you're telling me?' Her voice trembled.

She dropped the phone then fumbled to hand it back.

'I don't think so,' Hannah said.

Phoebe swallowed. 'Good, because I thought for a moment we were going to have to...'

Hannah watched her, she seemed genuinely upset.

'The groundskeeper thinks a tool was used,' Hannah said, then waited a long moment in silence.

Phoebe's eyes went wide and her hand went to her throat. 'You mean...' She stood up. 'You think *I* did this? Brodie thought I tried to dig up my own son?'

Hannah stood as well, put her hands out. 'I'm just trying to find out what happened.'

Phoebe's body shook like an electric current was passing through it.

'Maybe Brodie did it,' Phoebe said. 'He discovered it, right, not this groundskeeper?'

Her parents appeared at the doorway. Her dad, Raymond, was a big man with a barrel chest and beard, but a kind face.

'What's going on?' he said, soft and calm.

Hannah spoke to Phoebe. 'Why would Brodie have done anything like this?'

'Done what?' Amanda said, wringing a tea towel in her hands. 'Phoebs, what's happened?'

'Someone's been messing with Jack's grave,' she said, voice trembling.

Raymond stepped into the room. 'What?'

Phoebe stared at Hannah. 'You know that Brodie still keeps in touch with Jack, right?'

Hannah knew he'd set up an email address for the boy, sometimes sent messages. It wasn't so different from the wind phone.

'The emails, yes.'

Phoebe shook her head. 'Not just that. He hears voices.'

Hannah thought about the lecture earlier on IIF, panpsychism, hearing voices. 'A lot of people hear the voice of a loved one after they're gone.'

Phoebe flexed her fingers. 'Not like this. It's not just Jack's voice, there are lots of them. Telling him to do things. Bad things. I couldn't handle it.'

Hannah felt Raymond's hand gently on her elbow.

'I think you should leave, miss.'

9
DOROTHY

Camilla Curzon sat at the table in the overheated kitchen smiling at Dorothy. Camilla was amongst the first wave of people to take in a Ukrainian family at the outbreak of the war, and she'd been supporting the Kovalenkos since. She'd put up Yana, her two kids and mother-in-law Veronika in the granny flat of her Merchiston Place house. Dorothy looked around, it was actually a converted and extended double garage, must've cost a few hundred grand and was already worth twice that. And that wasn't even considering the main house alongside.

Veronika also sat at the table, a cup of herbal tea in front of her.

'I'm so glad you've come,' Camilla said, glancing at Veronika. 'We've been worried sick.'

Camilla wore a green velvet jumpsuit and multi-coloured scarf, big feathery earrings, Bohemian air about her.

Dorothy sipped her own tea, too fruity. 'So how long has Yana been missing?'

Camilla looked at Veronika, but the woman didn't speak. She was in her early sixties, wearing pink sweatpants and matching sweatshirt.

Dorothy wondered about the Kovalenkos' experience of war, if they had to flee with no possessions, what their journey to Scotland was like. Veronika's son had died in the war not long after they arrived here. What must that be like, your son dying thousands of miles away and not even being there to grieve?

'Two days,' Veronika said eventually. 'We haven't seen.'

Camilla touched Veronika's arm, which made the woman

flinch. 'Her English isn't great, why should it be? Better than our Ukrainian, right?'

Dorothy smiled. Camilla meant well, but she seemed a little too much for Veronika.

'And you spoke to the police?'

'They were useless,' Camilla said. 'Because she's not a UK citizen, they didn't give a shit. Excuse my language.'

People went missing all the time and the police didn't have the resources to find most of them. But a young woman with two kids would usually raise a flag.

'Police not care,' Veronika said. She raised her tea, sniffed it, put it back down again.

Dorothy wondered what her relationship with Yana was like. The cliché of the interfering mother-in-law, or loving and supportive?

'And you've tried tracking her phone.'

Camilla nodded. 'Nothing.'

Dorothy would speak to the police, find out if they'd checked phone and bank cards. She would've taken it to Thomas in the past, now she wasn't so sure.

'How was she before she vanished? Happy?'

'My Fedir is dead,' Veronika said. 'Her husband. Of course she was not happy.'

Dorothy placed her palms together. 'I'm sorry, I just meant did she seem any different?'

Camilla shook her head. 'I don't think so. Veronika?'

The woman shrugged.

Camilla sipped more tea. 'There's always the worry about immigration. These poor people have been through so much and they have the Home Office hanging over them. Like, they could be deported anytime.'

Veronika sucked her teeth. 'Why would Yana leave children?'

Something Dorothy had been thinking herself. Leaving two young kids behind in a foreign city.

The sound of the front door opening made everyone sit up.

'Roman and Olena,' Camilla said. 'We're trying not to let them see we're worried.'

A boy about twelve years old came in, looking at his phone, his younger sister lagging behind, both of them in bright-blue Bruntsfield Primary School sweatshirts, black trousers. They automatically kissed Veronika, who hugged them.

'School OK?' she said.

'Fine,' Roman said, not looking up from his phone.

Olena pulled her sweatshirt away from her chest to show her gran. 'I got a gold star for tidying up.'

'Good girl.'

They had strong accents but their English was clear. How easily the young adapt. They grabbed packets of crisps from the cupboard and disappeared, all three women watching them go.

Dorothy heard footsteps up the stairs and thought of something. 'I just need to use your bathroom.'

Camilla stood. 'Upstairs, first on the left.'

Dorothy went up and looked around the bedrooms. The first room had two single beds in it, for Yana and Veronika, judging by the clothes scattered around. She went to the next room, bunkbeds, both kids lying on their beds eating crisps.

'Hi,' Dorothy said.

Olena looked up and smiled, Roman did the same eventually.

'Who are you?' Olena said.

'My name is Dorothy.' She stepped into the room. 'I'm here about your mum.'

Olena frowned. 'She's away.'

Dorothy watched Roman, playing on his phone.

'Do you know where?'

Olena kicked the underside of Roman's bunk and he leaned over and scowled at her, then turned to Dorothy.

'They think we don't understand,' he said. 'But she ran away. She left us.'

'Why would she do that?' Dorothy said.

Olena was waving a socked foot up at her brother. He swiped it away with a fist.

'Maybe she got fed up,' Roman said, frowning down at Olena.

'Of what?'

Olena shrugged. 'Life.'

They shared a look. There was something here Dorothy wasn't getting. She pulled a business card from her pocket and held it out to Olena.

'Here,' she said. 'If you want to talk. About anything.'

Olena looked at her brother for approval, but he was back on his phone. Dorothy offered it again. Olena took it and threw it on her bed.

Dorothy smiled. She was going to get a call, she knew it.

᠄᠄

It was getting dark as she walked into her driveway. She was halfway to the house when she jumped at a creak behind her. She turned to see Thomas leaving the wind phone, the hinges of the door groaning.

'Christ, Thomas, you scared me.'

He stood for a moment then walked over to her, kissed her on the cheek. She held on for a hug but he pulled away. She wondered who he'd been talking to in the wind phone. His wife Morag most likely, we all have different ghosts.

'How are you doing?' She'd got fed up asking him if he was OK, the weight of that phrase. She'd Googled a less invasive question to ask, but this didn't seem much better.

Thomas ran a hand over his hair. 'Benny Low is dead.'

'What?'

One of the two police officers awaiting trial for various crimes. Low hadn't been guilty of Thomas's assault, that was all down to Webster, but he'd been involved with Webster in the abuse of young women. Webster was the ringleader, for sure, but Low was a willing accomplice.

'I just heard.'

Dorothy glanced behind him at the wind phone, had the crazy notion that Thomas got the message from beyond the grave.

Thomas's eyes seemed to shine in the dark as he spoke. 'Griffiths called from the station. Apparent suicide. They found him in his garage, car engine running.'

'Jesus.'

Thomas shook his head. 'Don't feel sorry for him, Dorothy.'

Dorothy stared at him in the gloom. 'I don't, but he was a human being.'

'He was a rapist and a murderer. Maybe he couldn't handle what he'd done.'

'Are they sure it was suicide?'

Thomas shifted his feet. 'They'll do a post mortem, they have to. But I'm sure it was suicide.'

'Why are you so sure?'

Thomas stuck his lip out. 'Because he was always spineless. Always did what Webster told him to. All this time at home, thinking about what he did. I'm sure he couldn't stand it.'

'Thomas.'

Thomas straightened his shoulders. 'What? Don't speak ill of the dead, is that what you're telling me?'

Dorothy reached out but he stepped back.

'I just think...'

She didn't know how to finish that sentence. He had every right to be angry. Webster almost killed him. Almost killed Dorothy. The corrupt cops had done so much damage. Dorothy *should* hate them. She still had nightmares about Webster pointing a gun at her. Pictured herself shooting him in the stomach in self-defence.

But Benny Low was someone's son, someone's brother, someone's husband, no matter what he did.

'You have to pick a side, Dorothy,' Thomas said.

She was shocked at his tone. 'It's not about sides.'

'It is, and you have to pick.'

'Then I'm on your side, of course. Thomas, come inside, let's talk about this.'

She knew his answer before he spoke.

'No, I have to go.'

10

JENNY

Jenny watched Hannah and Indy prepping dinner like an old couple, so comfortable in each other's company. Hannah held out her pinkie covered in sauce for Indy to taste. Indy smiled and nodded, and Hannah placed the chilli-sauce dish on the table alongside all the other stuff for the fish tacos – crispy haddock, tortillas, salad and slaw, a ton of sides.

Schrödinger mooched around the table eyeing up the plate of fish, tail raised.

'No,' Hannah said, carrying him to the beaten-up armchair at the window.

Dorothy came in and Jenny looked behind her.

'Thomas not joining us?'

'No.' Dorothy went to the table and poured a glass of Ramato. 'Everything OK?'

Dorothy took a big slug. 'I'm worried about him.'

'Have things got worse?'

Hannah and Indy were paying attention while they set the table.

Dorothy shook her head. 'He's so cold.'

Hannah placed a last plate of something spicy on the table and sat. 'He went through a lot, Gran.'

'We all did.'

Jenny smiled. 'Maybe we're more used to it. We've seen a lot of weird shit.'

'He was a cop, Jen,' Dorothy said.

Indy sat too, poured water and wine. 'I'm sure he'll come round.'

They ate, Jenny taking a moment to appreciate what she had. She'd been so low in the last few years. Thanks to Dorothy and Hannah she now had purpose. She would never take it for granted, sitting together like this.

The eating slowed eventually. Hannah tapped the table and Schrödinger leapt over, was given some leftover fish.

'You'll never guess what happened at the funeral this morning,' Jenny said.

She'd been sitting on this all day, had told Archie not to mention it, didn't want the others to worry. She laid it out now, played down the pepper spray, accentuated the weirdness. She talked about the Fultons and Conways, where the case had already taken her. She felt alive, a thrum in her belly. She got disapproving looks from Hannah and Dorothy.

'Mum, what the hell, you're messing with gangsters.'

Indy nodded. 'Taking that case was risky.'

Jenny put her hands out. 'It's fine. If anything, I'm the peacemaker.'

Dorothy straightened her shoulders and drank more wine. 'And what if the Conways are responsible, what will the Fultons do?'

'Take it to the police?'

Hannah scoffed. 'You know they won't.'

Jenny walked to the whiteboard on the wall behind her. 'Surely it's better if they know for sure who it was, rather than going postal on a hunch.'

She wrote *Fraser Fulton* on the board, then all the other people underneath – *Ellen, Harvey and Warren, Marina and Jez Conway, Callum Conway.* She was excited looking at it, she relished the challenge.

Indy pointed at the board. 'So what's your next move?'

Jenny underlined Callum's name. 'Give this guy a visit.'

'In Saughton?' Hannah said. 'Mum, be careful.'

'I always am.'

Hannah didn't share her smile.

'Speaking of new cases,' Dorothy said, pushing her chair back. She was a little tipsy, not something Jenny was used to. She took the marker pen from Jenny, wrote *Yana Kovalenko*, then a few more names underneath.

'From the band?' Indy said.

Dorothy blinked a few times. 'She's missing. I went to her place, they haven't seen her for days.'

Hannah picked up Schrödinger, who let himself be petted while he nibbled haddock. 'She's got kids, right?'

'At Bruntsfield Primary, currently being looked after by Yana's mother-in-law and Camilla, their kind-of landlady.'

Indy started clearing plates away. 'You think something's happened to her.'

It wasn't a question. Refugees and asylum seekers, especially attractive young women, were very vulnerable.

'That's what I'm hoping to find out,' Dorothy said.

Indy placed the dirty plates on the kitchen worktop, got a large tub of Mackie's honeycomb ice cream out the freezer to thaw, bowls and spoons from the cupboard. She gave Hannah a look.

'Are you going to tell them?' she said.

'What?' Jenny said.

Dorothy took another swig of her wine. Jenny felt an ache in her chest. The business with Thomas was taking its toll on her mum.

Hannah glowered at Indy, who was spooning out ice cream. 'I have to now, don't I?'

Jenny glanced out of the window, streetlights shimmering in Bruntsfield Links, the castle lit up like a cartoon. She remembered being in this room a few years ago, alone with her ex-husband Craig, when she discovered what kind of man he really was. She touched the scar tissue on her stomach now, felt the rubbery flesh through her T-shirt, remembered the knife sliding inside her so easily, thought about how little stands between us and the grave.

'It's Brodie,' Hannah said. 'Someone's disturbed Jack's grave.'

Dorothy put her wine glass down with a thunk. 'His Jack, at Craigmillar?'

Hannah nodded. 'Not a wild animal, according to the groundskeeper. A tool was used.'

Jenny shook her head. 'What the hell?'

Indy nodded. 'Exactly.'

Hannah ran a hand through her hair. 'I went to see his ex, Phoebe.'

Jenny watched Schrödinger sniffing around under the table. 'And?'

'She seemed legit. Sad but sweet. She mentioned something about Brodie hearing voices.'

'Talking to Jack,' Dorothy said. 'We know about that.'

'Bad voices.'

Jenny cleared her throat. 'Oh.'

Dorothy sipped more wine. 'Do you want me to talk to him?'

Hannah shook her head. 'It's OK, Gran. I'll do it.'

'I feel like he's my responsibility.'

Indy placed her hand over Hannah's on the table. 'It might be better coming from us.'

Jenny frowned. 'Do you know what you're doing?'

'As much as anyone,' Hannah said, taking a spoonful of her ice cream.

Jenny had no authority to tell anyone how to conduct themselves. She looked around the table at her whole world, and hoped they didn't get themselves in the kind of shit they couldn't get out of.

11

DOROTHY

She straightened up, felt an ache in her back and breathed deeply. She smelled the salt of the sea. They were upwind of the sewage-treatment facility, but it didn't smell much in autumn anyway, was only a problem on sticky summer days. This wasn't the ideal place for a cemetery, but beggars can't be choosers. Dorothy had purchased the derelict site from the council a year ago, and the Skelfs were turning it into Seafield Memorial Woods.

She imagined herself a rock in a stream, fifty primary-school children flowing around her, full of chatter, laughing and shouting and running. They were from Towerbank and Duddingston, all in high-vis vests, brought here by Green Cities, an environmental charity that rewilded derelict spaces. Dorothy had given some money for saplings, and the charity organised the kids.

They were planting two thousand this morning, a variety of native species. The charity workers and the kids' teachers were trying to marshal the children into a production line, some digging holes, others planting the saplings along with a support cane, someone else filling in the hole. Needless to say it was utter chaos, and Dorothy loved it.

She took a drink of water and looked around. It was already much improved from a year ago, when it was just rough dirt full of rocks and bricks, fly-tipped crap in piles. Now the earth had been turned over, rocks removed, wild grasses had been seeded and grown, weeds sweeping in on the wind and welcome too. A weed is just a plant in the wrong place at the wrong time, after all.

And trees. They already had a few thousand planted further

from the road, near the rusty, old railway lines. Along with these ones being planted now, the place would be a forest in a hundred years. Ash, beech, silver birch, rowan, hazel and oak, pine and fir and spruce. Dorothy wouldn't see it, but she felt warm to know it would be here.

Archie joined her for a rest and a drink of water. They both leaned on their shovels and Dorothy imagined they were a pair of old gravediggers. She watched the kids shove their saplings into the holes, or use them as swords, or wave them like magic wands. They would remember this, and that was important.

'This makes me think of the Future Library project,' Archie said.

'What?'

'A Scottish artist, Katie Paterson, came up with it. They're commissioning new books by writers, every year for a hundred years. The books won't be read by anyone until 2114. Margaret Atwood did one. At the same time, they planted a thousand trees in Norway, and paper from the trees will be used to print limited editions of each book.'

'Wow.' Dorothy felt something shiver through her. 'It's an act of hope, planning for the future.'

'Exactly.'

Dorothy looked to the far corner of the land, where a digger sat and a couple of workmen were busy with wooden planks and metal sheets. That was to be their terramation facility when they got the legal go-ahead. Some people might baulk at human composting but it was an established practice in the US, and Dorothy wanted the Skelfs to be the first to offer it in the UK.

'Everything OK over there?' Dorothy said.

Archie nodded. 'I had a word this morning, they know what they're doing.'

Human composting was simple. Lay the body in a container with woodchip, grass and straw and, in the right conditions, the microbes did their work. A few weeks in the box, then a few weeks to cure the soil, and you had decent compost. Either the bereaved took it away or the Skelfs would use it here.

Dorothy's attention was drawn to a white car crawling along Marine Esplanade. Sunlight glinted off the windscreen, but it seemed like the driver was watching them.

'Who would've thought?' Archie waved a hand around. 'All this. When I met you, what, fourteen years ago? I was just a lost wee boy. Now look at us.'

'You were ill, Archie.'

'You saved me.'

She looked away, uncomfortable.

'It's true, Dorothy. I wouldn't be here if it wasn't for you.'

Dorothy shook her head. 'You would've found a way through.'

'No, I wouldn't.'

She'd spotted him coming to the funerals of strangers, just like Brodie a year ago. But Archie's reason was very different, he had something they finally got diagnosed as Cotard's Syndrome, which made him believe he was dead. She'd helped with doctors, medication, given him a job. They'd been on this journey together.

She glanced at the western edge of the site, where their first graves were nestled in the long grass. The first of thousands.

Nearby, two little girls were acting out a funeral, one lying on the ground with a sapling growing from her chest, the other pretending to cry. Dorothy and Archie had taken the kids to see the graves when they arrived, the teachers had agreed it beforehand. The Skelfs were making death more visible, more normal, a part of life.

She turned to Archie. 'I heard about the Fulton funeral.'

Archie shook his head. 'Nuts.'

'And Jenny chasing the case, reckless as usual.'

Archie narrowed his eyes. 'I don't think she's like that anymore, Dorothy.'

'Come on.'

Archie gave her a kind look. 'She's not the same person she was.'

'And yet she's hassling gangsters.'

'It wasn't like that,' Archie said. 'She wants to help. Wants to *stop* any violence, not walk into it. She's like you, Dorothy.'

Dorothy let out a laugh, then regretted it. His words had surprised her.

'I'm sorry,' she said. 'I don't think anyone's ever compared Jenny to me before.'

Archie had warmth in his voice. 'You're a lot more alike than you think.'

Dorothy cleared her throat. 'Have you got anywhere with the drone?'

Archie had kept the thing. All drones had to be registered and pilots needed a licence, so it should be traceable.

'It's not a commercially available one...' He paused. 'It might be nice to ask Thomas for some help.'

Dorothy tensed up then felt a wave of sadness. 'He's retired, Archie, you know that.'

'He must have contacts.'

'I don't think he's in the right place for that sort of thing.'

'Anything you want to talk about?'

Dorothy pressed her lips together, her chest tight. 'I don't think so.'

He put a hand on her shoulder. 'Dorothy, you know I'm here if you need to talk.'

Dorothy nodded, touched his hand with her own.

She looked at the charity workers and teachers, struggling to keep the kids in order.

'We should get back to it,' she said. 'This forest isn't going to plant itself.'

She lifted her shovel over her shoulder, and went to dig a hole for the future. But her attention was distracted again by the same white car coming back the other way along the road, slowing to a stop. The driver's window opened. It was a long way away, but she was pretty sure. It was Don Webster, smiling at her.

12

HANNAH

She went inside and grinned at Indy sitting at the reception desk. 'Babes.'

Indy had come over earlier to open up, Hannah staying in bed for a while. She was enjoying not having to study, no demands on her time. But she was already bored.

The Skelf house was a three-storey gothic Victorian pile, the ground floor where all the business happened, upstairs where Gran and Mum lived. A fire two years ago only damaged the ground floor, which now had a new look. Lighter wood, airier feel, but still the gravitas of a home carrying a century of ghosts.

Next to reception was the chapel, recently extended to house the S900 resomator for water cremation. The other resomator was through in the business end of the building, in case the bereaved didn't want to see their loved one heading into an outsized washing machine. Also on the ground floor were the preparation room and office, two viewing rooms, a discreet privacy room for distressed mourners, and the boardroom, where they met clients to arrange funerals.

They no longer had freshly cut bouquets on reception, but potted orchids flanked Indy instead.

Hannah blew her a kiss, which Indy pretended to catch. It was their sarcastic joke about a cheesy, happy marriage, but it really *was* just a cheesy, happy marriage.

'Where is he?' Hannah said, doing a joke sexy strut to the desk and running her finger along the surface.

Indy nodded to the door on Hannah's right. 'Prep room.'

Hannah sashayed away, glanced back to see Indy watching her, then pushed the door to the guts of the business.

The prep room had a grid of body fridges built into one wall, each metal door with a small whiteboard carrying the deceased's name and vital info. The other side of the room used to be for embalming, but they'd sold the equipment and disposed of the chemicals in a safe way. There were still three body trays here, used for prepping the deceased.

There was also a large stack of coffins, mostly biodegradable stuff like willow, cardboard, bamboo and wool. Then there were other sustainable woods, and lastly a couple of old-stock hard-wood ones for anyone who insisted.

They used to make up their own coffins in the old workshop across the hall, and Hannah had fond childhood memories of being in there with Grandpa, the smell of sawdust and varnish, dust motes in the air. These days, the workshop had been con-verted into an office for Archie, to use for land management. There was also a small plant nursery in there, where Archie ex-perimented with different things to grow in the memorial woods.

Brodie was in the prep room now, standing over a semi-dressed old man on the slab. He was barrel-chested and covered in grey body hair, like an old silverback.

'Hey,' Hannah said.

Brodie turned. 'Good timing, give me a hand.'

Hannah walked over and looked at the body. No obvious signs of how he'd died, but for old men most causes didn't show – heart disease, stroke, pneumonia.

His eyes were open from dehydration of the eyelids. They could glue them shut if need be, but preferred not to these days.

'Patrick Shaw,' Brodie said. 'Goes by Paddy.'

Paddy wore suit trousers and socks, his top half bare. Brodie had a white shirt, jacket and tie on the worktop.

'Help me get him up.'

They took a shoulder each and raised him, lifting his head upright.

'Do you want to hold or dress?' Brodie said.

'I'll dress.'

Brodie took the weight as Hannah lifted the shirt and put one arm through, then the other, pulling the back down. Brodie lowered him then they both did the buttons and cuffs. They lifted him again, did the same with the jacket, but kept it open until Hannah secured the tie, Brodie lifting Paddy's head while she looped it round.

After a few minutes they had him looking good.

'He was a plumber,' Brodie said. 'Bet he hasn't worn this suit in years.'

'Except to other people's funerals.'

Hannah thought about how it was weird that we felt we had to dress the dead up.

'So I spoke to Phoebe,' she said.

'And?' Brodie fussed with Paddy's tie, smoothed his jacket.

'She says she doesn't know anything about Jack's grave.'

'She would.'

'I believe her.'

Brodie glanced at Hannah then looked away. 'She's very good at that.'

'What?'

'Getting people to believe her.'

'What does that mean?'

'Doesn't matter.'

Hannah remembered first meeting him, at a stranger's funeral at Mortonhall Crem. He broke into tears when she challenged him outside. Confessed he wasn't well. She thought about Phoebe in Gilmerton, her family supporting her. Thought about who Brodie had.

'It seems crazy that you two...'

Brodie looked up. 'What?'

'You obviously still care about each other.'

'A lot of stuff was said, after Jack. Stuff that can't be forgotten.'

'Like what?'

Brodie moved around Paddy. The air in here was as cold as they could stand, to reduce decomposition. That was important now they weren't embalming. But they should still get him back into a fridge as soon as possible. Paddy looked OK, discoloured, but not too bad. His skin was waxy and pale, sunken eyes. Better than the make-up and fakery they used to do here. Hannah thought so, at least.

'It doesn't matter now.'

'You should talk to her yourself,' Hannah said.

Brodie shook his head.

'She said something else.' Hannah ran a hand along the body tray. 'About you. Hearing voices.'

Brodie blinked heavily.

'I told you about that,' he said. 'The email address I set up, how I send Jack messages.'

'That's not what Phoebe was talking about.'

Brodie swallowed, smoothed Paddy's thin hair down.

Hannah hated this. 'She said you heard voices. Jack's.'

'That's pretty common.'

'And others?'

'It's ... not a problem.'

'Phoebe said that the voices told you bad things.'

Brodie breathed shakily, lips pressed together. 'It's not like ... That makes it sound weird.'

'Are they talking to you now?'

Brodie laughed. 'You're making it sound ridiculous. "Are these people in the room with us now?" It's not like schizophrenia or anything.'

'So you *do* hear voices.'

'Yeah, but...' He sighed, sounded as frustrated as Hannah felt.

She couldn't work out what this had to do with anything, with Jack's grave or Phoebe or any of it.

'Help me understand,' she said.

Brodie kicked the brakes off the gurney and wheeled Paddy to the fridges.

Hannah walked with him. 'I want to understand.'

'You can't,' Brodie said. 'Unless you experience it.'

He opened a door and pulled the tray out. Hannah got a blast of cold air, shivers through her body.

They lifted and slid him onto the tray, pushed him in, closed the door.

'Do you think this has anything to do with Jack's grave?'

Brodie held the fridge door handle tight. 'You think I did it myself? That some psycho voices told me to dig up my own son?'

'Of course not.'

'I'm telling you, Phoebe knows more about this than she's letting on.'

'I can set up cameras at the grave, track movements of—'

'Look into Phoebe,' Brodie said, steel in his voice. 'I mean really look into her.'

He left the prep room without looking back, and Hannah stared at the wall of fridges, thought about all the people inside. She listened, in case any of them wanted to talk to her. But she heard nothing.

13

JENNY

The sign read *HMP Edinburgh* but everyone called it Saughton Prison. Jenny had her name and ID checked, went through the metal detectors into a waiting area, then was ushered into the visitors' room with all the wives and girlfriends.

She had a flashback to the last time she was here, confronting her ex. He'd goaded her into attacking him, the smirk on his face making her lose it. He was always in control of her, until she killed him. And even after that, for a long time. But not anymore.

She saw Callum Conway in the far corner and headed over. Black hair cropped short, stubble on a strong jaw, bright-blue eyes. He looked like a bad boy from a television crime drama, all cheekbones and smoulder. The kind of man Jenny would've jumped at a few years ago. She wondered about him and Marina.

'Marina warned me not to meet you,' he said as she reached the table.

'And yet here you are.'

Callum nodded for her to take a seat. 'I was interested to see what a private investigator looks like.'

'And?'

'Not what I was expecting.'

He was flirty and Jenny liked it. She was a little older than him, both grew up in Edinburgh. Maybe they used to dance in the same clubs as kids, brushed against each other at the bar, eyed each other across the dancefloor. Fucked in the same toilet cubicle at different times. Or maybe that was just her.

'Neither are you,' she said.

He smiled and it lit up his face, then he waved around the room. 'Not one of these grizzled old cunts, eh?'

He wore a black polo shirt with the prison name embossed on it, his tattooed muscles on show.

'I wanted to ask you about—'

'Fraser Fulton, I know. You're wasting your time. You think I organised a drone attack on the fucker's funeral from here? Why would I bother?'

'A final insult.'

Callum shrugged. 'No need. He's gone and his business is there for the taking. My guys are already moving in. The rest of that family are nothing without him. I don't need to fuck up his funeral.'

'His widow said your family were responsible.'

He laughed. 'Based on what?'

Jenny wondered about his life in here, how much control he had.

He leaned forward and Jenny caught his aftershave, spicy and expensive.

'Because the drone came from the direction of Saughton, you think it was me. You know how stupid that is?'

'We're analysing the drone,' Jenny said, trying to get a grip of this conversation. 'We'll find the owner soon enough.'

Callum sat back. 'I understand why the Fultons haven't gone to the cops. None of us want those fucks involved in our business. But what's in this for you?'

'It's just a job,' Jenny said. 'I investigate things.'

Callum grinned. 'I bet you do.'

'What does that mean?'

'I heard you begged the Fultons for this gig.'

Jenny felt blood rise to her cheeks. 'I don't know where you heard that, but—'

Callum lowered his voice. 'I know all about you, Jenny Skelf. Your husband was a murderer, on remand in here, escaped on the way to trial. He's a fucking legend for that, by the way.'

'Ex-husband.'

'And you wouldn't let it lie. He went to ground but you found him, set him on fire.'

'He would've killed me otherwise.'

'And that turned you on, right? The thrill of the chase. You thought your days of adventure were long gone, a woman your age. But you got your kicks hunting him down.'

'You know nothing about me,' Jenny said, trying to stay calm.

'You love a bad boy,' Callum said. 'That's all this is. You want to be a tourist in this world of gangsters, right? Women like you are ten a penny. Do you know how many pervy letters I get from desperate housewives? Details about what they'd like to do to me, what they want *me* to do to *them*. I bet you'd like all sorts of kinky shit, right?'

Jenny gripped the table tight and closed her eyes, waited for her rage to pass, wondered if it ever would.

❦

She was collecting her phone from the lockers at the front desk when a young guard approached her.

'Mrs Skelf?'

She scowled at the lad. 'Ms.'

'Governor Morrison would like a word.'

'What?'

'Follow me.'

Maybe a chat with the governor would be useful. She walked behind the guard. He was tall and skinny, shaving rash on his neck and spots on his forehead. She wondered how handy he would be in a riot.

They went upstairs to a corridor that was more corporate office than prison. Arrived at the governor's door, which the kid knocked on then opened, waving Jenny in.

Morrison was sitting at her desk, long brown hair in a ponytail, powder-blue blouse and navy suit, lanyard round her neck.

'Ms Skelf,' she said, waving at a chair. 'I'm Debbie Morrison.'

Jenny looked around. Filing cabinets on one side, framed aerial shot of the prison on the wall, a few commendations and awards on a shelf.

She sat. 'To what do I owe this honour?'

'The honour is all mine,' Debbie said. 'Not often we get a celebrity in here.'

'I'm not a celebrity.'

'You're known across town, shall we say.'

Jenny was already tired of this. 'Let's not say that.'

Debbie smiled an empty smile. 'And what's your interest in Mr Conway?'

'Just following up a case.'

'Anything the prison service needs to know about?'

'I don't think so.'

Debbie templed her fingers together, elbows on the desk. 'Presumably something to do with events at Saughton Cemetery yesterday, at Fraser Fulton's funeral.'

Christ, word got around fast in jail.

'Was Callum Conway present when Fraser Fulton died?' Jenny said, keeping her voice light.

'I presume you read the report from the mortuary?' Debbie said. 'Fulton had a heart attack, end of story.'

Jenny had read it, mortician Graham Chapel was Dorothy's mate. The report told her nothing, just that an unfit man had a heart attack.

'You didn't answer my question,' Jenny said. 'Was Callum there?'

Debbie sat forward, pressed her lips together for a moment. 'He was not.'

'Are you sure?'

'You think I don't know what goes on in my prison?'

'I have no idea.'

'I run a tight ship.'

Jenny glanced out of the window, which looked southeast towards the cemetery.

'Any problems with drones?'

'I presume you've read the tabloids. Wildly exaggerated. A few drones have attempted to smuggle contraband into prison but always been intercepted.'

'What about going the other way?'

'Is that really what you think?'

It wasn't, but Jenny honestly didn't have any other ideas. 'But the prisoners are very familiar with drone technology, right?'

'It's 2024,' Debbie said. 'Who isn't? But if you're suggesting I would allow a drone to be flown from inside these walls, you're very much mistaken.'

She stood up and waved at the door, as if this was all over.

'If you need to speak to any of my prisoners again, Ms Skelf, you'll need to come through me first.'

14

DOROTHY

Dorothy and Brodie stood in the prep room facing the wall of body fridges, the chill making Dorothy wrap her cardigan tighter around her shoulders. The fridge they were standing in front of had *CF #13* written on the whiteboard, along with *male, white, six foot one*.

'This is him,' Brodie said, opening the door and sliding the tray out. He unzipped the bag to reveal the man's face and torso. This was the thirteenth person they would bury through their Communal Funeral project, a homeless man, dead from a drug overdose in a Wester Hailes underpass. Apparently he'd been living rough for some time, but no one in the neighbourhood knew him. It broke Dorothy's heart how easily people could slip through the cracks.

She stared at his face then his tattoos, several on his upper arms and chest. Tattoos were often a way to find out about a person's past. A lot of the unknown dead were veterans, and the Skelfs could sometimes drum up a crowd through army and navy networks.

But this guy's tattoos were different. On one side of his chest was a thick, black, vertical line that looped round, stopped, started again to form a lower case *b*. On the other side was a jigsaw piece filled in black over his heart.

'Biffy Clyro,' Brodie said.

It rang a bell with Dorothy, a Scottish band, some of their songs were on a playlist her ex-drum student Abi sent her.

'Look.' Brodie lifted the man's left arm and Dorothy saw a line in cursive script: *Living is a problem...* He lowered the arm and lifted the other one: *...because everything dies*.

'It's from a song on their fourth album,' Brodie said. 'I Googled it.'

Dorothy stared at the man's face and realised something. The Multiverse would have to learn that song for his funeral.

ꝏ

Dorothy spent the next few hours at homeless shelters and refuges across the city with a picture of Yana in her hand. She often found herself in these places when she got a missing-person case. Dorothy knew a lot of the staff now, they were always under incredible pressure. She swapped some banter with the residents when they clocked her hearse.

Next she checked out foodbanks, still armed with Yana's picture. It was soul-destroying that the number of these places kept increasing, everyone full of desperation and embarrassment. There were no jokes in the foodbanks about the hearse, all humour gone from these people's lives. That this was happening in a rich city like Edinburgh made Dorothy sick.

She turned into Dalmeny Street and parked the hearse across from the Ukrainian Catholic Church. It was an odd building, sitting on the corner with Buchanan Street, three front façades giving the impression that it was hexagonal. Dorothy knew that Yana had come to services here, maybe it was worth a shout. Yana was in a Catholic minority in Ukraine compared to the majority Eastern Orthodox, and Dorothy wondered if that had anything to do with why she was missing.

Next to the church was the Out of the Blue Drill Hall. The Multiverse were playing their charity show there in a couple of days, and Dorothy wondered about the weird coincidences in a city this small, like neurons from different parts of the brain connecting and creating something new. She had a sense of the city as a living organism, constantly renewing itself.

She crossed the road and stopped outside the church. A small blue sign read: *Our Lady of Pochayiv & Saint Andrew UCC*, underneath a blue-and-yellow flag.

She walked inside, saw the wooden pews, light-blue walls, a large painting of Christ behind the altar. There were banners, crosses and other depictions of Jesus and Mary either side of the church, a chandelier casting sharp light into the corners.

A young man in a black cassock walked towards her from an arched doorway to the side of the altar. His cassock looked uncomfortable, heavy drapery swishing round his ankles.

She introduced herself, got the usual raised eyebrow at her credentials. But Father Maxim Koval took her seriously when she showed him a picture of Yana.

'I have been worried about her also,' he said, accent a mix of Ukrainian rolled consonants and softer Edinburgh. 'She has not been to mass recently. We have a strong community here and she was very welcome. It is not easy, what is happening back home.'

'Do you know much about her?'

'I know she is a widow. Her husband died in the early days of the war. She used to bring the children here.'

'What about her mother-in-law, Veronika?'

'I don't think there was ever an older woman. Perhaps she is not Catholic?'

Dorothy glanced around the church, as if Yana might leap out from behind a crucifix.

'Did she ever take confession?'

Maxim gave her a look. 'You know I cannot speak of anything said during confession.'

Dorothy held her palms out. 'I know, but did she?'

'Yes, I heard her confession.'

'Did she say anything that made you concerned?'

Maxim considered this. 'I don't think so.'

'Can you think why she might leave her children?'

'She was grieving for her husband. For our country.'

Dorothy straightened her shoulders. 'You think she might've gone back to fight? Without telling anyone?'

'I'm not saying that.'

'Then what?'

'These are very distressing times,' Maxim said, pulling at his cuffs.

'You think she might've harmed herself?'

'I am not saying anything. Confession is sacrosanct.'

Dorothy ran her tongue around her teeth. 'Because if she didn't have a reason to leave, I'm very worried she's been taken. She's young and pretty, you know what I'm talking about.'

'Then that is surely a matter for the police.'

'And you think the police here will help a refugee?'

Maxim placed his hands together, like this was the end of the conversation. 'I will pray for her safe return.'

Dorothy frowned. She was going to do a damn sight more than pray.

❧

Outside the church, she noticed that the hearse was blocked from leaving its parking space by a doubled-parked car. A white car. As she approached, the car door opened and the driver got out slowly and stretched, then turned and leaned against the hearse.

Webster.

Dorothy breathed, touched the hearse roof across from him. He was smiling but looked tired. He was still a handsome man with an arrogant air, but he needed a shave and a haircut, looked like he wasn't sleeping. She remembered him in that bunker on Cramond Island, how he would've killed her and Thomas if Brodie and Hannah hadn't intervened. The smell of the sea air, her terror.

'You're breaking your bail conditions,' she said, voice level.

He looked up and down the street. 'Not if no one sees.'

'What do you want?'

He turned his palms to heaven. 'Just hanging out, no crime against that.'

She pictured him earlier today, at Seafield. His appearance again now meant that he'd followed her all day, either that or he was somehow tracking the hearse. Both possibilities sent the same message.

'This won't work,' Dorothy said.

'What?'

'Trying to intimidate me.'

He shook his head. 'You've got me all wrong, Dorothy.'

She would testify against him in court, no matter what. And she was sure the others would too. Then she thought about Thomas, his state of mind, and wondered.

'I heard about your friend,' she said.

He tensed his shoulders. 'What?'

'Benny Low. I'm sorry.'

He spat on the ground. 'You're not sorry. You wanted him dead.'

She wondered if his eyes were bloodshot from crying, not lack of sleep.

'No,' she said firmly. 'I would never want that.'

'Tell that to your boyfriend.'

'What?'

He stared at her then slammed the roof of the hearse hard, making her jump. Then he turned and got in the car, drove off.

Dorothy stood by the hearse for a long time, staring at Webster's handprint fading from the roof, her body trembling.

15

HANNAH

Following someone always made Hannah feel dishonest. She wandered around the St James Quarter a distance behind Phoebe Sweet and her boyfriend as they went into designer shops Hannah had never heard of, coming out with more bags, laughing and touching each other, drinking bubble tea. She watched them eat overpriced street food in the hall upstairs, while she chewed on some spicy crab of her own. She followed them into Harvey Nicks, Hannah flicking through clothes racks, avoiding the staff, blinking at the insane prices. She thought about Brodie back at the house, working with the dead all day. Maybe it had been a mistake, inviting him into the funeral business, given he was still grieving. She needed to talk to Dorothy about it.

She followed Phoebe and her guy down the escalator. The boyfriend was annoyingly rugged and ripped. Brodie was a good-looking guy but he was tall and gangly, had a vulnerability about him. This guy was alpha male, tight muscle Ts and slip-on shoes. He didn't look like he was into self-reflection and grief. But then Phoebe didn't look that way right now either. Hannah chastised herself for judging.

She followed them out of Harvey Nicks and up the road, where they walked into the Gleneagles Townhouse. She watched them sit at a window and pick up cocktail menus, then realised she'd had enough. Phoebe was enjoying life, spending money, flirting and getting drinks, not digging up graves.

Hannah walked into the Old Town, up The Mound, over George IV Bridge and along Lauriston Place to the EFI. She asked for Rachel Tanaka's room at reception, then took the stairs and went along the corridor. The building was a mix of up-to-the-minute design and Victorian bones, oak panelling lining a funky break-out space filled with pastel-coloured ergonomic chairs and throw cushions, exposed brick alongside a curvy herbal-tea station.

She found the room and knocked on the door, wondered what she was doing here.

'Come.'

Inside, Rachel Tanaka was at her desk, blonde wood with curved corners, matching bookshelves behind. In amongst the hardback textbooks were a statue of Buddha, a phrenology head and a Voodoo doll with pins sticking out of it.

'Astrophysics,' Rachel said, pointing her fingers like guns at Hannah.

Hannah was surprised she remembered. 'Sorry to bother you.'

Rachel waved her in. 'No, no, I am drowning in admin, please save me.'

'If you're sure.'

'Sit. Can I get you anything? There's an insane tea thing outside. I can recommend the Thai blue.'

Hannah sat. 'I'm fine.'

Rachel leaned back in her chair and smiled. She was in a light floral blouse, several necklaces jangling, green cotton trousers. She had an easy style about her that Hannah had only seen in Gran before. Maybe this was what enlightenment looked like, decades of Buddhist glow.

'I wasn't expecting to see you again so soon,' Rachel said, closing her laptop.

'But you *were* expecting to see me?'

Rachel shrugged. 'Sure.'

Hannah looked out of the window. The office faced the front of the building, a view of the manicured lawns and grey turrets of George Heriot's private school. It was home time, hundreds of pupils in blue uniforms pouring out of the gates like microscopic organisms. Hannah imagined they were cells in the body of the city, each one alive and conscious, each with agency, intent.

'I think you've ruined me, Professor Tanaka,' she said, a laugh in her voice.

'I told you, it's Rachel. And I'm sure I haven't.'

'I can't stop thinking about panpsychism,' Hannah said. 'I feel like I've always had an inkling about it. My wife is from a Hindu family, though she never practised. She sometimes talks about inanimate objects having consciousness. I suppose I always thought like that too, just never realised I was doing it.'

Rachel held up her pen. 'It's not as if this is going to jump out of my hand of its own free will,' she said, grinning. 'But it *is* a useful way to think of the world. It makes you move through life in a more considered way.'

Hannah nodded. 'And the idea that science and maths can back it up...'

'To a point,' Rachel said, flicking the pen between her fingers like a drummer.

Hannah had a flash of Gran twirling a drumstick. She imagined the books on Rachel's shelves speaking to her, a cacophony of voices, accents and opinions. She pictured Buddha shouting at the Voodoo doll, the phrenology head tutting at their nonsense, the whole universe an animated maelstrom of life.

'You mentioned hearing voices,' she said.

'Ah.'

'What does that mean?'

'I wondered if you were another one.'

'What?'

Rachel leaned forward. 'When we met the other day, I wondered if maybe it was happening to you.'

Hannah shook her head. 'No, not me. Do *you* hear voices?'

Rachel smiled. 'Yes.'

'Can you describe it?'

'I've experienced it for decades now, since I was a teenager. It's been hard, but my Japanese background helped. We have a culture of animism. In the West, the voices people hear tend to be negative, violent and destructive. In other cultures, where the idea is more accepted, voices are usually more benign.'

Hannah struggled to get her head around it. 'But they're hallucinations, right?'

Rachel shrugged. 'It's definitely an experience I have. It's real to me.'

'But...'

'You're struggling, I get that. You're a scientist. Empirical data, objective reality, all that stuff. This undermines it.'

'No, I don't think my experience is the only valid one. I just...'

She couldn't put it into words. Maybe she *wanted* the books on the shelf to talk to her. Maybe she wanted her body's cells to start behaving crazily. Maybe she wanted some more *life* in her life.

'It's my friend,' she said eventually. 'Brodie. He works at my family's undertakers.'

Rachel's eyebrows went up. 'Lots of opportunity to hear voices there.'

'I think it started when his son was stillborn.'

Rachel nodded. 'It can often be triggered by trauma or grief. That was certainly the case for me.'

'Will you talk to him?' Hannah said. 'Will you speak with Brodie?'

'The Hearing Voices Network have loads of resources, they're a terrific support to people in his position.'

'I'm worried that he won't seek help.'

She looked out of the window again. Just the last few school pupils out there, the rest had dispersed into the city, countless individual lives and consciousnesses and spirits flowing through the energy of Edinburgh.

'Sure,' Rachel said. 'I'll speak to him.'

16
JENNY

It was a cliché that the best Chinese restaurant in town was the one full of Chinese people. But Edinburgh had such a big Chinese population that, especially in the Southside, the streets were full of great places to eat, all rammed with Chinese Scots.

Archie held the door of Sichuan House open for Jenny. The room was small and bright, and Jenny had a memory of being here before in its previous incarnation as an Italian café. The turnover of these places was crazy, and living in Edinburgh her whole life gave Jenny a gift. She saw ghosts everywhere, this Chinese place was an Italian café, before that a fried-chicken place, an Irish pub, a stationery shop, and on and on.

They were greeted by a tiny woman younger than Hannah, black hair, big glasses and bigger smile. An older woman spoke to her in a language Jenny didn't understand and the young woman nodded, pointing Archie and Jenny to a seat near the kitchen, a tiny table squeezed into the corner.

She handed them menus and beamed. 'My mother says you are such a beautiful couple.'

Archie blushed through his beard, seemed flustered. 'Oh, we're not a couple.'

More chat from the owner behind the till and the young woman nodded.

'Well, she thinks you should be.'

Jenny enjoyed watching Archie squirm. She didn't mind being mistaken for a couple. Their friendship had grown steadily and, now that things were less chaotic, maybe there was more to this. Or maybe she was just horny, having not had a fuck in over a year.

She watched Archie now, imagined what he might be like in bed, and couldn't picture it. Maybe that was a good thing.

They ordered weird soft drinks and green tea. Jenny tried to imagine herself three years ago, dining out without alcohol. She would've been half-cut before she even got here. She was still drinking, but her life didn't depend on it anymore.

This meal was part of their adventures together. They went on long walks around the city, always coming across something new, undiscovered vennels and closes, dead ends and ancient corners. Then they would visit a restaurant they'd never been to before.

They ordered randomly from the menu – a spicy hotpot, pickled fish, a tofu and egg surprise and some chicken gizzards.

'So,' Jenny said, clinking drink cans with him across the table. 'A couple, eh?'

'Don't.'

Jenny shrugged. She wanted to say she could think of worse things, but she was scared. She loved what they had now, didn't want to fuck it up.

'How was today?' Archie said, changing the subject.

'Gotta love a trip to prison,' Jenny said, swigging what turned out to be a rice-pudding-flavoured drink.

'Not your first.'

'And it probably won't be my last.'

They swapped sips of their drinks, Archie had something with lychees and an unidentified berry on the front. Tasted bitter and sweet at the same time.

'Callum Conway was interesting,' Jenny said. 'Very handsome.'

She said that to see how Archie took it, but he just raised his eyebrows. He knew what she was up to. It was nice to be seen for who you really were.

'Surprised you managed to control yourself in the visitors' room,' he said.

'Who says I did?'

Archie stuck his lip out. 'I'm sure I would've heard about it on the news if you were caught fucking in Saughton.'

Jenny shrugged, suddenly tired of the game. 'Him and his missus both deny any knowledge of the drone.'

'They would.'

'But I watched each one of them when I mentioned it. I genuinely think they had nothing to do with it.'

Their food arrived, steaming and sizzling. The spicy hotpot looked like the trash compactor from *Star Wars*, tentacles floating in a murky gunk. She sampled something chewy and fiery, wasn't sure if it was meat or not. Fucking delicious.

'I got called up to see the governor,' Jenny said. 'At Saughton.'

'Like a naughty pupil.' Archie shoved a green egg in his mouth. 'And?'

Jenny tried the gizzards, spicy and sour. She took a drink.

'Just a brick wall. She reckoned Callum was nowhere near Fraser when he died, and he has no access to drone stuff inside.' She pointed her chopsticks at Archie. 'Speaking of which...'

Archie shook his head. 'Still looking into it. All commercial drones have to be licensed, but this one isn't on the list. I did some asking around, snooping online. This is not one of your bog-standard drones.' He put down his chopsticks and dug out his phone, read from it in a silly voice. 'This is a Magni-X VTOL micro-UAS.'

Jenny swallowed a mouthful of amazing pickled fish. 'Say what now?'

'VTOL is just "vertical take-off and landing". UAS is "unmanned aircraft system". The military love acronyms.'

'Military?'

'Not necessarily, but something like that. This is not the kind of thing you order off Amazon. But leave it with me, I know a guy I can ask.'

Archie always knew a guy. He'd been a plumber, gardener and handyman before starting at the Skelfs, then learned embalming, built coffins, drove the hearse. An all-round utility man. Now he'd taught himself how to manage a cemetery, learned all the most progressive processes in the funeral industry. Dorothy's right-hand man, maybe Jenny's too.

She watched him now, expertly using chopsticks to pop fish in his mouth. Thought about the owner of this place mistaking them for a couple. Smiled to herself.

'Here, try some gizzards,' she said. 'They'll knock your fucking head off.'

17

DOROTHY

Thomas cleared away their plates and Dorothy put on the moka pot for coffee. They'd eaten mostly in silence. Thomas loaded stuff into the dishwasher and she watched him in frustration. Since he walked away last night, she'd been worrying over him.

'Thomas, please sit,' she said, voice as calm as she could make it.

'Just a minute.' He continued to faff with the dishes, then turned and sat at the table.

They were lit by candles which highlighted the lines under his eyes and on his forehead. Or maybe he was just bone-tired.

She reached out and took his hands, rubbed her thumbs over his skin.

'We need to talk,' she said softly.

Thomas's eyes briefly sparkled with a joke. 'Are you breaking up with me?' He was mimicking those cheesy American teen dramas.

'Yeah, I'm in love with Johnny next door.'

They both smiled and Thomas slipped his hand out and took a drink of Malbec. He was drinking more than he used to, but she'd done the same after Jim died. There are a million coping mechanisms, some better than others.

'About Benny Low.' She pictured Don Webster's smiling face at Seafield, then outside the Ukrainian church.

Thomas frowned and took another drink. 'I don't want to waste any breath on him.'

Dorothy took his hand again, held firm. 'You don't want to talk, you don't want to spend time together, you're miserable all the time. It's so obvious you're suffering from PTSD—'

'How can I have PTSD?' Thomas said. 'You went through much worse and you're fine.'

Dorothy straightened her shoulders. 'It's not a competition, Thomas, we're meant to support each other.'

'We do.'

'No, we don't. I've been scared to talk to you for months, frightened of you shutting me out. I've been walking on eggshells, and I've had enough. We're both old enough to know we won't get many more chances at this. So if you want to hold on to this thing, you're going to have to talk to me.'

'So you *are* threatening to break up with me?' Thomas ran a hand over his hair and Dorothy wondered if it was just an excuse to stop holding hands.

'Thomas, I don't think you're coping well. Maybe you need help.'

'I was a police officer for decades, I can handle myself.'

'One thing has nothing to do with the other. You don't have to be perfect.'

'I'm fine.'

'So talk to me about Benny Low and Don Webster.'

Dorothy had wondered earlier whether to mention Webster's appearances, but it would only make things worse. That's what Webster wanted, to sow discord amongst them all.

'One of them is dead, the other will soon be behind bars.'

'You don't think that's enough, do you?'

'What?'

'For what he did to us. To those young women. To the reputation of the police. You think Webster deserves worse.'

'He deserves justice.'

Dorothy felt Schrödinger's fur against her leg under the table. She picked him up and stroked him, she needed something to hold on to. 'Did they confirm Low's death was suicide?'

Thomas glanced out of the window at the darkness. 'Not yet.'

'You're happy he's dead, though.'

Thomas got more animated. 'We can't all be saints like you, Dorothy. We can't all see the good in everyone, some of us live in the real world.'

'Do I need to be worried, Thomas?'

Schrödinger slid to the floor, slinked off to the armchair at the window.

'About what?'

Dorothy sucked her teeth. 'Come on. You giving all your stuff away. The way you hardly look me in the eye anymore. I know about Swedish death cleaning, it's the latest trend amongst the same hipsters who got excited about hygge. When people nearer the end of their life start giving away possessions, putting their affairs in order.'

Thomas shook his head. 'You think I'm going to kill myself?'

Dorothy let that hang in the air.

'I'm not suicidal,' he said leaning forward. He looked as if he was going to pick an argument, then his shoulders slumped.

'It's not like that,' Thomas said. '*Döstädning* is badly named. It's not about death, it's just organising your life for when...'

Dorothy still didn't speak. She picked up her Malbec and took a sip. He was a changed man, but the real Thomas was still in there, she was sure of it.

Eventually he looked up. 'It's therapeutic, to be honest. Getting rid of all this junk I've accumulated. Stuff I don't care about. It lets me focus on the things in my life that are still important. Like you.'

She held out her hands across the table. 'So I don't have to worry?'

'I promise.' He lifted her hands and kissed them.

Dorothy's phone rang on the table and they both jumped, then laughed at themselves. She looked at the screen, not a number she recognised. Thought of leaving it, but it could be someone in need of a funeral, or help.

'Answer it,' Thomas said.

She took the call. 'Hello?'

Just the sound of breathing down the phone.

'Hello, who is this?' Dorothy said.

'Is that Dorothy Skelf?' A young girl whispering, Ukrainian accent. Yana's daughter.

'Olena, is that you?'

She wondered why the girl was trying to be quiet.

'Mama is OK,' she said eventually.

Dorothy frowned. 'How do you know?'

'Mama is coming for us.' Dorothy heard voices in the background. 'I have to go.'

'Olena, wait, please.'

The line went dead.

18

HANNAH

Hannah preferred sunny funerals. The dramatic funeral cliché was of someone standing rain-soaked over the grave, tears and raindrops mingling as they fell. But a bright, fresh autumn day like today was perfect for saying goodbye and celebrating the life of the deceased.

She sat with Indy at the back of the chapel in the Skelf house, both in their funeral outfits. They'd discussed within the business whether they should get rid of the black suits but had decided to ask the bereaved on a case-by-case basis, letting the clients choose.

They were saying goodbye to Paddy Shaw, in his own nice suit in the coffin at the front. Behind him, the large patio doors opened onto the front garden, and Hannah heard sparrows chittering in the trees. A breeze moved around the room and Hannah imagined it was Paddy's spirit.

The minister was talking at the plinth next to Paddy's body. Behind him was the resomator, which they would put Paddy into once everyone left. His widow, Sorcha, had opted for water cremation, but still wanted to have him looking traditional, in a suit in a coffin. But coffins didn't go into the resomator, neither did non-biodegradable clothes. Paddy would be stripped and wrapped in a wool shroud to go into the machine, so Indy had recommended doing it later. The coffin and clothes could be recycled or returned to the family.

They were still negotiating all this new territory with the bereaved. Hannah was proud of them for moving this way, dreaded to think how much pollution they'd put into the land and sky over the last century.

The minister was a man of Paddy's age and girth, and seemed to know him well. The place was full of similar men, plumbers like Paddy, joiners, roofers, electricians, people who did things with their hands. Hannah compared it to her studies, esoteric stuff about astrophysics and exoplanets, and now panpsychism. She wondered what they would make of that. But that was presumptuous, she could appreciate *their* work, surely they could appreciate hers too.

The minister finished and one of Paddy's friends gave a eulogy, tight-lipped, shoulders straight. Paddy sounded like one of the good guys, always helping others, working extra for free for those in need over Christmas, a doting parent and grandparent, loving husband. We can all be summarised, but that didn't even scratch the surface of a life, did it?

When Paddy's friend sat down, Indy played The Proclaimers over the PA, 'Sunshine on Leith'. Paddy was a Hibby but the song had a resonance beyond football.

'Have you seen Brodie today?' Hannah said under her breath.

Indy nodded, kept an eye on the playlist on her phone. 'Gone on a pick-up with Archie, to the Marie Curie Hospice.'

They'd already talked about him in bed last night. The disturbance at Jack's grave made them both feel queasy. But Hannah felt even weirder at the thought that he might've had something to do with it himself, and maybe didn't realise or remember.

She'd spent yesterday evening checking her spy cameras, dumping old data onto a hard drive and wiping them for use. Hundreds of hours of footage that no one would ever watch, but you never threw anything out, just in case.

The plan was to set up a camera at Jack's grave, which felt icky. Maybe put another camera at Phoebe's house, though Hannah wasn't sure how that would help. Hannah had floated the idea of monitoring Brodie's behaviour at work, but Indy said that was a step too far, and she was right.

The playlist switched to 'Once in a Lifetime' by Talking Heads.

'How did he seem?' Hannah said.

'Did he seem crazy, do you mean?'

'Come on, babes.'

Indy shrugged. 'Did he look like someone who would have a psychotic episode and try to dig up his dead son then forget about it?'

Indy was much more on Brodie's side, Hannah was keeping her options open.

'I was just asking.'

Indy smiled and Hannah felt relieved.

David Byrne was singing over the funk, but Hannah heard another noise.

She looked around the chapel, others had noticed it too. She glanced at Indy, who shrugged.

Then a drone flew into the chapel through the open doors to the garden, black and sleek, four small rotors, landing legs spread like an insect's.

The congregation were out of their seats but unsure what to do.

Hannah and Indy shared a look.

'This is fucked up,' Indy said, grabbing a long pole with a hook on the end, something they used to open the high windows at the back of the chapel.

Hannah ran behind her as she approached the drone, which hovered over Paddy's body, turning left and right. Hannah saw a camera mounted on the underside alongside a canister and nozzle.

Indy swiped at the drone with the pole, but it manoeuvred out of range. Then there was a fizzing noise and the nozzle sprayed liquid in all directions around the chapel.

It took a brief moment for Hannah to register the smell, manure or fertiliser, brown liquid shooting in a fine spray over the congregation, the pews and the altar, and Paddy in the coffin, the white cotton lining staining instantly.

The congregation ran from the chapel, hands over mouths, as Indy jumped onto a pew and leapt, swinging the pole, bringing it down on the back of the drone so that it tipped and dropped, clattering off the edge of the coffin and tumbling to the floor.

Hannah stared at Indy, dripping in shit or whatever it was, a mixture of disgust and triumph on her face.

19
JENNY

The stench burned her nostrils, even up here in the first-floor kitchen with the door closed. Jenny looked across the table at Dorothy. They'd been in crisis mode for the last few hours, dealing with the immediate problem of a funeral home that stank of shit, a congregation covered in some kind of chemical fertiliser, and a dead body needing to be cleaned.

They'd had to postpone the funeral. Paddy's friends and family went home to wash themselves and their clothes, or maybe throw them out. Once they'd all left, Hannah and Indy stripped in the garden and Jenny hosed them down. Their clothes were rinsed on the grass then chucked in the washing machine, spurring memory flashes for Jenny, nappy disasters when Hannah was a baby, or the projectile vomiting bug she had aged eight, spewing all over her bed, carpet and walls. Jenny didn't think of herself as a natural mother – who was? – but she'd dealt with it all without fuss, because that's what you did. Resorted to an enormous glass of wine after the chaos subsided.

Hannah and Indy were now both taking umpteen showers. Meanwhile Archie got hold of an emergency extreme-cleaning company, folk he knew who normally handled crime scenes. They were downstairs now dealing with the chapel. Archie and Brodie took Paddy Shaw back to the prep room, stripped him, cleaned his body and put him back in a fridge. They chucked the coffin lining out and Archie power washed the coffin in the back garden, so hopefully it could be used for the funeral re-run.

Jenny felt sorry for the Shaws, but something else was burning a hole in her. 'Someone is fucking with us.'

Dorothy nodded.

Schrödinger jumped onto the table, then off again, and slunk into a corner. Maybe the smell was driving him mad as well.

Jenny walked to the PI whiteboard, looked at the names around Fraser Fulton. She turned back to Dorothy. 'We need to think logically.'

Dorothy put the kettle on. Jenny fancied something stronger but she wasn't about to go down that road again.

'There are two options,' she said.

Dorothy waved a hand to give her the floor.

Jenny raised a finger. 'One: I was right about the Conways being responsible for the attack on Fraser Fulton's funeral. And me talking to Marina and Callum has got their backs up, so they decided to warn me off with a second drone.'

Dorothy nodded, started making a pot of tea.

'One thing we can rule out is that someone else had a vendetta against Fraser Fulton besides the Conways. Because if it was someone else, they would have no reason for all this.'

Dorothy brought the teapot and mugs to the table, got milk from the fridge.

'And the second option?' she said.

Jenny raised another finger. 'Two: this isn't about the Fultons and Conways at all. It's about us.'

Dorothy poured tea and sighed.

Jenny looked at the PI whiteboard. The Fulton case, Yana Kovalenko missing, Brodie and Jack's grave. She peered at the surface, smears of old pen marks in the corners, smudges here and there. Thought about all the cases they'd taken on over the years, all those people, maybe some carrying a grudge. Then she looked at the undertaker board, all the funerals they had on the slate. Maybe a former client had a bone to pick. Then she thought of the way the business was moving, maybe another funeral director wanted them out of business, wanted to sabotage their reputation.

She turned to Dorothy. 'So who's out to get us?'

Dorothy was sitting at the table, hands wrapped around a mug of tea. The smell of fertiliser from downstairs was now mixed with bleach and some cleaning chemical Jenny didn't want to think about.

'Don Webster,' Dorothy said, keeping her head down.

Jenny watched her as she sipped tea. 'Is there something you're not telling me?'

Eventually Dorothy raised her head. 'Benny Low is dead.'

'What?'

Dorothy looked out of the window. 'Thomas told me the other night. Suicide, apparently, though they haven't done the post mortem yet.'

'Christ. When were you going to tell me?'

'I'm telling you now.'

Jenny chewed that over. Low had enough dirt on Webster to sink him. His death was pretty convenient for Webster.

'Are they sure it was suicide?'

Dorothy had a pained look on her face. 'That's what I asked. This is all second hand from Thomas.'

Jenny remembered something else, from last night.

'The drone,' she said. 'Archie said it was unusual, not commercial. He thought maybe military. But what if it was a police drone?'

Dorothy shook her head. 'I thought this was all behind us. Things never end, do they?'

Jenny didn't like the defeated sound of her mum's voice.

'We need to tell the police,' she said. 'If Webster was behind this, he's breaching his bail conditions.'

'He's already breaching bail conditions.'

Jenny frowned. 'What do you mean?'

Dorothy sighed. 'I saw him yesterday. Once at Seafield, then in Leith.'

'He was following you? Christ, Mum.'

'He's just trying to intimidate us.'

'What did he say?'

Dorothy shook her head, as if she wanted no part of this. 'Nothing important.'

'Mum, we have to tell the police, they'll arrest him.'

Jenny waited for Dorothy to say something, but she just sipped tea and looked out of the window. Jenny swallowed and realised she might have to take charge.

20

DOROTHY

It felt odd to be sitting in St Leonard's police station knowing Thomas wasn't upstairs anymore. Dorothy had tried calling him earlier, could've used his moral support and sway within the department, but he hadn't answered.

She looked at the young woman PC on reception and wondered what sort of career she had ahead of her. Another two constables came from the back and walked out the front door, glancing at her. Then the door opened again and there was DS Zara Griffiths. Dorothy had last met her a year ago outside Brewdog on Lothian Road, when she'd been looking for Thomas. Zara had dealt with the Skelfs before, investigating the whole business with Jenny and Craig. She was the closest thing Dorothy could think of to a friendly face in the department, now that Thomas wasn't here.

'Dorothy,' she said, offering her hand.

Dorothy shook it and took her in. Blonde hair in a tight pony, smart suit, light-blue blouse that matched her eyes. She'd always struck Dorothy as no-nonsense, broadly on the right side of things. She wouldn't cover for bad colleagues, at least Dorothy hoped so.

'DS Griffiths.'

Griffiths smiled. 'It's DI now.'

'Congratulations.' Dorothy wondered if that worked in her favour or not.

'Come on through.'

They went to an interview room at the back of the building, one Dorothy hadn't been in before. She'd given plenty of statements at the station, but mostly to Thomas in his former office upstairs. She'd taken advantage of his position and felt guilty for that now.

The room was anonymous, scratchy carpet, walls covered in crime-prevention posters, metal table and plastic chairs. A view of police vehicles out of the window, a high wall covered in razor wire behind.

'So,' Griffiths said. 'How's Olsson?'

It was weird how cops referred to each other by surname. Olsson was her Thomas, Griffiths was Zara, Webster and Low were Don and Benny. It felt dehumanising, somehow.

'He's surviving.'

Griffiths knew what he'd gone through with Webster on Cramond Island a year ago, but she didn't know about the nightmares and cold sweats, the distancing and death cleaning.

'Yeah, it's all we can do, right?'

Griffiths' tone was amicable enough, but she was no doubt conflicted about one cop hurting another, cops accused of rape and murder, a colleague dying by suicide.

She straightened her shoulders. 'I presume you're not here with good news.'

Dorothy laid out what had happened. The first drone attack, their assumption it was to do with the Fultons, Jenny's enquiries, then the second attack this morning. She could still smell the fertiliser in her nose, a chemical burn at the back of her throat. Whoever used it knew it would linger.

Dorothy explained what Archie had found out since this morning, that the drones were, until recently, used by Police Scotland for surveillance and crowd control. They'd been decommissioned two years ago, replaced by something cheaper and easier. Maybe, therefore, they had been easy for Webster to get hold of.

Dorothy petered out as she realised she didn't yet have any real evidence against Don Webster for the attacks.

But Griffiths' face said she was treating it seriously.

A year ago, she'd taken the statement from Ruby, one of Webster and Low's assault victims. But now Ruby and the other travellers had moved on from Cramond, another reason Dorothy was dreading the court case. Some things would surely stick, like the attempted murder of Thomas and Dorothy, but the other stuff might get negotiated down. That had depressed Thomas when the prosecuting solicitor outlined it. Plus the fact it was notoriously hard to get a conviction against a cop, no matter what they did. Juries liked them.

'This is not a lot to go on,' Griffiths said. 'You'll need to hand the drones over to forensics, of course.'

'I want a guarantee they'll be safe.'

Griffiths knew what Dorothy was implying but didn't bristle. 'As much as I can.'

Dorothy mulled that over.

Griffiths steepled her fingers. 'I'll need contact info for the bereaved at both funerals. Just to follow up.'

Dorothy nodded. 'There's something else.'

She told Griffiths about Webster's two visits yesterday, breaking bail conditions. Implied threats.

Griffiths sighed, no one wanted to investigate a dodgy former colleague. 'I'll speak to him.'

'That's it?'

'It'll be your word against his,' Griffiths said. 'Unless we can find some CCTV of either event.'

'So he can just do what he wants?'

Griffiths waved a hand around the room. 'It's not as if we have a ton of evidence yet. And he's smart. He could accuse *us* of harassment if we go in guns blazing. He'll claim that he's grieving for Low.'

Low was a colleague of Griffiths too, they were all connected.

'I wondered if that might have something to do with it,' Dorothy said.

'What do you mean?'

'When did Low die? Maybe his suicide sent Webster over the edge.'

'It's not useful to start attributing motives to something we have no idea about,' Griffiths said. 'That's not how we do things.'

Dorothy frowned. It might not be how the police worked, but it was how the Skelfs got shit done.

Griffiths glanced at the empty chair next to Dorothy. 'I'm surprised Olsson didn't come with you for this.'

That crawled under Dorothy's skin, no matter how much she tried to stop it.

21
HANNAH

Hannah pressed her fingers to her nostrils, was sure she could still smell fertiliser on her skin. She watched Brodie finishing his food across the table then she smiled at Indy and shared a nervous laugh, the pair of them shaking their heads. This was something to tell their grandkids about. Remember that time someone sprayed shit on us in the chapel? The cleaners were still working back there, one of the reasons they'd come out for lunch.

The three of them were at a table outside Söderberg on Middle Meadow Walk, great for people-watching, the Meadows a constant stream of students and office workers, schoolchildren from Heriot's, random artsy types, builders from the site up the road and a million other flavours of Edinburger. She watched two young men in splattered overalls demolish sausage rolls from Greggs as they walked past, caught a snippet of their conversation about some friend, how she was too good for that arsehole she'd been dating, he was probably sleeping around behind her back and they should tell her.

On the table were their three empty plates. Goat's cheese sandwich for Indy, artichoke pizza for Brodie and salmon omelette for Hannah, all gone. Something about the craziness of earlier had made Hannah ravenous.

Brodie's phone buzzed and he checked it. 'Archie says the cleaners are finished.'

Indy raised her eyebrows. 'Reckon they'll ever get rid of the smell?'

Brodie shook his head. 'I still can't believe it.'

'You didn't get covered in it.'

He looked genuinely concerned at Indy then Hannah. 'Are you two OK?'

Hannah nodded and smelled her fingers again. She'd showered three times but still felt dirty. She wondered about the others in the chapel, how they were getting on, what conversations they were having at home.

A tall, skinny server took their plates away. As he left, Hannah spotted Rachel Tanaka walking through the small vennel from Quartermile, where the EFI building was.

Hannah waved, and Rachel beamed, walked over to them. Hannah pulled a chair out and did the introductions.

'Brodie, this is the woman I was talking about.'

She'd thought it best to pre-warn him, it would be crazy to ambush him about this. She'd spoken to him first thing this morning before all the insanity at the chapel, her voice low and quiet, explaining that Rachel was a friend who also heard voices. He seemed doubtful but had still come along. Hannah had also promised Brodie she would chase up Phoebe and her boyfriend, and place that spycam at Jack's headstone, which seemed to sway him. If she did all that for him, he would do this for her.

There was something about Rachel's energy, Hannah felt it the first time in that lecture hall, and when they spoke in her office. She was instantly calming, made you feel at ease.

'How was your morning,' she said.

Hannah, Indy and Brodie laughed, and Rachel looked confused.

'Can you smell anything?' Indy said, throwing a look around the table.

'Like what?' Rachel made a display of breathing in deeply, holding it, then out again. 'Did one of you just have salmon?'

They laughed again and Rachel looked even more bemused.

'Sorry,' Hannah said, grinning. 'It doesn't matter.'

Rachel was sitting across the table from Brodie. 'How are you, Brodie?'

'Fine.'

'Did Hannah tell you about me?'

'Yeah.'

'Good.' She smiled around the table. 'I'm not here in any official capacity, you understand that. I'm just someone who can maybe understand a little of what you're going through.'

Brodie lowered his head.

'But I can appreciate,' Rachel continued, 'that it's a very difficult thing to talk about. Especially for the first time.'

'OK.'

Rachel sat quietly.

Hannah was desperate to fill the void, but knew she shouldn't speak.

Rachel cleared her throat. 'Maybe it's easiest if I talk about my own experience.'

Brodie gave the faintest of nods, looked at Hannah and Indy, eyes darting around like he would rather be anywhere but here.

'When I was twelve, my grandmother died. I didn't know her well, I was brought up in Vancouver while she lived in Kyoto. I went to Japan with my parents for the funeral, which was a culture shock. I'd been a number of times before but I didn't speak the language, and the formality of the funeral was disturbing. Plus, I was going through puberty at the time. I was confused and lonely, old Japanese people randomly coming up and holding my hand. I didn't really feel much in the way of grief and I felt bad about that, that I hadn't known my grandmother better, that my mom was upset when I wasn't, all that stuff. Anyway, I escaped from the wake for a while, went for a walk through a park, and they just started talking to me.'

'Who?' Indy said.

'The trees. I would love to say they were cherry blossom, but that would be too neat. I don't remember what they were, but I do remember it all seemed so natural. They weren't telling me bad things, they were consoling me, telling me that Gran had gone to a better place, she was at peace now, all the things that my relatives were saying. But somehow from the trees it seemed more real. I can't explain it.'

Brodie was listening closely, they all were, Rachel had that kind of vibe.

'When I came home to Vancouver, it increased. Not just trees, any plants or animals, then inanimate things, rocks, the beach, the sea used to shout at me and I didn't like it. And as the years went on, they became more nasty, telling me I was worthless and should kill myself, that I should do terrible things to my family, to random people in the street.'

Indy sat forward. 'That must've been terrifying.'

'How did you cope?' Hannah said.

'I told my parents but they didn't understand. That's one thing that's so important, I've come to realise. That people really understand what you're going through.' She looked at Brodie, who held her gaze. 'Which is the main reason I agreed to come and talk to you today.'

'How did you get the bad voices to calm down?' Brodie said, his voice heavy.

Rachel looked at him. 'Acceptance is the key. For a long time, when I came back to Vancouver, I fought it. I got drunk and high a lot, took various prescription meds, tried CBT. My mom almost put me in a psych ward. But it was the whole idea that it had to be *cured* that made it worse, paradoxically. As soon as I realised that the voices were just another part of me, that helped. I spoke to people in a support group, others like me who heard things, and that really started my recovery.'

She put her hand on top of Brodie's, and Hannah thought he would pull away, but he didn't.

'It doesn't matter why it starts,' she said softly. 'Grief, trauma, bullying, insomnia. Physical illness, drugs, stress. What matters is that you accept it as part of your life, as part of you. That doesn't mean you'll have them forever, many people stop hearing voices.

For some, it only lasts a short time. But personally, I would feel a little lost if my voices disappeared completely. I'm so used to them now.'

Brodie pressed his lips together into a thin smile, and Rachel beamed around the table. Her laidback and friendly vibe flew in the face of the idea that this was about mentally ill people struggling to cope. She was a beacon pointing a way forward for Brodie, and that was why Hannah had wanted them to meet. This had started out to do with Jack's grave, and she still had to solve that case, but it had become something bigger, about how Brodie lived his life.

Hannah sat back and closed her eyes, tried to smell the fertiliser of earlier, but all she could smell was fresh air.

22

DOROTHY

Camilla Curzon looked flustered as she answered the door, took a second to remember who Dorothy was.

'Oh, wow,' she said, touching her hair, earrings jangling. 'That's a coincidence.'

'What?'

Camilla waved Dorothy through the door. 'Have you found Yana? Do you know anything?'

She didn't wait for an answer, just bustled Dorothy down the hall to the kitchen. It was crowded, Veronika sitting at the island with two large men in matching black leather jackets and dark jeans, all three with cups of tea.

The two men stood automatically, one of them gesturing to his stool, which Dorothy declined.

Camilla drifted in and stood at the sink.

'This is Bohdan and Marko,' she said, a nervous trill in her voice. The two men nodded.

'Are you sure you would not like to sit,' Marko said, but Dorothy shook her head.

Marko was the bulkier of the two, dark skinhead and a busted and reset nose. Bohdan was taller, blond buzzcut, kind smile. The two of them seemed to take up all the room in the kitchen, and Dorothy thought they must be too hot in their jackets.

Camilla cleared her throat. 'Bohdan and Marko were in Fedir's unit, they were there when...'

Marko nodded. 'We are on leave for the first time since the invasion.' His accent was crisp and clear. 'We came to see Yana, give her Fedir's belongings.'

He looked at a kit bag sitting on the floor in the corner, then glanced at Bohdan. 'But we arrive to find that she is missing.' He looked at Veronika. 'And Fedir's mama is very worried. The children have no father, and their mother is gone.'

Dorothy thought about Olena on the phone last night. She'd come here to try to speak to the girl alone, but that didn't seem likely now. Part of her wanted to tell Camilla and Veronika what Olena said last night, that her mum was safe. But she worried that the reason Olena had called late at night and spoken in whispers had something to do with what was going on here. Dorothy didn't want to make things worse and couldn't work out her next move.

'Have you found her?' Camilla said, rubbing her hands together. 'Is she OK?'

Dorothy shook her head. 'I don't know where she is. I spent time yesterday going around homeless shelters and foodbanks. I went to the church she attends.'

She looked at Veronika, whose face turned into a frown. It wasn't her church. Veronika glanced at the two men, who shared a look, and Dorothy wondered what religion they were, what religion Fedir was, whether Veronika didn't approve of the marriage. Families were such a tricky landscape to negotiate, especially with religion in the mix.

Marko looked down at the kit bag in the corner, then around the room.

'I do not understand,' he said. 'I do not think a young mother would leave her children. Which means she must have been taken.'

The implication was clear enough and the tone of Marko's voice suggested he'd seen some bad things in his time. Women and children were vulnerable in every corner of the world, doubly so in a war zone. The first to be abused, tortured or killed. Dorothy wasn't stupid, she knew bad things happened to good people, here in Edinburgh as much as anywhere else. Her trip around the shelters and foodbanks yesterday was proof of that. But Olena's voice on the phone stuck in her mind. She should tell these people everything, that was the sensible thing to do. But her gut said no, so she stayed quiet.

Bohdan and Marko looked at each other then stood.

'We will leave Fedir's belongings here,' Marko said. 'But we are in the city for three days, staying in a hostel on Market Street.'

He looked at Camilla, and Dorothy thought there was something like suspicion in his face. Did they think Camilla had something to do with this? Did *Dorothy* think that? She wasn't ruling anything out.

'You have my number,' Marko said to Camilla. 'Please call if you find out anything.'

He took Veronika's hands in his and spoke to her softly in Ukrainian, nodded around the room and left, Bohdan copying him and following.

The kitchen seemed suddenly huge without the two soldiers in it, and Camilla gave a sigh as if this was all too much.

'I was actually hoping to talk to the children,' Dorothy said to Camilla. 'Are they around?'

Veronika and Camilla frowned at each other.

'Why?' Veronika said.

Dorothy looked at her. 'They might know something. Have you asked them?'

Camilla stepped forward to the kitchen island, now there was space. 'We've only reassured them that nothing bad has happened.'

'We do not know that,' Veronika said, hands clutching her cup of tea. 'As Marko said, a young mother would not leave her children. Not in a strange country.' She scowled at Camilla.

Dorothy understood, she would be miserable if her son had died after she'd been shipped to a foreign country, then her daughter-in-law had gone missing, leaving her with two grandkids and a heart full of grief.

'Are they here?' Dorothy asked again, looking out the kitchen to the hall.

She was already wondering how she would negotiate speaking to them alone. She didn't want Camilla and Veronika standing over them.

As if by magic, the front door opened and the kids came in, laughing and play fighting, swinging schoolbags at each other as they scuffed down the hall. Behind then was a young man, curly fair hair, lean figure but six feet tall, friendly face. Baggy T-shirt and cargo trousers with loads of pockets. Dorothy compared him in her mind to the two soldiers who'd just left, all of them men but very different in outlook and experience.

The kids spotted Dorothy in the kitchen and Olena's face dropped, Roman glancing at her. They were both out of breath from mucking around as they dumped their bags and kissed their gran.

'Took them for ice cream,' the young man said to Camilla.

Camilla hugged him and turned to Dorothy. 'My son, Oliver. He's great with the little ones.'

'Ach, they're lovely.'

Camilla grinned. 'This is Dorothy, she's helping us look for Yana.'

Camilla side-eyed the kids as she said Yana's name, and Olena glanced at Dorothy as she opened the fridge.

'Oh, yeah?' Oliver said. 'Anything?'

Dorothy shook her head and looked at Fedir's kit bag. Her natural curiosity meant she wanted to open it.

'Actually, I wanted to talk to Roman and Olena about that,' she said.

Roman stared at her with his face tight, Olena moved slowly as she poured herself a glass of milk and put the carton back in the fridge.

'I really don't know what they can tell you,' Camilla said.

'Let them speak,' Veronika said, strength in her voice.

Dorothy watched while the kids settled at the island. They glanced at each other more than once, maybe just sibling stuff, maybe something else. Olena didn't look at Dorothy the whole time, raised her milk glass to cover her face, drank slowly.

'So,' Dorothy said. 'You both know that your mother has gone missing.'

Camilla flinched.

Roman nodded, Olena put her glass down and wiped her top lip.

There were already secrets here. None of the adults knew that Dorothy had spoken to the kids upstairs on her previous visit. And none of them knew that Olena called Dorothy. She wondered if Roman knew, if he was there when she called. What else he might know.

Olena finally looked at Dorothy and swallowed hard. It was clear what the look meant. *Please don't tell them I called you.* Roman watched her the whole time, it was also clear that he knew about the call, that they both knew more than they would say in front of the adults.

Dorothy went through the motions. 'Is there anything you can think of, anything at all, that might help us find your mom?'

Olena flicked a look around everyone in the room with a straight face, Roman still watching her. Dorothy could see something between them. It was obvious was she was going to have to speak to them alone somehow.

'No,' Olena said confidently, looking at Roman. 'Nothing at all.'

Roman just nodded then looked at the floor.

23

HANNAH

It felt weird setting up a spy camera in a graveyard, though Hannah had done it before. The Skelfs had an array of modern cameras for indoor and outdoor use, day and night vision, ones that could be hidden in smoke alarms or car keys, or worn on the body.

Jack Sweet's grave posed a small problem. There was no tree coverage nearby and no row of headstones facing Jack's, because his grave was so recent. Another problem with placing a spycam here was that all the headstones were small, to match the graves and the deceased buried beneath the surface. Anything bulky was sure to stand out.

So Hannah had brought a small toy truck with her, which she set at the foot of the headstone. As she did so, she noticed that the signs of disturbance at Jack's grave had been smoothed over by the groundskeeper. She checked the coverage on her phone, moved it a little, checked again. Not ideal, a shot from this low down, and there was always the danger that the lens would get wet or dirty. But there was enough clarity to work with, so she synched it up and walked away.

She would keep an eye on alerts, but the vast majority would be other mourners passing by, the groundskeeper, or local wildlife. Rabbits were frolicking just up the hill right now. There would be foxes and badgers at night, cats prowling, sometimes hedgehogs. It was amazing the stuff that went on in cemeteries after dark.

Hannah didn't think of the New Town as *real* Edinburgh, it felt to her like it was the domain of trust-fund students, high-class offices and Airbnbs. She was here, sitting in the van outside 4 Heriot Row, waiting for Zane Underhill to emerge from his flat. She'd found Phoebe's boyfriend's name on her socials, then got lucky with the Land Registry, he owned the property himself, which meant he was loaded. To be fair, she could already have assumed that from the way he spent money in Harvey Nicks with Phoebe. Judging by his socials, he seemed more like an ordinary Edinburgh guy than a trust-funder, dressing up to go clubbing with his mates on a Friday night, dinner with Phoebe another night, football, both playing sevens and watching Hearts.

She'd been here for an hour. She didn't think she could follow Phoebe much more without being recognised, and the boyfriend was the only other angle she had on this thing. She'd already established he was in when she got here, buzzing his flat then giving the excuse of a wrong address. Now she just hoped he wasn't staying in all day.

Another twenty minutes of waiting and her wish came true when Zane emerged from the front door, phone cradled in the crook of his neck as he threw on a jacket and walked to the corner of Dundas Street, then headed up the hill into town. All these streets were named after dead white guys, the ones who ran the empire, who fucked over countless poor people. That was how you got statues in your honour, or streets or private schools named after you.

Zane was animated on the phone as he strode up the hill and Hannah began to feel the burn in her calves as she tried to keep up. She was young and should be fit, but sport had never really been her thing.

They were on Hanover Street now, delivery vans trundling over the cobbles, the view of Princes Street and The Mound appearing as Hannah approached the top of the rise at George Street. Another statue of an old white guy stood in the middle of the junction, looking down over the city. Hannah couldn't see from this side who he was, just flowing robes and curly hair. She glanced behind her. The statue guy was looking the wrong way, missing the view to the Firth of Forth and Fife beyond.

She turned back to see Zane stepping into All Bar One on the corner of George Street. It was an anodyne pub space, big windows, long bar, bright and airy.

Hannah stopped before she got to the pub's windows facing Hanover Street, and waited a few minutes for him to get served at the bar. Then she walked slowly up the last part of the hill, keeping a close eye on the tables at the window, but she didn't see him.

She kept walking, round the corner then into the bar, stood inside getting her eyes acclimatised to the light and space. Down the bottom end near the toilets, she spotted Zane with a pint of lager, settling himself on a bar stool, clinking glasses with another guy holding a pint. The other guy smiled at Zane and turned a little, and Hannah frowned.

She knew that face well, had seen it a few hours ago at lunch.

Brodie.

She was trying to get her head around all this when she felt her phone buzz in her pocket. She retreated to the pub entrance, pulled it out, saw the first notification for the gravecam in Craigmillar. She opened the file and frowned, then had to lean against the wall for support.

Crouching in front of Jack Sweet's grave, smiling and waving right at the camera in the toy truck, was Don Webster.

24

JENNY

Trinity wasn't a part of town Jenny knew well, but she recognised Edinburgh affluence when she saw it. The area as a whole was the usual mixed bag for the city, Jenny had driven past tenements and terraces, new-build neighbourhoods and run-down estates on the way here. But Laverockbank Terrace was sturdy old Victorian brick, mostly detached houses with big gardens. Not the kind of place you could afford on a detective sergeant's wages, which made her think.

She found number eleven, parked the older of the Skelfs' two vans under a giant weeping willow and got out. She could smell the salt of the sea, Newhaven Harbour wasn't far from here, just over the back of this place. Sitting on this hill, the house must have spectacular views over the Forth.

Jenny tugged her blouse to straighten it, cleared her throat, then walked up the path and rang the doorbell. Above the door, the lintel had the words *Free Church Manse* carved into it. These big houses all had a weird history. She wondered if the ghosts of the old churchmen still haunted the place, frowning austerely at the current inhabitants and their sinful ways.

This place did not make sense as Don Webster's home.

The door opened and a tall, beautiful woman with sharp Middle Eastern features stood there, baby girl on her hip. She had jet-black hair in a rough fringe and deep-blue eyes.

'I'm sorry,' Jenny said, looking around and already backing away. 'I think I have the wrong house.'

The woman narrowed her eyes while the girl gurgled. She had the same black hair as her mum, same eyes too, lucky kid.

'I know who you are,' the woman said.

'Sorry?'

'Jenny Skelf, right? I recognise you from your picture in the papers.'

Great, the paparazzi never took a complimentary shot. The few that Jenny had glanced at, back when she was the talk of the town, made her look ten years older, thirty pounds heavier, and deranged. But then she *had* just killed her murderous ex-husband, so smiling for the camera wasn't her top priority.

'You're in the right place,' the woman said. 'If you're looking for my Donnie.'

Jenny noticed wedding and engagement rings on the woman's finger. So Webster was married to this beauty and had a gorgeous baby daughter. Jenny had never bothered to find out about his home life, had assumed from his actions and demeanour that he lived alone in a man-cave fuck-palace.

'I'm looking for Don Webster,' Jenny said.

'My husband is not in just now,' the woman said slowly. 'But would you like to come in for a moment?'

Jenny shook her head. 'No, just...'

She didn't know how to finish. She'd weaselled Webster's address out of Thomas months ago, when he was vulnerable and depressed and still had access to the police database. She never thought she'd use it, it was just an insurance policy.

But now Webster was attacking Skelf funerals with drones, spraying the mourners with pepper spray and fertiliser. Dorothy had gone to the police but Jenny had zero confidence. Since when did a cop investigating another cop ever turn up anything? The original court case didn't even have a date yet, kicked into the long grass while they 'gathered evidence'. How much gathering did they need to do? Webster had attacked and beaten Thomas and Dorothy, had murdered poor Billie, threatened and coerced other young women into performing sex acts.

'Please,' the woman said. 'I insist.'

'No, I—'

'Come.' The woman took Jenny's elbow, and she let herself be guided through the house and into a large living room. A baby's play gym was set up on the floor and the woman placed the girl on it. She gurgled and swung her little fists at the soft elephant hanging above her.

Jenny remembered Hannah at that age, when Jenny was absolutely besotted, not just with her new daughter but also with Craig, her loving and devoted husband. Nothing would ever separate them, they would always support each other, until death. Well, they got that bit right anyway.

'I'm Lena,' the woman said, waving for Jenny to sit. 'And this little bundle of joy is Maisie.'

Jenny was surprised there wasn't more anger in Lena's voice. From Lena's point of view, the Skelfs were ruining her husband's life. But surely Lena would realise what kind of man her husband was, after even a cursory glance at the evidence in the case. Jenny thought of her own marriage and how that panned out. And she thought of the countless other wives who stood by their husbands while they did despicable things.

She saw a wedding photo on the mantelpiece, Lena and Don Webster a few years ago, Lena even more gorgeous, Webster dashing in a dark kilt. Both of them beaming about the future ahead of them.

She turned to Lena and didn't know where to start.

'Nice home,' she said, feeling sick about how meek her voice sounded.

Lena smiled. 'What you mean is, how the hell does a detective sergeant afford a place like this?'

She was sharper than Jenny had given her credit for. Jenny had made the classic misogynist assumption, that because she was beautiful she must be stupid.

'No.'

Lena held her hands out. 'Not that it's any of your business, but I'm a partner in a law firm and come from a very wealthy family of merchants.'

'Right.'

Lena angled her head. 'Does it surprise you that a man like Donnie would be attracted to a strong, smart, independent woman like me?'

'It surprises me that you're attracted to him, if I'm honest.'

'He's a good man.'

Jenny balled her hands into fists and leaned forward in her seat. Lowered her voice. 'He is absolutely not a good man, and you know it.'

Lena glanced at Maisie on the play mat. 'There's no proof of any of these terrible things he's been accused of.'

'No proof.' Jenny couldn't help raising her voice. 'I was fucking there.'

'So you saw your mother shoot my husband.'

The truth was that Jenny hadn't seen that, had been on another part of Cramond Island when that went down. But she saw the immediate aftermath, Dorothy and Hannah beaten, Thomas half dead.

'I saw Don raping that young girl Ruby, along with those other guys.'

'Ah yes, the itinerant lady who has since moved away from Edinburgh, and who the police can now find no trace of.'

That stuck in Jenny's craw. The police obviously weren't that interested in tracking down a traveller who was a vital witness in the case.

'I saw your statement,' Lena continued, kneeling down to play with the mobile above Maisie's head. The baby gurgled. 'That my Donnie was apparently with three other men, according to this missing girl. One of whom, my good friend Benjamin Low, has succumbed to suicide because of the allegations against him.'

Jenny shook her head and stood up.

'You're not an idiot,' she said. 'There's no way you can believe your husband's side of the story. He killed Billie Rae because she wasn't going to put up with his abuse any longer, she was about to grass him up.'

Lena smiled. 'And where's the evidence for that? As far as I'm aware, forensics didn't find anything that linked my Donnie to that girl's death.'

Jenny tried to keep a lid on her rage. 'You just can't believe him.'

Lena looked at Jenny as if she felt sorry for her. She picked up Maisie and stood, nestled the baby on her shoulder.

'I know all about you,' she said to Jenny, her voice light and airy. 'I read all about you in the newspapers. Just because you made the mistake of marrying a lying, murderous prick, you think all men are the same. You and your ridiculous family have had it in for my Donnie from the start of all this. He's just an honest police officer trying to do his bit to improve life in this city, and you have gone out of your way to ruin his reputation, so much so that I...'

'What?' This could be something Jenny could use.

Lena tickled Maisie's chin then turned to Jenny.

'Let's just say, I'm worried that Donnie might go the same way as Benjamin.'

'You're worried about suicide?' Jenny said. 'With a guy like Don? You're fucking delusional.'

Lena didn't even look at her, was too preoccupied with her daughter. 'I think you should go now.'

25
DOROTHY

She found Brodie at a laptop in the back room amongst the sustainable coffins.

'Hey,' Brodie said, energised. 'Come and check this out.'

He was weirdly upbeat, given everything that was going on. As she got closer, Dorothy smelled alcohol on his breath. She wondered about mentioning it, he was at work, after all, though there were no more funerals to conduct today and no driving to do. Decided to leave it for now, we all have different ways of dealing with stress.

He turned the laptop and showed her. He was on a subreddit page, thousands of members, long threads of conversations that she skimmed, then she saw the name at the top.

'All Biffy Clyro fans,' Brodie said. 'I went on a bunch of forums about our communal-funeral guy. Posted pictures of his tattoos and a few folk recognised them. Some had met him at gigs, said he was a good guy. Nobody has a full name but they all knew him as Ewan.'

He tapped the screen and turned the laptop back towards himself. 'So much love for the guy out there and he didn't even know it.'

'That's kind of sad,' Dorothy said.

Brodie stuck his lip out. 'But beautiful too, right?'

'Yes, beautiful.'

'It's going to be a busy funeral. I posted up the details, loads of people have said they'll come. Should be a great party.'

Dorothy was sweating and her arms ached. This Biffy Clyro song started with strings then muted electric guitar, then a collection of seemingly random staccato stabs of bass and drums. It was all in 4/4, but they began on the second eighth note of the first bar, then switched to the first beat in the second bar, then reversed the order for the next two. It was meant to be unsettling and Dorothy kind of loved that. When the song finally exploded it was powerful, not the kind of thing she was used to drumming, but she enjoyed letting go, opening the hi-hats more than usual, bigger fills, more crash hits on the pull-and-push vibe of the pre-chorus, then opening out for the half-speed chorus. It was glorious. Then back into a staccato middle eight, once more round the houses and they were done.

It was going to be a nightmare to try to teach this to the rest of the band. The timing was bad enough but the chord sequences were complex too. The musicians in The Multiverse were good, but it would be a challenge. But life was about challenges, and it was the least they could do for Ewan.

She looked around the studio in the fading light. She could smell her own sweat, liked that fact because it meant she'd been working. She thought about their new sign outside the house, which said they were undertakers rather than funeral directors. She thought about the comparison to drumming. What she did behind the kit was an undertaking too, she was always working in service of the song, doing what was necessary without attracting attention to herself, serving the greater good of the band. Drummers were the undertakers of music.

She flicked through some of Abi's playlists. The girl sent her new music all the time and Dorothy tried to keep up. The music was getting heavier as Abi got older. Dorothy found a playlist called *Strong Female Character*, a joke phrase they'd shared after Dorothy recommended comedian Fern Brady's memoir to Abi. The playlist was all female-fronted indie rock, mostly American, bands Dorothy had never heard of before like Alvvays, boygenius,

The Linda Lindas and, Dorothy's favourite name, Mannequin Pussy.

She put the playlist on, started drumming to 'Hot Rotten Grass Smell' by a band called Wednesday. It wasn't too taxing but great to thrash along to, the singer moaning then screaming, the band simmering then exploding. Dorothy had plenty of scope to smash the crap out of her kit, not caring about the noise and the neighbours and the mess of the world. So many angry young women out there, and why the hell shouldn't they be? #MeToo had come and gone, but what had changed?

Dorothy thought about all the bullshit flying around them and their house at the moment. She still got whiffs of fertiliser from this morning, despite the best efforts of the cleaning crew.

She thought about Don Webster, walking freely around the city, smiling smugly at all the shit he was throwing at them. She thought of all the abuse he'd meted out to young women like the singer she was listening to now, fronting a band called Bully, livid about the state of the world.

Dorothy thought about Thomas, how she could possibly help him. Then, as if she'd conjured him from thin air, Thomas was standing in the doorway smiling at her. She pulled off her headphones and put down the sticks. Wiped sweat from her forehead with the back of her hand. Thomas stared at her and Dorothy wondered what she looked like, a sweaty septuagenarian hunched over a drumkit, panting heavily and desperate for a drink of water.

'We need to talk,' Thomas said, and a cloud came over his face.

26

HANNAH

She let herself in the front door. The businesses were closed for the day and Indy was tidying her desk, folding her laptop and sticking it in a drawer. Hannah watched her for a moment, the thrill of her body in that suit. They weren't a dressing-up couple, strictly loungewear around their flat, so there was something about seeing her wife in a tight skirt and blouse.

'Hey.'

Indy turned and beamed. 'Hey, babes.'

'Is Brodie about?' Hannah said, glancing at the door to the back of the building.

Indy shook her head. 'Already gone.'

She walked over and kissed Hannah, more than just a peck, touching her hips. Kissed her again.

'Why?' Indy said after a few more. 'Something going on with his case?'

'The weirdest thing,' Hannah said. 'I was following Phoebe's boyfriend—'

Indy grinned. 'You have the strangest job.'

'It's not even really my job.'

'But you love it,' Indy said, 'sneaking around like James Bond. Spycams and shit.'

Hannah laughed. 'For a start, James Bond *never* sneaks around. Have you seen any of those movies?'

Indy shook her head.

'Seriously? How did I never know that about you?'

'When have *you* seen a James Bond movie?'

'They're full of explosions and car chases. He swans about in a tux drawing attention to himself the whole time. It's ridiculous.'

'Aaanyway,' Indy drawled. 'About Brodie?'

'Yeah, I was trailing Zane Underhill, Phoebe's boyfriend.'

'Zane Underhill?'

'Lives in the New Town,' Hannah said, by way of explanation.

'Ah, OK.'

'I followed him up the hill to George Street, where he popped into All Bar One.'

'God.'

'Yeah, he was meeting someone.' Hannah raised her eyebrows. 'Brodie. Just two blokes having a pint.'

'That's very weird.'

'Very. Meeting his ex-girlfriend's boyfriend, what the hell?'

Hannah pictured Webster's face on her phone right after that discovery, thought of telling Indy and decided not to. Indy was the natural worrier of the two of them.

There was a knock on the front door.

Indy and Hannah shared a look then Indy opened the door to two police officers, a woman Hannah recognised at the front, a big lump of meat behind her.

'Griffiths, right?' Hannah said.

Griffiths angled her head. 'And this is PC Parks.'

Even from those few words, Hannah knew this wasn't going to be a pleasant visit.

'Is this about Don Webster?' Hannah pictured the look on his face from earlier, shuddered as she remembered how he'd attacked her a year ago.

'Not exactly,' Griffiths said, looking behind them. 'Mind if we come in?'

Indy let them into the reception area. In the brighter light, Griffiths looked tired. Parks' complexion was ruddy, pockmarked skin on his cheeks, thick hands. Hannah wondered why Griffiths needed back up.

'Is Thomas here?'

'I don't think so,' Hannah said.

Indy nodded at the staircase. 'He's upstairs with Dorothy.'

Hannah frowned. 'What is this about?'

'I think it's best if I speak to Thomas.'

'Did you go and see Webster?' Hannah said. 'What did he have to say?'

Indy touched her shoulder. 'Hannah.'

She shrugged it off. 'He's targeting us, terrorising the bereaved at our funerals.' She could feel her cheeks getting warm. 'I can still smell that shit in my nose from this morning. It's bullying and intimidation.'

Griffiths put out a hand. 'I'm sorry, I need to speak to Thomas.'

She walked upstairs, Parks in her wake, Hannah and Indy behind. At the top of the stairs, Griffiths knocked on the open kitchen door then went in.

Dorothy and Thomas were holding hands, whiskies on the table in front of them. It looked as if Griffiths was interrupting something important. The air in the room was electric, Schrödinger slinking past Hannah's legs to leave.

Dorothy seemed surprised at the sudden mass of people filling her kitchen but Thomas looked as if he'd been expecting them.

'Thomas,' Griffiths said.

'Zara.'

Dorothy stood and walked to Griffiths, glancing at Parks. His presence here was a sign.

'Thomas,' Griffiths said, 'can you come down to the station for a minute, answer some questions?'

Thomas sucked his teeth then pressed his lips together. He didn't seem to know what to do with his hands. 'I don't think so.'

Griffiths glanced at Parks, then back at Thomas. 'Come on, sir. Let's not make this difficult.'

'No need for the sir,' Thomas said. 'I'm retired, remember?'

Dorothy straightened her shoulders. 'What is this about? Webster?'

'This is not about Don Webster,' Griffiths said.

'Then what?'

Griffiths looked at Thomas. 'Do you want to tell her?'

Thomas just sat there, his hands now in fists on the table top. He glanced at Parks.

'OK,' Griffiths said. 'Let's do this the hard way.' She cleared her throat. 'Thomas Olsson, I'm arresting you in connection with the death of Benjamin Low. You are not required—'

'Low?' Hannah said. 'But that was suicide.'

Dorothy was staring at Thomas, who kept his head down. He looked defeated, like all the bullshit of life had got the better of him.

'That's not in question,' Griffiths said to Hannah. 'But some new evidence has come to light.'

'What sort of evidence?' Dorothy said, her eyes still on Thomas.

Griffiths waited again, giving Thomas a chance to speak, but he didn't.

'A good deal of communication between Thomas and Benny,' Griffiths said eventually. 'While the act of suicide is not illegal itself, it is a serious crime to encourage or assist someone in suicide. But you know that, Thomas, don't you?'

Thomas shook his head. 'That's not what I was doing.'

'You shouldn't have been in touch with him at all,' Griffiths said in a low voice. 'Fuck's sake, Thomas.'

Thomas bolted upright from his seat, fists clenched, his chair scraping across the floorboards. He looked like he might try to run for the door, but Parks was standing there, arms folded.

'Thomas?' Dorothy said. 'What is this?'

Thomas didn't look at her, just let himself be led out of the room by Griffiths, who threw an apologetic look around the women then left, Parks close behind.

27

JENNY

She didn't want this to be a big deal but the flutter in her chest told her different. She lay in bed, diffuse morning light through the curtain, shadows of the trees outside dancing across the wall. She looked at Archie, still asleep in her bed. After last night.

They'd been at a local Greek place for dinner when Jenny got the call from Hannah about Thomas. They paid up and hurried back to the house, where Dorothy was just heading out to the station. With no news and nothing happening, Hannah and Indy had headed home to their flat in Argyle Place. Leaving Jenny and Archie in the kitchen, both kicking with adrenaline and nowhere to put it. So, a couple of drinks later, they'd kissed then come to bed. Archie was gentle with her, and she couldn't remember the last time she'd had sex that wasn't angry or self-destructive. Sex that was about mutual pleasure, that felt relaxed, as if they knew their way around each other's bodies already. Archie was a larger guy than she was used to, but he moved with consideration and grace.

She didn't know what this was and she dreaded him waking up. She was about to ease herself from under the covers when his eyes opened and he smiled.

'Hey,' he said.

'Hey.'

'So, last night.'

Jenny was a rabbit in the headlights, panic rising in her chest. She tried to quell her instinct to run. 'Yeah.'

She kissed him quickly and got out of bed, self-conscious in her underwear. It was stupid, after last night, but she felt like a teenage girl in the school changing room.

'Mum will need me this morning,' she said.

He nodded. 'I should get going.'

He started getting dressed, and Jenny felt crushed by embarrassment. But she also didn't want him to leave.

She hadn't heard Dorothy coming back last night, wondered if she'd spent all night at the station.

'I don't know what...'

There was so much she didn't know, about Dorothy and Thomas, about this thing with Archie.

Archie had his jeans and shirt on, was pulling socks on his feet and grinning.

'Jenny, it's OK. This doesn't have to be...'

Such a handsome face, such kind eyes. A genuinely good person, she didn't deserve that. And she didn't want to spoil their friendship.

'This can be anything you want,' Archie said, putting his shoes on. 'Or nothing.'

'OK.' Jenny threw on joggers and an old Napier Uni sweatshirt, flicked her hair into a bun, glanced in the mirror. She was surprised to see herself smiling, looking contented. She hadn't felt like that in a long time. Not bad for a woman approaching fifty who'd been through what she had.

Archie walked past her to the bedroom door and she clumsily kissed him, felt the reassuring touch of his lips, his beard, the firmness of his arm under her fingers. He was a solid man, and she liked that.

They were both in the hall when Dorothy came out of her bedroom in a kimono and smiled at them.

Jenny felt like a teenager again, sneaking around her parents' house.

'Join us for breakfast, Archie,' Dorothy said, and headed for the kitchen.

Jenny looked at him and they shared a grin and a shrug, then followed Dorothy.

'Mum, sit down, I can do this,' Jenny said, watching Dorothy fuss with the toaster and kettle, look in the fridge. 'Mum.'

Dorothy seemed half asleep, blinked too much. 'What?'

'Sit down,' Jenny said, pulling out a chair.

She sat opposite and Archie took over on the breakfast front.

'Tell us about Thomas,' Jenny said.

She heard the front door open and close then footsteps, recognised the youthful leaps of Hannah and Indy. Then they appeared in the kitchen, Schrödinger flouncing in behind.

'There's nothing to tell.' Dorothy picked up Schrödinger and stroked him.

Jenny looked from her to Hannah sitting at the table, then Indy helping Archie with cereal and bowls, milk and cranberry juice.

Dorothy buried her nose in the scruff of Schrödinger's neck for a moment then straightened up.

'I went to the station and waited in reception. Eventually Griffiths came out and told me to go home. She said that Thomas had waived the right to a solicitor and he was staying in the cells overnight. I asked if I could see him but she said no. She wouldn't tell me anything. So I came home.'

Her voice caught in her throat and her eyes were wet. Jenny went round the table and hugged her awkwardly as she sat with Schrödinger on her lap. She felt Dorothy's breath heaving against her chest. This was crazy. Thomas was the most dependable of all of them, the one they relied on. Or he had been until a year ago. But he'd been an empty shell since the attack. Maybe not so empty after all, given what he was accused of.

Dorothy took a deep breath and Jenny released her, sat down.

'Tell me about something else,' she said, looking around the room, stopping on Archie for a long moment, then at Jenny. 'Take my mind off it.'

Jenny looked at the whiteboards. She'd made a big song and dance about the Fultons and Conways, and now she felt like a fool. With Webster's other appearances, it was obvious the drone attacks were him. She got up and put a line through all the old names on the board, then wrote *Don Webster* and *Benny Low*.

Hannah checked the doorway to the kitchen before speaking. 'I saw Brodie meeting Phoebe's boyfriend for a drink yesterday.'

Jenny frowned. 'His ex's new guy? Why?'

'That's what I need to ask him. And I popped a gravecam at Jack's headstone.' She glanced at her phone. 'The only hits so far have been horny bunnies. And one other.' She looked at Dorothy. 'It was Webster.'

Indy frowned. 'What?'

'He knew the camera was there,' Hannah said to Dorothy. 'So he must've followed me.'

Dorothy shook her head. 'He's trying his best to get to us.'

'Well, it's working,' Indy said.

'No,' Dorothy said firmly. 'We can't let him win.'

She breathed heavily then looked at the whiteboard again.

'I met two Ukrainian soldiers yesterday,' she said. 'Looking for Yana. Comrades of her husband.'

Jenny shared a look with Hannah. Mum was avoiding the hard stuff, and maybe they needed to let her do that for now.

'Do you think they have something to do with her going missing?' Hannah said.

'I have no idea. I tried to speak to the kids, but I need to get them on their own. They definitely know something.'

The way she spoke, she sounded half present, her mind obviously chewing over what Thomas might have done.

'Maybe I should speak to them,' Jenny said. 'If you're not up to it.'

Dorothy waved this away as Archie and Indy started putting food on the table – cereal, toast, fruit, cold meat and cheese, some leftover curry and roti.

'No,' she said. 'I need to keep occupied. Besides, I already know them. If you barge in, I doubt they'll talk to you.'

Jenny rankled at that. 'I wouldn't *barge in*, Mum.'

But she remembered speaking to Webster's wife yesterday, what was that if not barging in like the old Jenny?

'I'm sorry,' Dorothy said, then Jenny felt bad.

Archie cleared his throat. 'Besides, Jen, we have the funeral today, remember? Our first mushroom suit.'

Jenny looked at the food on the table, imagined that all this had been grown and fertilised by the remains of loved ones. What better way to celebrate the deceased than by consuming them, making them a part of you. She looked around the busy kitchen, realised that these people were already a part of her.

28

HANNAH

She left Indy at reception and went to the business end of the building. Her phone buzzed again and she flinched. Apart from Webster's face that one time, all her other gravecam alerts had been rabbits snuffling around the headstones, tails bobbing. She swiped her phone but it wasn't rabbits or Webster, instead it was the groundskeeper walking past with a rake, just a couple of seconds of footage.

She walked to the prep room, where Mum and Archie were getting the deceased ready for today's funeral. A woman called Clover Snowball, which was an impossibly good name. Clover had researched and bought a mushroom suit for her natural burial after she was diagnosed with inoperable liver cancer.

The mushroom suit that Archie and Jenny were currently struggling to get Clover into was made of biodegradable cotton and laced with spores from a mushroom which was expert at metabolising toxins. It looked like thermal underwear covered in lightning strikes, white zig-zag lines across Clover's body. The mushrooms would accelerate her body's decomposition and producing toxin-free, nutrient-rich soil.

Hannah watched Archie and Jenny carefully manipulate Clover into the suit. There was something intimate about it, and between Mum and Archie too. The way they moved around each other, touching shoulders and hips and hands and not realising. Hannah wondered about that.

She walked on past Archie's office to the garage, where Brodie was washing the hearse. It was a silver Mercedes, more modern than typical black ones, but it showed up dirt more quickly.

The garage door was open to the garden and Hannah saw the wind phone in the corner flanked by hedges. She'd mostly used it to speak to Grandpa, gone four and a half years now, and it felt like she'd never got enough time with him. He'd dedicated himself to the business and had less time for his family as a result. This work was intense and took you over, so sometimes Hannah needed space from all the death.

'Hey,' she said to Brodie.

He looked up and grinned. 'Hi.' He held a fat yellow sponge soaked in soapy water in his fist, was running it over the back windows. He was in a hoodie and joggers, wet patches all over him. 'I could use a hand if you're not busy?'

She took another sponge and soaked it from the bucket, ran it over the roof, scrubbing at some hardened bird shit.

'Crazy about Thomas, right?' Brodie said.

'Yeah.'

'How's Dorothy coping?'

Brodie had been there on Cramond Island a year ago. He fought Webster in that abandoned building, distracted him enough that Dorothy got the gun, shot Webster in self-defence. Hannah was there too. They already had this history together, this bond.

'We've all been through a lot.'

'For sure.'

Hannah thought about the first time she ever saw him, when he asked for help. She wanted to help then, and wanted to help now.

'I set up the camera at Jack's grave,' she said.

Brodie had some foam on his cheek. He wiped it away and placed his sponge on the roof of the hearse.

'And?'

'Nothing yet,' Hannah said. 'Just a lot of rabbits. But I did some other work on the case too.'

He waited.

'I followed Zane Underhill.'

He blinked a few times, nodded to himself, rested his hands on the roof. 'Yeah?'

Hannah put her hands out, one with the sponge still in it, waiting for an explanation.

He coughed, picked up his sponge.

'Brodie, for God's sake. You asked me to look into this. So I followed your ex's boyfriend and saw him having a cosy pint with you. What's that about?'

Brodie put the sponge down again, stared at Hannah for a long time, and she held his gaze. Eventually his face fell.

'I don't know how to explain it,' he said. 'It sounds too weird.'

'Try me.'

Brodie leaned against the car, a wet line soaking his hoodie. 'Phoebe and I split up because of what happened with Jack, right?'

Hannah nodded.

'Apparently it happens a lot. A couple lose a child and they can't stand to look at each other. Some people said that because Jack was stillborn, it shouldn't matter so much. That made it worse, to hear that kind of shit. Everyone supported Phoebe, she was the one who lost a son in childbirth. I had no one. No parents, no friends. Everyone we knew was her family and friends, all they cared about was her.'

He blinked again, sighed.

'When we broke up, I felt we were alone *together*, you know what I mean? We'd suffered the same loss, felt the same thing. We were grieving for Jack, we would always have that in common. Then I found out she was seeing someone else, had put it all behind her. What the fuck? That's when I *really* felt lost.' He shook his head. 'I got jealous. But worse, I just couldn't understand. I found out about this guy from her socials. A handsome, rich kid called Zane, for fuck's sake. What the hell were they doing together? Had Phoebe even told him about Jack? About our past?'

'What did you do?'

Brodie shrugged. 'It's easy to get to know someone. I joined his gym. Started chatting. I knew what he was into, so I made myself into someone he would like. I hoped he'd be a fucking prick, making comments about girls at the gym, cheating on her maybe, an arrogant, entitled dickhead.'

'But?'

'He's a nice guy, that's the worst thing.'

'So you're *friends* now?'

Brodie laughed and it sounded like a cry of despair. 'I don't have any friends, you know? And we get on.'

Hannah shook her head. 'Brodie, this is crazy. How does Phoebe not know?'

'I use a fake name.'

'How do you think this is going to end, exactly?'

'Why does it have to end?'

'You don't think Zane will want you to meet his girlfriend? That Phoebe might be interested in her boyfriend's sudden new gym buddy?'

Brodie looked her in the eye. 'I told you it sounded weird.'

29

DOROTHY

She stood in the garden with her eyes closed, concentrating on her other senses. Sparrows chattered in the trees, the trill of their wings at the feeders. A dog barked in Bruntsfield Links, the shouts of young children in the park. Beyond that, the traffic rumble of Bruntsfield Road in the distance. The breeze on her forehead, sunshine warm on her face. The smell of cut grass from a neighbour's garden, a mulchy odour.

She opened her eyes, heard a yelp from one of the kids in the park. Sounded like they were playing rounders. They would be on top of Jim, his ashes scattered on the level grass, the rest of the park undulating as if the plague dead buried five hundred years ago were trying to rise up again. She'd tasted some of Jim's ashes when he was cremated, mixed their atoms so that he could never leave her. But she'd replaced him with Thomas in her bed within a couple of years. She'd thought Thomas was a good man, so hard to find at any age, let alone in her eighth decade.

She walked to the wind phone, stared at the wood grain, flecks of rust on the metal handle, imperfections in the weathered white paint. She stepped inside the phone box and lifted the receiver, held it to her face.

'I'm sorry, Jim, I owe you an apology. It seems like a dream that we were together for fifty years. How can that be possible, when I'm still the teenage girl who met you on Pismo Beach. You were so pale, your Scottish body used to rain and gloom. You looked ridiculous on the beach, squinting in the sunshine. But such a beautiful smile. Such an easy way with yourself, as if you already knew who you were. All the other boys I met back then were exactly that, just little boys, no sense of community, connection, empathy. But I could see all that in you. You were a good man, determined, focused.

'I thought I'd found those qualities again in Thomas. You could've been friends, or that's what I used to think. I don't know now. They say you should stand by your friends through thick and thin. But what if they've done something that makes you see them in a new light. What if Thomas is not the man I thought he was?'

She laughed self-consciously and raised a hand to her mouth.

'I'm a cheeky bitch talking to my dead husband about my boy-friend. But there's no one else I can speak to about this, no one else whose opinion I value. You were always such a good judge of character, Jim, and I miss that. I feel lost without you.'

She waited for an answer. Closed her eyes and listened, the outside world muffled by the phone box. She pressed the handset against her ear until it was hot, then removed it and stared at it.

Eventually she put the phone down and left.

She checked the time then walked out of the garden and through the park. She'd been right about the kids playing rounders on Jim's ashes. She went across the Meadows and into Quartermile. Came round the corner and spotted Thomas sitting at a table outside the Söderberg Pavilion. This wasn't their usual Söderberg and she wondered if that was deliberate on his part, to put her off her stride. The café was in the shadow of an office block, opposite a Malaysian restaurant and a bubble-tea place. Fewer people around, a sterile feel to the development despite a handful of the old hospital buildings surviving.

He saw her approach and stood, kissed her then sat. He looked around for a waitress, avoiding her eye.

'Thomas.'

He stopped and looked at her.

'Are you all right?' she said. 'What happened at the station?'

He looked around again, pretending he wanted to order something.

'Thomas, talk to me. I waited for hours at St Leonard's.'

'There was no need to do that.'

'I know there was no *need*, but I care about you, I wanted to be there.'

He avoided her gaze some more until she grew frustrated.

'For God's sake, Thomas, just tell me what happened.'

'I was questioned about the suicide of Benny Low, released on bail this morning.'

She reached for his hand but he turned to look for a server again.

'Can't get a damn coffee,' he said.

'Christ almighty.'

Thomas's chest rose and fell and he blinked too much.

'Why did they question you, *exactly*?' Dorothy said.

He shrugged, which annoyed her more than anything.

'Thomas, you were a cop for decades. Don't pretend you don't know what's going on.'

He placed his hands under his legs, sat forward. 'They think I encouraged him to kill himself.'

'Why would they think that?'

Thomas's eyes darted around, settled on the sugar bowl. 'Emails.'

'What sort of emails?'

'Nothing, really.'

'You sent him emails, then, they're not making that up?'

He waited a long time before answering. 'I was in touch with him.'

'Christ.' Dorothy stared at him. 'Why?'

Thomas shook his head. 'I just wanted him to think about what he'd done.'

Dorothy leaned forward. 'But you must've known that would jeopardise the case against him and Webster. We can't be in contact, we're key witnesses against them.'

Thomas pressed his lips together.

Dorothy felt sick. '*Did* you encourage him to kill himself?'

He waited too long to answer. 'No.'

'Shit,' Dorothy said. 'I can't believe this is happening.'

'It's not happening to you,' he said, anger in his voice.

She stared at him. 'Don't you dare. This involves all of us.'

He looked around and she felt a shift inside her. He was acting pathetically, PTSD or not, and he was endangering them.

'Have you been in touch with Webster as well?' she said.

His silence killed her.

'How could you?' She waited for an answer but knew he didn't have one. 'Thomas?'

Eventually he sat back and looked her in the eye. 'I'm breaking up with you.'

30

JENNY

Jenny felt like a teenager, wondering what a boy thought of her. She had to quell the urge to talk at Archie, fill the space between them in the hearse as Archie negotiated Southside traffic then headed round Salisbury Crags and through Holyrood Park. This was a longer route to Seafield, but it avoided all the roadworks in town.

She looked at him as they turned left at Jock's Lodge, headed through Lochend then Restalrig. He was so comfortable in silence, and she kind of resented that. So comfortable in his own skin too. He was a long way from the lost soul Dorothy took under her wing fourteen years ago. Jenny wasn't involved in the business back then, had her own shit to deal with. But she'd known about Archie, the guy with Cotard's Syndrome who Dorothy found hanging around cemeteries and funerals because he thought he was dead. He always said Dorothy had saved him.

She wanted to talk to him about last night, but simultaneously she did not want to have that conversation. She remembered him being tender and tentative to begin with, then more assured.

When she'd been together with Craig, they existed in a kind of banter bubble, swapping quips and one-liners, slagging off people they saw around them as if they were superior to it all, living beyond the ordinary. She realised now that was one of the reasons he was able to behave the way he did, because he thought he *was* above it all. In comparison, Archie was definitely one of the people, part of the teeming mass of humanity. Maybe it would be nice to spend a little time swimming in those waters.

She eventually succumbed to the need to speak, waffling about the traffic and the weather.

'What?' Jenny said, catching a look on his face.

'You're so funny when you're nervous.'

'I'm not nervous.'

Archie shrugged. 'That was two minutes of the most boring chit-chat I've ever heard.'

Her laughter broke the tension. 'Fuck you.'

'That's what you did last night.'

Jenny put her head in her hands. 'Oh my God.'

Archie slowed at a junction, stopped at the lights.

'Look, we're both grown-ups,' Archie said. 'Last night was fun.'

Jenny raised her eyebrows. 'You make it sound like go-karting or something.'

'I mean, it wasn't as much fun as go-karting.'

She punched him on the arm. 'Fuck you, I was great.'

He glanced at her as he put the car in gear. 'You were.'

His suddenly seriousness made her blush and she had to cover it with a joke. 'You were not bad yourself.'

Archie stuck out his bottom lip. 'I practise a lot on my own.'

'Yeah, I thought that.'

'Are you calling me a wanker?'

'If the cock fits.'

She looked at him, smiling. Part of her worried that they would shrug this off, chalk it up to a mistake. She didn't want that. Rather, she wasn't sure what she wanted, but she did want to have options. She hated in books when characters knew what they wanted all the time. In real life, who has a fucking clue?

They reached Seafield Memorial Woods, Jenny smiling at the sign standing in front of a large patch of dirt and grass, a few graves, and thousands of saplings recently planted by schoolkids. Trust Dorothy to arrange that, so community minded, such a part of things. *Be more Dorothy*, Jenny thought for the millionth time. But maybe there was room for a sarcastic and confused middle-aged cow as well.

They drove the hearse into the waiting area and parked. The

cemetery still needed so much work, yet people were keen to be buried here, to have their remains disposed of environmentally. But they needed parking spaces that weren't just muddy puddles, a waiting-room building in case of terrible weather, a toilet for old folk who might get caught short.

Jenny looked at the thin grass, the saplings, the graves. One day this would be a mighty forest but for now it was just scrubby land next to the sewage works.

There were some cars parked in the clearing, more on the road outside. People were gathered in small groups, some smoking weed. Clover Snowball worked for a youth charity which helped with everything from literacy and numeracy to finding homes, outdoor activities, music and art classes.

Jenny looked at Clover's body in the back of the hearse. She was in her black mushroom suit, lines of spores embedded in the material.

Archie went to speak to the bereaved, came back with Clover's two sisters, who helped Archie and Jenny slide Clover out of the hearse. She was on a metal tray, no coffin, arms folded across her chest. They walked with her to the open grave, pile of muddy earth next to it, and placed her alongside.

The sisters were both sturdy women like Clover, from Northumbrian farming stock. Along with Archie, they tied a hemp rope around her ankles, another under and through her armpits. They laid the ropes down.

Jenny looked around. Bright-blue sky, fresh wind off the sea, traffic in the distance. She breathed in, couldn't smell the sewage plant. A hundred people were at Clover's grave now, all in bright clothes as she'd requested. The presence of a lot of younger people gave the crowd a nervous energy, they weren't as used to death as the older ones.

One of the sisters acted as a humanist celebrant, said beautiful things about Clover, how she'd dedicated her life to the service of others. Jenny thought about that. She'd been a self-centred and self-destructive bitch for so long, but at least now she was aware of it. She was trying to help others, right? That's what being an undertaker was.

The sister finished talking then someone cued up 'Dancing Queen' by ABBA on their phone, played through a smart speaker, those piano trills incongruous in a big open graveyard by the sea.

There was no mention of the mushroom suit and Jenny wondered how Clover had come by this thing. She wasn't a campaigner or an environmentalist. But maybe that was even better, that the information was just out there now.

The sisters took a rope at each end of Clover's body and lowered her into the ground, their muscles straining as they took the weight. But they managed it smoothly, placing the ropes in the hole alongside her. They would decompose along with her, the suit, all of it. Feeding fungi, detoxifying her body, creating life. Continuing on into the future. Wasn't that what we all wanted?

Jenny watched the sisters throw handfuls of dirt on top of Clover and hoped that she could keep going, keep helping. Keep living.

31

HANNAH

Hannah sat in the kitchen of the big house with Indy, their bellies full of a mushroom frittata that Indy had just made. She'd told Indy over lunch about Brodie and his friendship with Zane.

'How does he think that's going to end?' Indy said.

'That's what I said.'

'And what's it got to do with him hearing voices?'

Hannah shrugged.

Schrödinger mooched over to their table in search of scraps but they had clean plates. Hannah cuddled him, even if he didn't want it.

'And what's hearing voices got to do with Jack's grave?' Indy said.

'I. Don't. Know.' She said it with a smile in her voice, but the case hadn't coalesced yet, she couldn't get a handle on it.

A noise started upstairs, Dorothy drumming. Sharp thumps at seemingly random moments, interspersed with silence. This went on for a while then eventually it whipped into a full-on thrash.

Schrödinger made for the door then downstairs, away from the disturbance.

Indy raised her eyebrows. 'She's getting something out of her system.'

'What did Thomas say earlier?' Hannah said.

'She never said. But it seems insane that Thomas would've done what he's accused of.'

'I don't know. He's been lost since last year. And he refused to see a counsellor.'

Whatever song Dorothy was playing had a break, more weird off-time stabs, then full-on rock again.

'At least Gran has that therapy,' Hannah said, pointing at the ceiling.

She felt her phone buzz and pulled it out, opened the gravecam app. On the screen were an older couple, on their knees in front of Jack's grave, placing an assortment of toys against the headstone.

Hannah recognised them, showed the screen to Indy.

'Phoebe's parents,' she said.

They both watched as the couple bowed their heads.

'Are they praying?' Indy said.

There was an audio track with the video but it was windy today, Hannah could only hear the noise of the breeze.

The couple sat so still in front of the grave that the footage ended. It was motion activated, and if it didn't get a signal for a few moments, it stopped recording.

Hannah looked at Indy, then at the clock on the wall. It was about ten minutes from here to there. 'Fancy a drive over?'

Indy shook her head. 'Someone has to be at reception.'

Hannah kissed her harder than she needed to then ran downstairs and grabbed the keys, went outside and into the van.

Her phone buzzed again when she was driving and she checked it. They were still there, shifting positions. Were they meditating? They still weren't speaking, or she couldn't hear anything, at least. She could analyse the audio later.

She arrived at Craigmillar Cemetery, drove down the central lane, turned at the far car park and headed back, pulling in a short distance away with a view of the couple facing the grave. She looked out of the window, then at her phone, trying to work this out.

Amanda Sweet took a piece of paper out of her pocket and read it out loud. A poem about babies who die before their time. There was a whole part of the internet where you could get this sort of thing.

Hannah watched them, wondering where Phoebe was. Brodie had been upset when Jack died because everyone rallied around her as the mother, and he felt left out. But what about everyone else who'd been expecting to welcome a new life into the world? Grandparents' grief must be tough, they're expecting a new generation to play with, to make them feel young again, to pass on to whatever crumbs of knowledge they might have. Then it just doesn't happen. They have their own grief, and have to watch their child grieving too.

Amanda pulled a small backpack from behind her and unzipped it. She took out a blanket, laid it out and began putting stuff on top, sandwiches, cans of juice, crisps, apples, a flask of something hot. She poured two little cups from the flask and they both blew on their drinks.

Hannah was reminded of the Victorian trend of spending a Sunday afternoon in the graveyard catching up with your loved ones, socialising with other mourners at the neighbouring graves. Not such a bad idea, and something that other cultures were much better at. How did people here get so detached from the idea of spending time with their dead relatives?

Hannah watched the Sweets munch their sandwiches and sip tea as they sat at the graveside of their first grandchild, who they never got a chance to meet.

She wondered about her dad's ashes. They'd resomated him this time last year and handed over his remains to his sister Stella, the last remaining relative he had apart from Hannah. Hannah had wanted nothing more to do with him. He'd murdered her friend Mel, pregnant with his baby, then tried to kill Jenny and Dorothy when he was found out. So Hannah was shocked to find tears in her eyes as she thought of him. He didn't deserve that, he'd never cried over what he did to her and the others. That was the logical attitude, of course, but tears rolled down her cheeks all the same.

32

DOROTHY

She got funny looks from passers-by as she walked down Bruntsfield Place. A woman in her seventies, eyes narrowed in concentration, drumming with her palms on her thighs, trying to nail down the timing of that damned Biffy Clyro song. She turned the volume up in her earbuds to combat the noise of taxis and vans rolling past. Went back to the start of the song, waited for the first blast of noise on the guitar. She almost had it, just a little more practice.

She checked her watch as she turned the corner, heading towards Bruntsfield Primary School at the bottom of the road. It was a big, old, pink sandstone building, imposing turrets and balconies on the upper floors that were surely a health and safety nightmare these days. As she reached the gates, she spotted the entrances either side of the main building, *Girls* and *Boys* etched in stone above.

Kids were already milling around in the tarmac playground, mucking about on the few colourful benches and games painted on the ground. Dorothy had checked the school's website for times, knew that the youngest children got out a little earlier than the older kids.

She got looks from waiting parents as she went back and started listening to the song again, determined it wasn't going to beat her. She thought about Ewan in the fridge back at the house. Homeless, friendless, no one who really knew him. She couldn't believe it was so easy to fall through the cracks. He must be someone's son, someone's brother, a cousin or nephew.

She thought about Thomas, felt her body tense. How dare he act as if there was nothing between them? Part of her wanted to help him with what he was going through, so obviously in need of therapy, maybe meds. Anything to shake him out of this insane spiral. But at the same time, he might be responsible for Benny Low's death. He'd targeted a vulnerable person and manipulated him, punished him, destroyed him.

Even the fact that Thomas had been in contact with Low and Webster was ridiculous. Dorothy didn't have huge faith in the police, but you had to try to work within the system, otherwise this was the result. More people dead in a world full of death. The whole legal case in jeopardy. And now all this shit with Webster retaliating with intimidation. Archie had handed over the drones to Griffiths after confirming they were decommissioned police ones with the serial numbers scraped off. Dorothy just had to trust that Griffiths would do her job.

She realised she'd completely ignored the whole Biffy song in her earbuds and cursed, drawing stares from two young mums with their arms folded next to her.

Then she spotted Olena coming out of the main entrance with three other girls, all of them skipping and laughing. She got to the school gates and looked around, and Dorothy caught her eye.

'Olena.' Dorothy didn't know how to play this or what she was even doing here. But the kids were the key to finding Yana, she felt that in her bones.

The girl frowned but came towards her.

One of the mums next to Dorothy frowned too. It was obvious from Dorothy's tentative call and Olena's body language that they weren't related.

'Excuse me,' the woman said. 'Who are you?'

Dorothy put on her nicest old-lady smile. 'I'm a friend of Olena's Nana Veronika. She asked me to pick up her and Roman.'

The use of Veronika's and the kids' names made the woman relax her shoulders. She looked at Olena for confirmation.

'Hi,' Olena said to Dorothy, which was as far as she would commit.

'Where's your brother?' Dorothy said, smiling at the woman and manoeuvring Olena away from her.

Olena shrugged.

Dorothy crouched down and lowered her voice. 'We don't have much time, Olena. Why did you call me the other night?'

Olena looked at her shoes. They were pretty new, and Dorothy wondered if Camilla Curzon had paid for them.

'Olena, if there's something I need to know about your mum, you have to tell me. Now.' Dorothy's voice sounded harsh and she didn't like that. She breathed deeply. She was hunkering down and her knees hurt. 'Olena, you said she was safe. What do you know?'

She held the girl's shoulders, maybe too tightly. But she had to solve this, had to have some control in her life, and this was the only thing she could control, a puzzle that needed to be solved.

'Olena.'

There were tears in the girl's eyes and Dorothy realised she was out of order, none of this was good. She'd turned up here to hassle a little girl, for God's sake, what was wrong with her?

'Hey.'

Dorothy looked up to see Oliver, Camilla's teenage boy, walking towards them with Roman. They were both angry.

'What the hell are you doing?' Oliver said.

Dorothy straightened up.

Roman went to Olena, gave her a hug, threw a stare Dorothy's way.

'Just chatting,' Dorothy said, sounding pathetic.

'It looked like you were harassing her.'

Oliver's voice was loud and Dorothy felt the other mums and dads in the street staring at them.

'She knows something,' Dorothy said.

Oliver pushed his chest out. 'Leave them alone. If I see you near them again without permission, I'll call the police.'

It was crazy being chastised by a teenage boy but Dorothy deserved it.

She turned and walked away from the school, tears in her eyes, wondering what the hell was happening to her.

33
JENNY

Jenny wandered around the kitchen while the kettle boiled. She stopped at the funeral whiteboard and wiped off Clover Snowball's name. Looked at the other dead people, thought about their lives, whether they had anyone who loved them. One read *Ewan* and had *CF #13* underneath, the next communal funeral. Brodie was usually pretty good at rustling up a congregation, but she wondered if his eye was on the ball, given everything that Hannah had said about him.

The kettle clicked off and she made a mug of tea, realised there was no milk in the fridge. Turned when she heard Schrödinger's claws on the floor behind her. It was a strange feeling, being here in the kitchen alone. Archie, Brodie and Indy were running things downstairs. That felt comforting, knowing there were three people the Skelfs could count on. She thought about being with Archie last night. She didn't regret it at all, but it was complicated. She'd had her heart broken so badly in the past, couldn't bear it happening again. He'd been her friend all the way through her appalling behaviour, he knew things about her that she didn't want to know about herself.

She sighed, grabbed her jacket and went downstairs.

'Off to get milk,' she said to Indy at reception. 'Need anything?'

'Chocolate,' Indy said. 'Surprise me.'

She went out and along the drive, glanced at the wind phone, thought about all the ghosts hanging around waiting for a call. Went through the gateposts to the road, heading towards Sainsbury's. Birds chirping in the trees, little kids mucking about after school, a fresh breeze on the air.

Halfway along Bruntsfield Terrace she heard a car door open and close behind her. Then footsteps. Someone going into one of the houses, she assumed. But the steps got louder and faster, then someone grabbed her arm, hard. She felt something sharp press against the back of her jacket.

She turned. Don Webster with his face close to hers.

She looked down. A knife.

He smiled at her. 'Fancy a drink?'

She tried to pull away, felt the blade go through her clothes, touch her skin. She looked around, no one nearby. He tightened his grip on her arm and hauled her across the road to the park, doubled back to walk through the Links.

She thought about screaming out, wondered about the knife at her back. He wouldn't do it, wouldn't stab her in broad daylight in the middle of Edinburgh. But there was something in his face, his manic energy, his nervous sweat. She'd seen people at the end of their ropes before, knew that energy. She had a thick scar on her belly from the last time. She had a sudden flash of Craig's face as he slid a knife into her, like it gave him some relief from his torture.

'You've lost your fucking mind,' she said.

He shook his head, looking around, making sure they didn't go near anyone else in the park. 'It's amazing what you can get away with, I've discovered.'

She tried to yank her arm away, but he had it tight.

'If you don't join me for a wee tipple,' he said, 'I will come back here when you're not around and it'll be your mum or daughter next.'

He dragged her across the putting green into The Golf Tavern, an ancient place that was now a sports bar, empty this time of day. They went to the bar, the knife hidden from view by Webster's body pressed close to hers. She could shout out at any time, get the barmaid to call the police, but she knew what he said was true, he would continue to harass the Skelfs if she broke free. This wouldn't be over.

He ordered two double gin and tonics and made her pick them up, take them to a dark booth at the back facing away from the bar, and pushed in behind her. Only then did he ease the pressure of the knife against her. He'd boxed her in.

'Cheers,' he said, clinking the glasses together.

She stared at him. Slicked-back black hair, gym body in a tight T-shirt under his leather jacket. Danger in his blue eyes.

She glanced at her drink, condensation dripping down the outside, making a ring on the wooden table. She wanted it so bad. Her crutch under stress was booze, always had been.

'You realise you're implicating yourself in all sorts of shit.' She nodded at the knife he was still holding under the table. 'Plus committing a bunch of new crimes.'

She tried to sound cocky, but he was someone who'd killed, tortured and raped. He hadn't been convicted yet, but she knew. All the Skelfs knew. Thomas knew. It was a disgrace that he was allowed to be here, doing this. Sometimes, though, life was fucking disgraceful.

She tried to think. She had her phone in her pocket, if she could work out how to unlock it, record him. There must be CCTV in the pub, but what would that prove?

Webster shook his head. 'I'm not implicated in anything. I just came from St Leonard's. Griffiths is a fucking joke. She thinks she can pin something on me? They have nothing and they know it.'

'What about the drones?'

He laughed. 'What about them? Could've come from any-where.'

'They're ex-police.'

'There are hundreds of decommissioned ones out there. They get into the hands of all sorts of people.'

She watched him sip his gin and looked at her own glass. Blinked heavily then picked it up, felt the buzz of it on her lips, the tingle down her throat, so fucking good.

'That's it,' he said, and the tone of his voice made her feel dirty.

She closed her eyes for a moment, imagined she was somewhere nice with Archie, then opened them and lowered her drink.

'What's this about?' She tried to keep her voice level.

He smiled at her. 'Like you don't fucking know.'

She put on a stupid face as if to say, *explain it to me, then*.

He moved close and she smelled his breath. 'You came to my fucking home. You spoke to my wife.'

'Lovely baby,' Jenny said.

He threw a fist into her side, which made her double over, gasping for breath.

He glanced behind at the bar, no one was watching.

'Let me make this as clear as humanly fucking possible. If you mess with my family again in any way, I will fucking kill you, and I will make it long and painful.'

Jenny eventually got her breath back, looked at her gin.

'I can get to you anytime,' Webster said. 'Any of you. Your mum, your daughter. The police won't save you. Nothing will save you.'

Jenny swallowed hard. 'You're going down for the stuff at Cramond. There's nothing you can do about that.'

Webster looked happy that she'd spoken back to him. 'You have no idea how this works, do you? I have the best solicitor in the country. Witnesses and evidence go missing all the time. Cutbacks at Police Scotland mean that the force is not what it used to be. Mistakes get made. Why do you think I'm out on bail? Even if it goes to trial, which I doubt, there's no way a jury will find a nice upstanding cop like me guilty.'

He was grandstanding and he loved it. She wondered about getting his knife off him, burying it deep in his guts.

He finished his gin and slammed it on the table, pressed the knife against her body again, and she flinched despite herself.

'Just remember,' he said softly. 'I can get you Skelfs anytime I want. Understand?'

34

DOROTHY

She was just about to turn into Bruntsfield Terrace when her phone buzzed. She got it out and saw a text message from a number she didn't recognise:

Please follow us

She checked the number against her recent calls, it was Olena.

She looked around, thought about what to do. She'd left them and Oliver about five minutes ago.

Then another buzz:

In Sainsbury's rn, follow us after

She turned and walked back past the record shop and pharmacy, had to skip onto the road at the busy bus stop, saw the Sainsbury's on the corner, which was swarming with schoolkids. She stopped ten yards away, making sure she could see the entrance.

She waited a few minutes, wondered if she'd missed them. Was about to step towards the shop when she saw Olena, Roman and Oliver coming out, the girl clutching a bag of Haribo in her fist, popping a couple into her mouth, offering the bag to the other two.

Dorothy remembered something. The first time she met the kids, they'd come into the house in Merchiston on their own, without Oliver. Yet here he was, picking them up.

They turned to head towards the house in Merchiston, walked for a while, slaloming between other pedestrians, then stopping before the bend in the road to cross to the other side. Dorothy turned her face away while they looked down the road, stared at the window of the bagel place she was facing. Waited a few moments then turned back. They were across the road with their backs to her again.

She wondered if Olena had spotted her. If Roman was in on it. What Oliver's role was in all this.

She followed them into Merchiston Place. This looked like a non-starter, they were just heading back to the house with Veronika and Camilla.

Then they turned into Merchiston Park, heading north. The pavements were less busy so she left more space between her and them, crossed over the road but kept them in her sights. The houses here were the same big, expensive places to begin with, but as they headed further along the road the detached houses were replaced by terraces, then tenements by the time they got to the other end of the street.

They turned right into a mews, then left, Dorothy losing them for a bit before catching them round the corner. She noticed Olena lagging behind the others for a moment, glancing round. Oliver turned back too and Dorothy darted behind a parked van and waited, her heart thudding in her chest.

She waited a long time then came out and couldn't see them anywhere. She hurried to the end of the street, past newer tenements, then it opened out to the Union Canal, Boroughmuir High School and new apartment blocks in orange and purple across the water. This used to be the brewery district, now all shiny and new. The city was always reinventing itself.

She looked both ways, spotted Oliver getting his keys out, opening the stairwell door at a tenement along the way, Roman and Olena following inside. Olena looked back, bag of sweets still in her hand, and this time Dorothy thought the girl saw her.

She waited, wondering what to do. Across the road, a handful of pupils from the secondary school were hanging around in the park. A woman walked past with her sausage dog on a lead.

Dorothy's phone buzzed.

Second floor

She walked to the doorway she'd seen them go into. Checked the buzzers. Curzon on there. She'd presumed Oliver was still living with his mum up the road. Seemed a bit odd for him to have a flat so close to his family home. But they clearly had plenty of money, and property in Edinburgh was the only investment guaranteed to make you wealthier.

She wondered whether she should press the buzzer. Sometimes it pays to just be direct. Her finger was hovering over the button when her phone went again.

Window

She stepped back as far as she could, pressed her back against the low barrier by the canal. Not much protection against little kids going into the water. She looked up, squinted her eyes, the sun from the west glinting off the windows. Examined the second floor. Checked the smaller windows first, then slowly scanned along to the bay window on the corner, the more expensive property, nice views over the water and beyond.

She waited, shading her eyes. Eventually she saw Olena standing there, putting more Haribo in her mouth, phone in her other hand. She smiled at Dorothy then spoke to someone else back in the room. She pointed out of the window to something in the distance, as if she wanted them to come and look.

Dorothy waited a few moments.

Then Olena was joined at the window by Yana, her arm around Oliver as they looked at whatever Olena was pretending to show them. Oliver kissed Yana on the cheek and ruffled Olena's hair.

Olena glanced at Dorothy then left the window.

Dorothy watched as Oliver and Yana turned to each other and kissed, hard, heavy, just like two people in love.

35

HANNAH

Standing outside the Sweets' house on Innes Crescent, she noticed the solar panels on the roof, that the grass of the lawn hadn't bedded in yet. She turned and looked at the fields between here and the bypass, how long until they were filled with similar houses?

She was about to ring the bell when Phoebe opened the door with a black staffie pulling on the end of its lead. She took in Hannah on the doorstep while the dog panted.

'What do you want?' Phoebe shifted her weight to account for the dog's pull.

'Are your parents in?'

'Why do you want to speak to them?'

Hannah didn't want to get into it here. 'Are they?'

'They're not here, and I'm just heading out with Tyson.'

Hannah made a face.

Phoebe rolled her eyes. 'I know, my dad named him.'

Hannah looked around the empty street. 'Can I come with you?'

'Why?'

'Just for a chat. Some fresh air.' Hannah felt stupid as she spoke.

Phoebe shrugged. 'If you can keep up.'

She closed the door and headed west, Hannah scuttling alongside.

They left the housing estate and turned along the main road out of town, then cut across a field and emerged at a path with a sign: *Loanhead Railway Path*.

'I didn't know this place existed,' Hannah said, looking round.

Phoebe shrugged again. 'Edinburgh has loads of secrets.'

They headed west, Phoebe keeping Tyson on the lead as cyclists sped past. They passed through a tunnel covered in graffiti that ran under the bypass, the rumble of traffic overhead drowning Hannah's thoughts. Out the other side, she saw the back end of an industrial estate on the left, skip hire, joiners, lots of low metal huts. Woodland on the right.

Phoebe took a path into the trees, let Tyson off the lead, the sudden quiet of the woods a shock after the noise of the road behind them.

'So, what's this about?' Phoebe said.

Tyson sniffed and peed, his stocky body bouncing down the path between ash and elm.

Hannah didn't know how to answer. 'It's a bit difficult.'

'What does that mean?'

They emerged at a pond, coots and moorhens stalking the reeds, two swans with a pair of cygnets gliding on the murky water.

Hannah saw another sign: *Straiton Pond Nature Reserve, Strictly No Fishing, Motor Vehicles, Firearms or Fires.* Beneath *Firearms* someone had written in pen *Why not?* Hannah had lived in Edinburgh her whole life but she still only knew a fraction of the city. She had a sudden sense that she would never understand it completely, felt a mix of dissatisfaction and relief about that, wondered if she would spend her life here or head off around the world with Indy, maybe never come back. But this city would always be home, it was where the Skelfs had lived and died. It was where they'd said goodbye to the dead for over a century and that meant something.

Phoebe stopped at the edge of the pond. 'Why did you ask about Mum and Dad earlier?'

Hannah pictured them picnicking at Jack's grave, wondered if Phoebe knew.

'Do you know where they are?'

'In town at the shops.'

Hannah glanced at Phoebe, high ponytail, neat jumper and jeans, all put together. 'What if I told you that earlier today they were having a picnic at Jack's grave.'

Phoebe tried to hide it but she was surprised. 'At Craigmillar?' She watched Tyson sniffing around some bushes, crows calling in warning from higher up. She shook her head. 'What makes you think that?'

'I have footage,' Hannah said. 'I can show you if you like.'

She took her phone from her pocket.

Phoebe looked at it like it was an alien artefact. 'You were spying on them?'

'I set up a camera at the grave.'

Phoebe stared at her. 'You're spying on *Jack*?'

'It's not like that.' But really it *was* like that.

'Who gave you permission?'

Hannah's scalp itched, the tickle of guilt up her spine. 'Technically, I don't need permission to—'

'He's my fucking son.'

Tyson turned and watched them both, tail pointing at the ground, ears pinned back. Hannah wondered what sort of damage a dog like that could do. She imagined Tyson digging up a grave.

'And Brodie's,' she said eventually.

Phoebe shook her head. 'Don't mention him to me.'

She started walking, Hannah followed.

One of the swans on the water flapped its wings at a duck getting too close to the cygnets. Just another parent protecting her young, natural as breathing.

'Why not?'

Phoebe played with the hook of the dog lead, clicking it open and closed with her fingers. 'Nothing.'

'Phoebe, last time I spoke to you, you said you still cared about him.'

'That was before...'

'Before what?'

They went into some trees then out the other side. Somewhere ahead of them was the soft rush of traffic.

Phoebe stopped and looked around for the dog. 'Tyson?'

She clicked the lead. The dog emerged from the undergrowth, stopping at scents here and there.

Phoebe turned to Hannah. 'Did you know?'

'Know what?'

Phoebe stared at her. 'You did, didn't you?'

'Phoebe, I don't know what you're talking about.'

Quacks from the ducks on the pond behind them.

'That creep made up an alias and befriended my boyfriend. Met him at the gym. How fucked up is that?'

'Oh.'

Phoebe's eyes went wide. 'So you *did* know.'

Hannah held her hands out as Phoebe started walking again.

'I didn't know when we spoke the other day,' Hannah said. 'I only just found out.'

'What do you mean, found out? Brodie didn't tell you?'

'No.'

Phoebe looked Hannah up and down.

'Wait,' she said. 'You were following Zane, weren't you?'

She waited for a reply, but Hannah just looked away.

'My God, you two are total creeps. What's wrong with you both? Zane is a good guy who has nothing to do with my past life, OK? Nothing to do with Jack. First Brodie stalks him, then you follow him. Then you're planting hidden cameras on my dead son's grave. What's the matter with you?'

She snorted in disgust and clicked her fingers at Tyson, who came towards them.

'And you have the brass neck to say my mum and dad are weird for wanting to spend time with their grandson. You should be ashamed.'

She attached the lead to Tyson's collar, waited to see if Hannah would say anything, but she stayed silent.

Phoebe turned and walked away, her ponytail bouncing in the sunshine, the noise of the bypass traffic suddenly a roar in Hannah's ears.

36

JENNY

She sat in the van watching the entrance to St Leonard's police station, fingers gripping the steering wheel. The adrenaline of her encounter with Webster earlier had worn off, leaving her shaking and incredulous that he'd had the nerve to pull a knife on her in broad daylight in the middle of fucking Edinburgh. But what he said was correct, you could get away with anything if you just had the balls to do it.

Webster hadn't specifically told her not to go to the police. Jenny didn't want to make this a formal complaint, that would only make things worse. But she needed someone to take this seriously. So she was here to speak to Griffiths off the record. Jenny had worked outside the law before, but that felt like a different version of her. She was trying so hard not to be the old Jenny. Sitting in The Golf Tavern with Webster's knife against her skin, she'd felt all the old rage and impotence she'd experienced with Craig. She kept trying to move on but her past kept sucking her back in.

She waited. Eventually she spotted Griffiths leaving alongside another female officer. She hardly recognised her with her hair down, a smile on her face and the top two buttons on her blouse unbuttoned.

Jenny stepped from the van and walked across the road. Griffiths said goodbye to the other officer, turned and spotted her. Her face dropped.

'I'm off duty,' she said as Jenny caught up with her.

'I know,' Jenny said. 'But I need a quick word.'

'Tomorrow.'

'This can't wait.'

'It'll have to.'

'Webster came to see me.'

Griffiths stared at her. Jenny put the palms of her hands together in a plead. Griffiths looked around, back at the station, up the road. Sighed.

'The High Dive,' she said nodding at the bar on the corner of Montague Street. 'You're buying.'

It was a hipster pizza place and bar, distressed frontage, uncomfortable stools, jazzy soul in the background. Jenny ordered two pornstar martinis while Griffiths texted someone. Jenny got paranoid, wondered if she was contacting Webster, if he would saunter through the door in a moment, run that knife through her belly right where her scar already was. Her stomach muscles hadn't knitted together so strongly after last time, it was the easiest way into her intestines, her vital organs. Maybe wiggle the blade about in there, eviscerate the pancreas, her liver.

They settled with the drinks, Jenny appreciating the hit and fizz of hers, Griffiths smacking her lips.

'Cheers,' Jenny said deadpan.

'So,' Griffiths said. 'Webster.'

Jenny looked around. The place was filling up, the tall and icy-cool waitress taking orders.

'He pulled a knife on me,' Jenny said.

Griffiths spluttered her cocktail. 'You need to report this.'

'What's the point? He said he could get to us at any time. Me, Mum, Hannah. And he's a hundred percent correct. What are the police going to do?'

'Well, nothing if you don't report it.'

'And nothing if I do.'

Griffiths gave her a look over the rim of her glass. 'Jenny, I know you don't have any time for the police.'

'Do you blame me?'

To her credit, Griffiths seemed to consider this.

Jenny waved her drink, got a little on her fingers, sticky and sweet as she sucked it. 'Webster hasn't even been chucked off the force yet. He's a murderer and a rapist, now he's intimidating my family, pulling knives in broad daylight. And long before him, the cops let my ex-husband escape from a prison van, never found him for years. I had to do that myself.'

Griffiths angled her head, her blonde hair swinging in a way Jenny didn't like, too cute. 'That would've technically been the prison service who let Craig escape, not the police.'

'Same thing. And don't bother saying "it's not".'

Griffiths held a finger up. 'It's not.'

Jenny sipped her drink, fuck it tasted good.

Griffiths drank too. 'Look, if you don't report this, we can't go and talk to him.'

'If you go and talk to him, he'll just come back and do the same to Hannah or Mum.'

Griffiths avoided her gaze for a moment, she knew that was true.

Jenny leaned in. 'Zara, you know him, he's your colleague. You know what he's like. He's absolutely convinced he's going to get away with all this.'

Griffiths cleared her throat, looked around, as if about to tell a secret. 'I do know what he's like, OK? That's why I wanted this investigation, to get him properly. But it has to be done by the book, a hundred percent, otherwise he'll just walk free. The odds are already stacked in his favour. The traveller witnesses disappeared. Low is dead, so we can't put pressure on him to give Webster up. We still don't know who the others involved were. But this stuff with the drones, this could fuck him up. The fact he's showing his hand means he's worried.'

She stopped to sip her martini, her eyes alive. She was two-thirds through hers, Jenny almost finished.

'But the knife thing is weird,' Griffiths said. 'Why be so obvious? I mean, the drone attacks are deniable, but turning up outside your house with a knife. There's probably CCTV we can pull. Why would he take a chance like that?'

Jenny swilled the dregs of her drink, tipped the last drops into her mouth.

Griffiths narrowed her eyes. 'What did you do?'

Jenny sighed. 'I went to his house. You were getting nowhere. We reported the drone stuff and nothing happened. He can't be allowed to get away with this.'

'What happened?'

Jenny pressed her lips together. 'He wasn't there.'

'But?'

'I spoke to his wife, Lena. Met their baby.'

'Christ.'

'How can a bastard like that have a smart wife, a beautiful daughter and a big house?'

'What did you say to her?'

'Nothing,' Jenny said, trying to remember. 'But she's sticking by him.'

'What do you expect? He's a charming motherfucker, and he's her husband. Some women are like that.'

'If I could only make her see what he's really like.'

Griffiths finished her martini and clunked the glass down too hard on the bar. 'Do not go back there.'

Jenny raised her hands. 'Why not? It's not as if the police are doing anything.'

'Stay away from Webster,' Griffiths said. 'Please, for the love of God.'

Jenny stood up, arched her back. The waitress drifted past with pizzas and Jenny felt suddenly hungry. 'I can't promise that.'

37

DOROTHY

It was impossible to focus on the gig. They were playing in the main area of the Out of the Blue Drill Hall, a community arts hub that was also a focus for refugee and immigrant support. The gig was a benefit for Medical Aid for Palestinians. None of the women in the choir had family in Gaza, but they knew what it was like to be under fire, to flee your home in fear of your life. The empathy that ran through the band, especially the choir members, made Dorothy's heart swell.

There were around two hundred people in the crowd, they'd be sure to raise a decent amount of money. It might not feel like they were making a difference, but Dorothy had learned in the undertaking business that even a tiny effort could have a huge effect on someone's wellbeing. Most of the audience were friends and family of the band members, plus some interested and kind-hearted other folk, but that just made it a more communal experience. A crowd that was on their side, willing them to play well and enjoy themselves, unlike some of the indifferent audiences at trendy indie shows Dorothy had been to over the years supporting her drum students for their first gigs.

But she couldn't get into it. They were playing 'Woman' by Karen O from the Yeah Yeah Yeahs, a pop romp with a retro Motown double-time snare. But all Dorothy could think about was Yana and Oliver, groping each other at the window of Oliver's flat like lovestruck teenagers. Oliver *was* a teenager, of course, but Yana must be over thirty.

Dorothy hadn't confronted her earlier, she needed time to think it over. Yana had run away from her mother-in-law but kept in touch with the kids. How long was that sustainable? Veronika didn't strike Dorothy as the kind of woman who would take kindly to her widowed daughter-in-law cavorting with a Scottish teenager. How long was it since Fedir had died? Dorothy had been in the same situation after Jim's death. She'd been friends with Thomas before that, then afterwards it gradually became more serious, much deeper, like love. Now she didn't know what to think. She pictured Thomas outside Söderberg, breaking up with her like *they* were the teenagers. But she still worried about him. His behaviour with Benny Low, the death cleaning, all of it.

The Karen O song was a good fit for The Multiverse, a call-and-response chorus, high energy but melodic too. They reached the middle eight breakdown, Dorothy doing the classic Phil Spector beat on the toms, rolling around the kit, splashing on the cymbals for effect. Then they were back up, a last romp to the end of the song.

The crowd loved it and Dorothy smiled at the grinning faces on stage. She looked around the dark hall, glass-paned roof and metal beams bouncing too much treble back into the room. A balcony along one wall and artists' studios in small side rooms, a tiny, volunteer-run bar at the back, Mike on the sound desk, everyone chipping in for free. The woman bouncer on the door, the guy selling home baking and handmade T-shirts, bassist Zack's flatmate Frankie doing a great job with the lights. All of it counted, every tiny interaction of your life mattered.

They started into 'S.O.S.' by Abba. They had an unwritten rule that at least a couple of the tunes in their set had to be crowd pleasers, songs that a majority would know. The band members came from such diverse backgrounds – different countries, religions, generations, musical tastes – that they were insanely eclectic. But everyone knew Abba, right? And the song was appropriate for a charity fundraiser, everyone needed help sometimes.

Dorothy watched the choir sing with beaming smiles, reflected in the audience. She hammered on the toms, building to the huge singalong chorus. So much joy in the room.

They finished and went straight into that Young Fathers song they'd rehearsed, Dorothy grinning at Gillian as she grappled with the two floor toms to the side. It was great to drum with another person, something primeval about it. The song was a joyous rattle and yell, angry and uplifting at the same time, simple on the drums but all the better for that, Dorothy finally managing to slip her mind into the space between the beats, disappear into the flow state, the place where the ego dissolved and there was only the beat of your heart and the company of others.

But the moment was over too quick. The crowd were cheering and sweating and grinning, and Dorothy and The Multiverse were all doing likewise. They had one more song, 'Transatlanticism' by Death Cab for Cutie, an epic singalong that started with simple piano chords by Gillian, a plaintive melody, sparse guitar. The drums didn't come in until three minutes in, and Dorothy sat and waited. She'd always tried to be a part of something, to help others. Sometimes she got it wrong but she always *attempted* to have empathy. She tried to see things from the point of view of Yana and Oliver, Veronika and Camilla. She tried to understand Thomas, as well as Griffiths, Webster and Low, their victims Billie and Ruby. All the countless dead across the city, the family and friends left behind, the ashes scattered in the soil creating another layer of the city's consciousness. And she tried to put herself in the shoes of Jenny, Hannah and Indy, Brodie and Archie. And Jim.

The choir were singing loud, the drums and guitars building and swelling, blossoming like a flower in the sun, the crowd urging the band onwards to something unattainable, something always just out of reach. But the point of life was reaching for it all the same, in 4/4 time together, calling to God or whatever you believed in, connecting to each other as if your lives depended on it.

38

HANNAH

The opulence of Dean Cemetery in the early-morning sunshine made Hannah feel uncomfortable. Giant trees loomed over extravagant graves, this was one of Edinburgh's oldest graveyards, used by the rich and famous for the last few hundred years. It was just up the hill from Dean Village, the Water of Leith running to the south, the Gallery of Modern Art over the wall. It was unusual to do a burial here in the twenty-first century, especially in the old part of the cemetery, but Audrey Abercorn was being laid in her family plot on top of a bunch of Abercorns, ranging from philanthropists to slave owners.

Beyond the congregation, Hannah could see monoliths and pyramids, giant crosses and mausoleums, weeping angels and chisel-chinned busts surrounded by Greek columns. All for what? These lord provosts and barons, earls and politicians, explorers and major-generals were all still dead. Their legacies didn't live on just because they had giant phallic monuments. They were worm food like everyone else.

Hannah frowned at Audrey's coffin, non-sustainable wood and burnished brass going into the ground was not the kind of thing she approved of. But the Skelfs had apparently been burying Abercorns for almost a century, and Dorothy had made an exception, though she'd still insisted that Audrey wasn't embalmed.

Audrey was ninety-three when she didn't wake up one morning, a pretty great way to die, Hannah thought. If only we could all have such a peaceful ending. She thought about some of the deaths she'd encountered, how shocking they'd been. She'd had enough of that to last a lifetime and she was only twenty-four.

Hannah had driven the hearse here. They'd come the long way through the West End from the Skelf house, avoided traffic carnage on Lothian Road. It wouldn't do to get stuck in a jam in the hearse, or pranged by a bus driver not watching where he was going. Hannah wondered how many times a Skelf hearse had been involved in an accident over the years.

She was standing a respectful distance from the mourners, next to the hearse parked on the gravel path. Jenny and Archie walked towards her from the grave, where they'd been helping to carry Audrey's coffin. Hannah watched them closely, there was something in their body language she couldn't quite untangle. Had something happened? Had they fallen out? She hoped not, her mum had been so *normal* recently, it was a huge relief.

Archie went to check over the funeral car and Jenny smiled at Hannah, though there was something in her eyes.

'Nice day for it,' Hannah said, waving a hand at the manicured lawn, the woodpigeons and ravens in the trees. Just another funeral in a world of death.

Jenny smiled then pressed her lips together, look at the treetops.

'You OK?' Hannah said carefully.

'Just had a flashback to the funeral at Saughton. That drone.'

Hannah had the same suddenly, picturing the drone flying in the open doors at the chapel. She caught a stink of fertiliser in her nostrils. She felt her body tense and realised this was the intended effect, that the Skelfs should be traumatised.

'Are we a hundred percent sure this is all Don Webster?' Hannah said.

Jenny let out a sarcastic laugh. 'Oh, we're sure.'

Hannah took her in for a moment, Jenny's shoulders stiff under her funeral suit. 'Did something happen?'

'Like what?'

'I don't know. You tell me.'

'Nothing happened. Except I spoke to Griffiths about Webster and she's doing nothing.'

'I'm sure she'll get there.'

Jenny raised her eyebrows. 'You think?'

Silence between them, the words of the minister standing over Audrey's grave, asking everyone to bow their heads. Hannah usually did that out of respect, despite the fact she wasn't into religion, but this time she kept her head up, watching the sky for drones. But all she saw was a sharp-beaked bird at the top of a pine tree, maybe a hawk. Plenty of hunting in a grassy space like this, and the river below.

'Did you see Gran this morning?' Hannah said.

Jenny shook her head. 'She was still in bed when I left.'

'Were you at the gig last night?'

'No, had other stuff to do.'

Did Hannah imagine it, or did Jenny glance at Archie leaning against the Mercedes? 'Pretty bad form that neither of us went.'

Jenny shrugged. 'How's Brodie's thing going?'

Hannah wasn't sure how to answer. 'Weird.'

'Weird how?'

'I'm not sure yet.'

She'd spent last night going over it with Indy, not really getting anywhere. She was still shaken by Phoebe's explosion yesterday, mostly because she was right, Hannah *was* out of order to record her parents at her son's grave. What was she thinking? She'd got so used to the idea of being a private investigator that she'd forgotten about people's feelings.

Jenny touched Hannah's arm, and Hannah was surprised to feel a shiver run through her.

'Have you heard of panpsychism?' Hannah said.

She was wary, her mum was the most sceptical person she knew. She hated anything that smelled of new-age mumbo-jumbo.

'No.'

Over at the graveside, some of Audrey's relatives were taking the strain on the ropes, lowering the coffin into the ground.

'It's the idea that consciousness is baked into everything,' Hannah said. 'Like, at a molecular level. There's some mathematical basis for it, apparently.'

Jenny looked at Hannah for a long time, a smile coming over her face.

'What?' Hannah said, punching her arm.

'I love how my daughter is sometimes a total mystery to me,' Jenny said, shaking her head. 'The way your brain works.'

'I'm not saying it's true, it's just an idea.'

Jenny laughed, then covered her mouth.

Audrey Abercorn's daughters threw dirt onto her coffin, dabbed at their noses with tissues.

Jenny fixed Hannah with a stare. 'I love you, Hannah Skelf.'

She didn't wait for a response, just walked towards the mourners.

Hannah watched her go, then spoke under her breath. 'Who are you, and what have you done with my mum?'

39

JENNY

'I need to talk to you,' Jenny said.

Archie paused, about to take a bite of pizza. 'That sounds ominous.'

Jenny looked round. Söderberg had been a Skelfs haunt for years, but Jenny always had reservations. Dorothy liked people-watching from these outdoor tables, and Hannah and Indy treated this place like a second home, but deep in her heart Jenny liked greasy spoons, places that still had a hint of old Edinburgh about them. She was a no-nonsense girl, her father's daughter. All that spiritual stuff Mum went on about, all the mind-bending science Hannah loved, those things didn't speak to her. She was a full fry-up, gin-and-tonic, basic bitch and she knew it.

She realised she still hadn't replied to Archie, frown lines on his forehead.

'No, nothing like that,' she said.

'Oh,' he said, finally taking a bite. A little smudge of sauce in his beard, which Jenny pointed out. It felt weird being this comfortable with someone, she wasn't used to it.

Archie finished chewing and wiped his mouth with a napkin. 'Because I meant what I said, this thing...' He waved at the pair of them. 'It can be whatever you want.'

She took his hand across the table and he seemed shocked by this. Jenny felt renewed energy moving through her today. The thing with Webster yesterday, then Griffiths, it felt like she now had permission. Permission to be herself, to get things done.

'You know I've been through a lot,' Jenny said.

Archie didn't speak, just stared at Jenny's hand on top of his.

'But you've been there,' she said. 'Through all of it. Never demanding anything, never judging. This thing.'

She dug the netsuke from her pocket. The fox was rubbed smooth in places, between the animal's ears, along its back, its front paws. It had been her version of rosary beads since he'd carved it for her.

'This is the best present I ever got.' She was surprised at the emotion in her own voice.

Archie shook his head.

She squeezed his hand. 'Honestly, I'm not kidding.'

He stared at her, then the fox.

'It reminded me of you,' she said. 'That you were there. That you've always been there. You gave it to me at the exact moment I needed something like that. When I was in the darkest hole. When I thought all men were bastards and I was done. When I was fucking and drinking and punching my way into oblivion. It was just this beautiful little piece of wood, but you made it because you cared. I can't even tell you what that meant. What it means.'

Archie nodded. She loved that about him, that he didn't just jump in.

She sat back. 'I've come to realise that I was always drawn to psychos, unhealthy bullshit. Therapy didn't fix that. You did. Time did. *This* did.'

She held the netsuke up and kissed it melodramatically, undercutting everything she'd just said because she was mortified at being so open and vulnerable.

Silence sat easy between them for a moment.

'So,' Archie said. 'What *did* you want to talk about?'

Jenny put the netsuke away, hesitated.

'Don Webster pulled a knife on me yesterday,' she said quietly.

She glanced at two students walking down Middle Meadow Walk, Asian girls in heavy puffa jackets, laughing and smiling, big glasses, neat backpacks, living their best lives.

She turned back to Archie, anger in his eyes.

'And you're just telling me now?' he said.

'It's no big deal.'

He shook his head. 'Don't do that, Jen, don't pretend it's nothing. You don't have to be that person with me.'

She ran her tongue around the inside of her mouth, chewed her cheek. 'It was just a warning, to show he could intimidate us. It didn't work.'

'Did you tell Dorothy or Hannah?'

She looked away, her eyes following a skateboarder heading down the slope towards the park.

'Jen,' Archie said. 'You have to tell them.'

'No, I don't.'

'They're your family,' Archie said, voice trembling. 'What I would give for…' He cleared his throat, didn't finish that sentence.

The Skelfs had buried his mother a few years ago in Binning Memorial Wood. Jenny had watched him dig the hole. Felt the rain on her cheeks. Hadn't in a million years imagined she would be here with him, like this. How easy it was to be blind to what was right in front of you.

'And the police?' Archie said, his voice more level.

'I spoke to Griffiths.' She didn't mention it was off the record. There was only so much idiotic truth she could admit to in one day.

'And?'

'She's looking into it.'

Archie stared at her.

She wanted to tell him she was going after Webster, that she was going to attend Benny Low's memorial service tomorrow and face him. But she didn't speak in case he tried to talk her out of it.

40

DOROTHY

Dorothy stood at the tenement entrance and looked at the buzzers. Curzon. She pressed and waited. Nothing for a long time. Pressed again then stepped back and looked at the corner window where she'd seen Oliver and Yana yesterday. Maybe she was imagining it, but she thought she saw the edge of a curtain shiver.

She looked behind her, over the canal to the school, a few older girls wandering out. Turned back to the door, tried a third time. Waited for the crackle of life from the intercom, but nothing.

She wasn't even sure what she was doing here, but she had to do something. She couldn't talk to Camilla or Veronika until she'd spoken to Yana. And she didn't want to interrogate the kids any more.

She pressed two buzzers on the third floor and someone came on the line quickly, an older female voice.

'Hello?'

'Delivery for Curzon on the second floor, just need to leave it on their doorstep.'

A pause while the woman considered it. Dorothy had put on her nicest old-lady voice.

The door unlocked with a click and Dorothy pushed it open, went upstairs. The stairwell was well kept, bikes padlocked at the bottom of the railing, flowers and boots outside some doors.

She got to the second floor and stood outside Oliver's door. Rang the doorbell, lifted the letterbox. Nothing to see inside, a coatrack on the wall, a painting she couldn't make out, some men's shoes.

'He's not in.' This was the woman from the intercom, leaning over the banister from the floor above, heavy-knit cardigan pulled tight. With the light from the skylight behind her she looked like a visiting angel, wispy white hair, bony hands on the rail.

Dorothy took a few steps towards her. 'Any idea where he is?'

'Hospital, I presume.'

'Why would he be in hospital?'

The woman peered at her like an inquisitive bird. She was maybe only ten years older than Dorothy but had the energy of a wizened tribe elder. Dorothy used to feel young, even a few years ago, but that was being overtaken by the weight of her years. Her body was slower in yoga, ached more, took longer to recover from everything. There was the psychological weight too – Thomas, Webster, all the deception and lies and violence and death.

'Who are you?' the woman said.

'I'm Dorothy, a friend of Camilla, his mum.'

The woman stuck her bottom lip out. 'Does that mean his mother doesn't know what's happened?'

Dorothy looked confused, laid it on thick. 'I don't think she does. I spoke to her earlier and she said I should pop in and see the boy, as I was passing.'

The woman tutted. 'She should've been informed.'

'What?'

'Those two big men yesterday.'

Dorothy breathed deeply. 'What about them?'

'Disgusting what they did.'

'*What?*'

The woman looked both ways as if about to reveal a secret.

'I heard a commotion, came out and there were two brutes beating him up, right on his doorstep.'

Dorothy looked at the door, noticed stains on the welcome mat, maybe blood.

'They were twice his size,' the woman said. 'I was scared they were going to kill him.'

Bohdan and Marko, Fedir's comrades. Presumably they found out about Oliver and Yana.

'I called the police and an ambulance,' the woman said. 'Told the bullies they were coming, so they left him lying there. The police didn't come for hours. The ambulance took ages too. What a world.'

'Was he OK?'

The woman shrugged. 'He could speak. Said he would be in touch with his mum, let her know. Obviously he hasn't.'

Presumably because he had a secret to keep.

'What about the woman?' Dorothy said.

'His fancy-woman, you mean?' The woman shook her head. 'I haven't seen her since yesterday.'

'And they took Oliver to hospital?'

The woman nodded. 'Terrible business, just terrible.'

❧

She bustled into the ward pretending to be Oliver's grandmother. It wasn't hard, just act like you know what you're doing. It was a secret Dorothy had only learned late in life, and she regretted all the wasted time being deferential and thinking she should stay in her lane.

Oliver was in the first bed in the ward, head bandaged, nose broken, eyes swollen and bruised. He had a cast on one arm, his bare chest purple and red with welts and bruises. He was breathing shallowly, eyes closed, hands gripping the sheets like he was holding on for his life.

'Oliver.'

His fists clenched but his eyes stayed shut. He cleared his throat and a hand went to his chest. He opened his eyes and looked confused. Eventually recognition crossed his face.

'You. From the school yesterday.'

'What happened, Oliver?'

He coughed and gripped his chest again. 'Broken ribs.'

'I'm sorry.'

He shook his head, blinked slowly. 'Is Mum here?'

'No.'

'Good. She can't know about this.'

Dorothy took him in. He was just a kid, really. His curly hair poking out from under his head bandage made him look like a sad clown. He wasn't built for this sort of thing.

'I spoke to your neighbour,' Dorothy said. 'I know what happened.'

Oliver started crying, breath shaking.

'It's OK,' Dorothy said. 'It's going to be OK.'

Oliver pressed his lips together.

'I presume this is about Yana,' Dorothy said.

Oliver glanced at her then looked down the ward. Three old men, various states of disrepair. Was this what Dorothy had to look forward to? Was this how we all ended, in a room full of dying strangers?

'I don't know what you're talking about.'

Dorothy looked at him, his eyes still wet, and wanted to hug him.

'I saw you with her,' Dorothy said. 'I know.'

He lowered his head. 'I don't...'

'Where is she, Oliver?'

He started crying again, which made him cough, and he gripped his ribs in agony, pressed a button on the bed control panel.

A young nurse arrived, pink hair, stern face, tattoos of dragons on her forearms.

'You need to leave,' she said to Dorothy.

41

HANNAH

She wasn't sure why she was here except she needed to think. And she loved listening to Rachel Tanaka talk, something about her mix of intellectualism and charisma made Hannah, and everyone else in the lecture theatre, want to be in her company. She thought about last year, how she'd become obsessed with a retired astronaut, how she was drawn to older, prestigious women. It was about the confidence and authority these people had, something she lacked. She felt kind of lost in her life at the moment, the PhD behind her and nothing in front of her, and she didn't know what to do with herself. She was reluctant to dedicate herself to the family business, could she handle all that death and grief for the rest of her life? She'd suffered depression and anxiety as a teenager, which wasn't that long ago. She'd been medicated but gradually weened herself off, but it was always in the back of her mind, and maybe working in the death industry was bad for her mental health.

She wondered about Brodie, if Dorothy had done the right thing bringing him into the Skelf fold. He'd just suffered the most intense grief, and to be suddenly thrown into undertaking, maybe it had sent him off the deep end. Hannah was seriously considering that Brodie had tried to dig up Jack himself, driven by the boy's voice in his mind. Grief can destroy you in infinite ways.

Rachel was talking about more theories of consciousness to a rapt audience of students. Hannah loved this environment, the dedication to ideas and how we lived our lives, how the mind works, how we can explain who we are. But she was massively out of her depth here. She longed for some simple astrophysics, something she had a background knowledge in. Talk of super-massive black holes, cosmic strings, exoplanets and nebulae seem esoteric to most people, but these were real things, albeit on an outlandish scale. However this stuff, the workings of the mind, seemed so abstract and out of reach. Rachel spoke about Global Network Theory, which tried to explain how the mind worked. Then Higher-Order Theories. Hannah couldn't get her head around it all. Rachel was talking now about a recent neuro-science experiment.

'In the study, participants could freely decide if they wanted to press a button with their right or left hand,' she said. 'Using a brain scanner to monitor patterns of activity, the researchers could predict which hand the participant would choose up to seven seconds *before* the participant was aware of the decision. So it seems that decision-making is largely an unconscious process. What we think of as consciousness is only the tip of the iceberg. Some have even suggested this has implications for freewill.'

Seven seconds. Hannah thought about Brodie's unconscious. About the voices in his head. In Rachel Tanaka's head. And ap-parently in one out of ten people walking down the street. There are a hundred billion neurons in a human brain, and a hundred trillion synaptic connections. That was more than all the stars in the Milky Way. It was impossible to think about all the ways the brain can work, all the ways we consciously or unconsciously make decisions, our gut reactions.

How can we ever understand our motivations if even our con-scious minds can't know?

All these mathematical theories of consciousness, thousands of research papers adding up to the fact that we don't know what we're doing and we don't know why we're doing it. You might as well say everything is conscious, the light switch on the wall, the slide on Rachel's presentation, the cloud outside the window, the dirt under Hannah's fingernails. We don't know what conscious-ness is, how it happens, what it's even for. Why not think of the whole universe as alive? It was better than the alternative, that it was a dead, lifeless place.

She made a decision, got up quietly from the back of the lecture theatre and left.

❦

She found Brodie in the chapel, stacking chairs and putting them in the corner. They were so busy these days, Hannah didn't even know whose funeral this was. The resomator in the other corner was humming, the noise of pressurised water jets coming from inside the machine. They'd considered draping something over the shiny chrome finish so as not to draw attention to it, but had all agreed that went against their ethos of being open and direct about death.

Hannah was sure she could still smell the fertiliser from the attack the other day. The patio doors were closed and Schrödinger was mooching outside in the garden, pausing to stare at a flower bed, following the flight of two sparrows along the top of the hedge.

'Hey,' Hannah said, just as Brodie had finished with the chairs.

'Hey.'

Hannah joined him at the resomator, placed a hand against the metal drum. It was a little warm and she knew that the temperature inside was a hundred and fifty degrees Celsius. What of this dead person's consciousness, where did it go? If consciousness was in everything, in every atom, quark and electron, eventually this person would be scattered across the universe. Would those atoms retain a memory of what it was like to be them? Did that mean that everyone on the planet was one big brain?

'Are you OK?' Brodie said.

Hannah looked through the small observation window at the front of the resomator.

'Who's this?'

'Cristina Iglesias,' Brodie said. 'She ran a plant shop in Dalry. Leukaemia. It was a lovely ceremony. She was young, lots of her friends said beautiful things. They're going to plant stuff in the community garden in her name.'

Brodie seemed so at home with all this already.

The view inside the resomator didn't show much, just the body wrapped in a winding sheet, jets of water and alkaline solution, steam billowing around as liquid filled the space, drops on the inside of the thickened glass. Soon Cristina would be liquid and ashes. Where would her consciousness be then? Her soul?

'That's nice,' Hannah said, then turned to Brodie. 'Look, I'm removing the camera from Jack's grave. I don't think I should be intruding on people's grief, it's not cool.'

'But what about the disturbance, how will we find out who did it?'

Hannah kept looking at Brodie, expecting him to turn away, but he didn't.

'I think maybe you did it,' she said. 'Without realising.'

42

DOROTHY

She stood amongst the trees lining the central boulevard of Morningside Cemetery and watched Thomas. He was standing at his wife's grave, shoulders slumped, staring at Morag's headstone. In one sense, Dorothy wanted to stay hidden amongst the pine trees forever. As long as she was just watching Thomas from a distance, nothing bad was going to happen. It was when they opened their mouths that trouble started.

She'd called him as soon as she left Oliver at the hospital. The sight of that poor boy in bed, beaten and bruised, reminded her of Thomas a year ago, after a similar beating by Webster. It was so obvious to her that Thomas needed support, therapy or counselling. Someone had to help him because he seemed beyond the point of helping himself.

He'd been distant on the phone earlier, insisting he didn't want anything to do with her anymore. She respected that, but knew their circumstances had contributed to his decision. In that sense, Webster had won. Thomas had eventually agreed to meet her in Morningside Cemetery. Meeting at his wife's grave was obviously a power play to put Dorothy off her stride, and she resented him for that, for all of this. She tried to see the positive in everyone, but she was struggling right now.

She stepped out of the trees and there was a bluster of crows from the branches above her. Thomas turned at the noise. She tried to understand the look on his face as she approached, but it was implacable. Like he'd just shut down the emotional part of his personality. She was out of her depth.

'Hi,' she said, glancing at Morag Olsson's gravestone. Dorothy and Thomas had always been careful about not trying to replace each other's dead partners, making it clear that this was its own thing. But now it felt like nothing, at least that's what Thomas seemed to want it to be.

He splayed his hands. 'You wanted to see me?'

'Thomas, please.' Dorothy felt on the verge of tears, and she felt stupid that she cared so much. 'Don't be like this.'

'I told you it's over,' he said, looking at Morag's grave, then around the graveyard as if an answer might jump out from behind a headstone.

Dorothy sighed. 'Look, I'm not some hysterical woman desperate for you to change your mind. We're not kids anymore, we both know how the world works. But we had something worth holding on to, I thought.'

She couldn't help looking at Morag's grave. She'd had a heart attack while riding her bike, some congenital thing, there was no way of predicting it. Dorothy's Jim had had a stroke on the toilet in the middle of the night. The simple desolation of these deaths, of every single death in this cemetery, in this city of the dead, on this goddamn planet, billions of them, utterly mundane in their details but profound for those left behind. That was the paradox at the heart of the human condition, none of this mattered but it was all absolutely vital at the same time. The weight of it all crushed Dorothy as she tried to work out what to say.

Thomas blinked in the fading light, the sun catching the top of the cemetery wall to the west. Dorothy wondered if the buried dead could feel when the ground warmed up, if they were comforted by it.

'I'm more concerned about you,' she said. 'You clearly need help. The man I knew was thoughtful, selfless, kind. I don't know what happened to him.'

Thomas pressed his lips together and shook his head, avoiding Dorothy's eye.

'That man was a lie,' he said eventually. He stared at Morag's grave. 'That man died the day she died.'

'Bullshit,' Dorothy said, and she was glad to see some emotion on his face at last. 'We were both grieving, sure, but we had a new life together. There were things worth doing because we were together. If you want to throw that away, fine, but don't pretend it was a lie. That insults us both.'

She wanted to bring up Webster, Low, everything. But she knew that would only make him shut down.

Thomas's face mellowed a little but he didn't speak, just sighed as if he wanted to be somewhere else.

'Look, if you won't speak to me, speak to someone else.'

She took a card from her pocket. It was for the counsellor who worked at the university, who'd helped Jenny when she was at her lowest. Jenny had turned around, maybe he was worth a go.

'Take it,' she said, shoving it in his hand when he made no attempt to move.

He took it eventually, put it in his pocket without looking.

Dorothy felt tears in her eyes. She looked around the graveyard at all the dead people with no future.

'I have to go,' she said.

She strode away, along the path and through the gates, wiping her eyes and blowing her nose. In Morningside Drive the big houses gave way to tenements then shops. She had an odd feeling, turned and looked around, couldn't see Thomas or anyone else. She turned onto Comiston Road then up Morningside Road, enjoying the anonymity of the busy street. She passed charity and gift shops, then the M&S Foodhall, then pressed the button at the pedestrian crossing at Waitrose. She waited for the green man and stepped out, heard a car engine revving, turned and got a quick glimpse of a white car accelerating in her direction, swerving towards her as she dived backward off the road, its front wing connecting with her hip and lifting her off her feet, sending her tumbling onto the pavement where she smacked her head on the concrete with a sickening thud.

43

HANNAH

The anxiety in the kitchen was palpable. Hannah helped Indy at the stove while she rustled up omelettes for supper, it was past midnight and none of them had eaten.

Jenny aggressively fussed over Dorothy on the sofa by the window, fluffing up pillows, tucking in a blanket, placing a glass of water on the table alongside.

'Do you need anything else?' she said.

'I'm fine,' Dorothy said calmly.

'I still think you should've stayed in overnight.' Jenny stood over Gran with her fists tight.

Schrödinger jumped onto Dorothy's lap and she smiled and stroked his back. He nestled into her, arching his back in response to her touch.

Dorothy closed her eyes briefly. 'You heard what the doctor said.'

'Are you OK?' Jenny said, leaning in. 'Headache?'

'Go and help with the food.'

They'd spent several hours in A&E waiting for Dorothy to be treated, after an initial assessment that her injuries weren't life threatening. A young woman had witnessed the hit and run on Morningside Road, and sat with Dorothy in the ambulance then the hospital until Hannah and Jenny arrived. Two police officers showed eventually, noted down what little Dorothy remembered, spoke to the young woman too, but she hadn't got the car's numberplate or make. The police said there would be CCTV, but didn't seem in a hurry to check it. Jenny mentioned Griffiths' name, then Webster's. They wrote them down but seemed nonplussed.

When Dorothy got seen, they'd checked for concussion and passed her to the X-ray department. More sitting in chilly waiting areas. The X-rays showed no broken bones, just a badly bruised hip where the car hit.

Jenny had urged Dorothy to stay overnight but they had no beds and Dorothy didn't want to anyway. So they were back home with a leaflet about concussion and some painkillers for the hip. They had to wake Dorothy tonight every couple of hours, to make sure she still knew where she was. Delayed brain injury, especially for someone her age, was a real possibility.

Hannah got why Mum was so edgy but Gran seemed fine, and worrying about her wasn't going to change anything.

'I can't believe this,' Jenny said under her breath as she got plates and cutlery from the drawer.

'She'll be fine,' Indy said. 'You know how strong she is.'

'She's not as strong as a fucking car. This was Webster.'

'We don't know that,' Hannah said, getting tomatoes from the fridge, chopping lettuce.

'You heard what that woman said.' Jenny clattered plates onto the table. 'It was definitely deliberate, which means it was Webster.'

'Mum, you need to calm down,' Hannah said, glancing at Dorothy. 'This isn't helping.'

Jenny gradually cooled as she put salt and pepper, hot sauce and ketchup on the table. She closed her eyes and Hannah watched her. Jenny breathed deeply, in and out, which reminded Hannah of Dorothy. Maybe they were all becoming their mothers. Jenny was turning into a calm, centred woman. What did that mean for Hannah, decades of turmoil and chaos ahead?

Indy melted cheese onto the first large omelette, cut it into slices and served it up. Hannah had Indy, she was married to a smart, sexy woman, whereas Jenny had been married to a psychopath. That made all the difference.

Hannah took a plate over to Dorothy but she refused it, instead shooing Schrödinger off her lap then pushing the blankets back and slowly standing.

'Mum,' Jenny said.

Dorothy waved that away. 'I'll sit at the table like everyone else.'

'But—'

'Stop fussing,' Dorothy said, but she was limping badly and placed a hand to her side where the car hit. No wonder. Hannah had seen the state of her hip at A&E, black and blue.

Indy offered her arm and Dorothy took it, smiling. Indy pulled a chair out and held on while Dorothy sat. Dorothy patted her hand as she let go.

Hannah thought about bleeds on the brain, how our bodies were more fragile and vulnerable as we got older. It all seemed so unfair that someone so young at heart was in a body that would eventually give up. Hannah felt ill thinking about it, ran her fingers along Indy's hip as she passed her and sat.

They ate in silence for a while, Hannah sharing looks with Indy, Jenny watching Dorothy closely, Dorothy pretending it wasn't happening.

Dorothy looked at Hannah. 'Where did you get to with the disturbance at Jack's grave?'

Jenny clunked her knife and fork down. 'Mum, we need to talk about Webster, this bastard is threatening our lives.'

Dorothy placed two fingers at her temples as if she was trying to read minds. 'I don't want to think about that just now.' She looked at Hannah. 'Well?'

Hannah swallowed. 'I think he did it himself.'

Dorothy frowned. 'I don't think so.'

'I can't find any other explanation.'

'Did you ask him?'

'He just denied it. But I'm not even sure he's aware. Voices are telling him things.'

Jenny turned. 'Maybe he's dangerous.'

Indy cleared her throat. 'You know, where my family came from, it was normal to hear the voices of your ancestors.'

Dorothy nodded. 'It's no different to the wind phone.'

Jenny seemed to have no answer.

Silence hung in the air and Hannah wondered when they would get back what they had.

'What about Yana,' Indy said out of nowhere. 'Did you get any-where?'

In all the fuss about Webster they hadn't had a chance to catch up on each other's cases, or the funerals, or life.

Dorothy nodded. 'I know where she is but I haven't spoken to her yet.'

'Where?' Jenny said.

'I'd rather not say until I've had a chance to speak to her.'

'Why would she leave her kids?' Jenny glanced at Hannah.

'That's what I want to talk to her about.'

Jenny narrowed her eyes. 'It's not dangerous, is it, Mum?'

Dorothy smiled. 'It's not dangerous.'

'Promise?'

'I promise.'

The way she said it, Hannah didn't believe her at all.

44

JENNY

Jenny stood in the memorial rose garden and raised her face to the morning sun, imagined she was one of the flowers striving for warmth and nourishment, soaking in good vibes. She would need them for what was coming, to be honest.

She looked at the neat rose bushes, the benches and memorial plaques, the industrial chimney of Warriston Crem nestling amongst the sprawl of buildings up the slope. Mourners gathered in the car park, men in suits and women in black dresses easing themselves out of their cars, shaking off the worst of their misery, swapping small talk about potholes and roadworks, the unusually sunny weather, the fact we're all going to die.

She watched everyone arrive, feeling invisible in the rose garden, no one aware of her existence. There were a lot of mourners, cars heading round the other side of the crem to the overspill car park. She walked a little to the right and saw the floral displays, *BENNY LOW* and *PERSEVERE* in large letters made of white roses, surrounded by green foliage. Must've been a good Leith boy, a Hibby. 'Persevere' had always struck Jenny as a downbeat motto for the Republic of Leith. Just keep going in the face of all the shit life throws at you, no matter what.

Benny Low hadn't managed it. But he had a good turnout, as they say, a large crowd of coppers. There might've been even more if he'd died in the line of duty, rather than suicide driven by shame. Jenny was guessing, of course, she had no idea why he killed himself. Or even if he really did. She wondered about the post mortem, about Thomas's arrest for assisting him by suggestion. Was that really a crime to tell someone what a total waste of space he was and convince him to end it all? She found it hard to feel sorry for Low.

But then she saw Low's young widow with two small children, one a toddler, the other just a baby in a buggy. Imagine having to explain it all to them when they got older.

She spotted Webster and his wife getting out of a car and she ducked behind an oak tree. Waited a while, peeked out and saw Webster looking around, taking a good sweep of the area like the paranoid cop he was. She shrunk back. Waited another few minutes until the car park was empty and she heard organ music start up, then walked smartly to the front of Lorimer Chapel, tugging on the hem of her jacket and the collar of her blouse as she walked in, head down, and took a seat at the back of the congregation.

She shouldn't be here. But the thing with Mum last night had outraged her so much that she had to see Webster's face today, confront him. It was one thing to pull a knife on her, something else entirely to try to kill her mum.

Benny Low's coffin was already on the plinth at the front, and the minister was talking about him. The minister was young and seemed to know him, maybe Benny was a good churchgoer. A few jokes at the expense of Hearts, some heartfelt platitudes, then Webster got up to speak. Jenny watched him closely, the face of a murderer, a rapist. She wondered what Dorothy would make of him now, if she would see his side of things, like she always tried to. What good side was there, loving father and husband? That didn't mean you couldn't also be a bad man through and through.

'What the hell are you doing here?'

Jenny jumped as Griffiths slid into the pew alongside her. Jenny took a moment to collect herself, checked around the chapel but no one had heard Griffiths' whisper.

'I might ask you the same question,' she said under her breath. 'You're investigating Webster and Low, isn't this a conflict of interest?'

Griffiths tugged at her cuffs and looked straight ahead. 'A fellow officer has died, I'm here to show my respects. Plus it's always interesting to see who shows up to these things and how they behave.' She gave Jenny a glance. '*You* should leave, though.'

Jenny pointed to the front. 'Did you hear about the hit and run?'

Griffiths nodded.

Webster was up there delivering anecdotes, to laughter and nods of recognition. He seemed to be enjoying himself, liked the attention. His wife was watching him closely, Low's widow too, like he was a stand-up comedian.

'That prick threatened my family,' Jenny said. 'I told you about it and you did nothing. Now he's tried to follow through on my mother. I'm not going to let that lie.'

'We don't know it was him,' Griffiths whispered.

'Like fuck we don't,' Jenny hissed. 'She was with Thomas beforehand, he was obviously following them, took his opportunity.'

'We're still gathering CCTV.'

'Fuck CCTV. He's standing up there a free man.' Jenny couldn't keep the vitriol from her voice, but was careful not to raise it. She wanted to confront Webster but not right now, not like this. And not with Griffiths watching. 'At least Low had the strength of character to kill himself.'

'No one here is guilty of anything, yet,' Griffiths said.

Jenny wanted Griffiths to feel on edge, maybe that would make her pull her finger out.

Webster was still talking at the lectern, hands in his pockets. He'd turned serious now, and looked around the chapel, making Jenny and Griffiths lower their heads. Webster paused as he looked at the door to the chapel and for a moment Jenny thought he'd spotted them. Instead he pointed down the aisle.

'You.'

Jenny turned and saw Thomas walking in, neat suit buttoned up, shoulders back like he was on parade, shined shoes on the soft carpet.

There were gasps from some of the congregation. Jenny held on to the pew as she stared.

'You fucking killed him,' Webster said. He stepped from behind the lectern, came off stage and strode down the aisle. Two burly guys from near the front stood and tried to stop him but he shrugged them off. Thomas stopped halfway down the aisle and unbuttoned his jacket, spread his arms wide as if waiting for a hug.

Webster reached him and swung a piledriving punch into his face, making Thomas stagger to the side and grip the nearest pew. He righted himself, smiling, and Webster rained blows down on him as the burly guys tried to pull him off, but he fought them and continued landing punches and kicks on Thomas, who didn't raise a hand in defence, smiling as blood spurted from his lip.

Griffiths got up and ran down the aisle as others joined the melee. Jenny stood and watched and saw Thomas's face as he stared at Webster and took his punishment. He looked serene and happy, and Jenny felt sick.

45

DOROTHY

Her hands and feet were cold and her head pounded. She looked at the light skimming the surface of the canal, the kids at Boroughmuir mucking around at break time, boys roughhousing each other, girls huddled in groups and vaping. She wondered about gender norms, had a feeling that things were better now, that kids didn't have to conform to all that bullshit that existed when she was a schoolkid in Pismo Beach. Those sunny days felt like a fever dream sometimes, as if they happened to someone else entirely. Your body replaced all its cells every eight years, which means she was almost a tenth-generation version of the girl she had been, growing up in 1960s California, her mind shaped by the colour and light, the warmth. Now here she was, standing outside an Edinburgh tenement on a cool autumn day in a different millennium.

As she watched the school playground across the canal she could pick out the non-conformers, the small groups of tomboys or geeks, the brightly dyed hair and Doc boots, girls in trousers, boys with long hair, the ones yet to find their tribe. School was a tough experience on anyone who didn't fit in, she knew that from Jenny, and Hannah more recently. She was proud that the Skelfs didn't fit in. She was in her mid-seventies now, was supposed to be narrowing her world, shrinking into herself, preparing for the grave. But she was out here chasing mysteries, playing drums, finding love. Though maybe not that last one. She wondered what Thomas would do if he knew about the hit and run.

She heard a noise and turned back to Oliver's front door. Spotted the postwoman disappearing inside, missed her chance to sneak in. She crossed the road and waited in the adjacent doorway for her to come out. A few minutes and the door clacked open, the postie heading the other way, earbuds playing metal so loud Dorothy could make out it was Metallica, stocky legs in shorts pounding down the canal side as Dorothy grabbed the closing door and ducked inside.

She went up to Oliver's place, hip aching, head throbbing. She'd been swallowing codeine since last night, which took the edge off. Jenny had stuck to her guns and woken Dorothy every two hours to check she wasn't dead, as she said straight-faced each time. Dorothy had weird dreams about Jim, the two of them on trial for murder and cannibalism, then Jim defending her from a gang of thugs who beat him stupid, Dorothy unable to move or speak, just having to watch as they tore him limb from limb, feasted on his flesh.

She knocked on the door. Waited and looked at the nameplate. Listened carefully. Knocked again. Waited. Opened the letterbox.

'I know you're in there, Yana,' she said. 'It's Dorothy from the band. I need to speak to you.'

Her back was aching as she bent over. She wondered if the neighbour would come out soon.

'Yana, I saw Oliver at the hospital, I know what happened. Please. I'm not here to cause any trouble or make you do anything. I just want to talk.'

More silence, maybe a sound inside the flat, but there was noise still coming from outside, kids hollering to each other in the playground.

Dorothy sighed, straightened her back, let the letterbox close. She rubbed her hip, felt the lump on her skull where her head kissed the pavement. Wondered about the blood vessels inside, if she would be OK. No concussion, but who knows what other damage had occurred, what was waiting for her down the line?

She rested her head against the door, felt the grain of the wood

under her thumb, imagined passing through the door magically.
'Yana, everyone is worried. Faiza and Ladan asked me to find you.'

Nothing.

She turned to leave, was three steps down the stairs when the
door opened and Yana stood there for a moment then turned into
the flat, lifting a hand for Dorothy to follow.

She straightened her shoulders and went inside, closed the
door, followed Yana to the living room, where she was standing
at the window watching the kids outside.

She turned. She had dark bags under her eyes but was still
beautiful, blonde hair tied up, sharp cheekbones, bright-green
eyes. She would've grown up with a lot of attention from men,
and Dorothy wondered about that. She was wearing baggy
joggers and a sweatshirt, the kind of clothes beautiful women
wear so as not to draw attention to themselves. Oliver seemed
like a boy in comparison. This was a woman who'd seen things,
who'd been forced to leave her home, her husband killed.

'I'm glad you're safe,' Dorothy said, joining her at the window.

'How did you find out?' Yana said, strong Ukrainian accent
but her English clear.

'Olena led me here,' she said, pointing outside. 'I saw you and
Oliver from down there.'

Yana shook her head. 'I don't know what we are thinking. This
is so stupid.'

She was on the verge of tears and Dorothy wanted to hug her.

'The only stupid thing was keeping it a secret.'

Yana's eyes widened. 'Do you think?'

'Tell me what happened.'

Yana looked out of the window again, then around the room.

'He's just a baby,' Yana said. 'This is such a mess.'

She started to cry. Dorothy pictured her standing in the choir
at rehearsals, face beaming, belting her lungs out, lost in the
moment. The power of communal music was the most under-
rated thing, let you feel part of something bigger.

Dorothy didn't speak, that old trick of leaving space.

Yana sighed. 'Of course, I met him when we came to stay with Camilla. A cute boy. So happy and simple. He helped out with the kids, was very good with them. They liked each other. He made them feel at home, I appreciated that. I came here with them a few times, enjoyed being out of that house. Away from Veronika.'

She paused, walked to a bookshelf filled with science fiction and fantasy, a shelf of manga and graphic novels. She ran a finger along the spines.

'Veronika is grieving for Fedir, I understand. Her son is dead, a hero, fighting in a just war. But I am done with that. Fedir and I ... we weren't so happy before the invasion. It sounds bad, but I was relieved when we were separated. I had to look after the children and he was gone. I didn't want him back.'

She wiped tears from her eyes, sniffed. Dorothy handed her a tissue and she wiped her nose and laughed self-consciously.

'It feels good to tell someone,' she said. 'You are a good listener.'

Dorothy shrugged. She should be, she'd done it her whole life.

'When he died ... I was sad, I suppose. But the weight of his death on Veronika and the children, I didn't feel that. I just wanted to start again. Forget all the horrible things...' She waved around the room. 'Then there was Oliver.'

Dorothy kept her face impassive.

'I know it is stupid,' Yana said. 'But his energy. His kindness. He is only a boy but he is a good person too. I just needed to be with someone good. You understand?'

Dorothy nodded.

Yana sniffed back more tears and dabbed at her nose with the tissue. 'But we can't be together.'

'Why not?'

'You saw him in hospital. They will kill him.'

'Bohdan and Marko?'

Yana sighed. 'They think only of Fedir. Of the disgrace to his honour. Am I supposed to grieve forever? How long is long enough?'

Dorothy had experienced this with Thomas after Jim died. 'You have to do what you feel is right. People will always disapprove.'

Yana cleared her throat. 'But it is complicated.'

Her expression changed, and Dorothy somehow knew what was coming.

Yana glanced down and laid a hand on her stomach. 'I'm having Oliver's baby.'

46

HANNAH

Hannah and Indy had brought their bagels and bubble teas from the shop around the corner to eat outside. The park was busy, kids from Gillespie's heading to and from the Greggs on the main road. Hannah had been in there at lunchtime before, grimaced at the one-in-one-out policy, the way the kids were treated like crap. But then a lot of school was like that. It was now seven years since she'd been at Porty High and she didn't miss it. Having to be *on* all day, pay attention to boring classes, avoid hassle from idiot boys, be sociable for much longer than she had energy for. University life had suited her better, along with the fact she'd found Indy during that time. But she wasn't a student anymore.

The grass was dry so they sat and watched the life all around them, taking messy bites of the bagels, bacon and brie for her, goat's cheese and beetroot for Indy. The bubble teas were ridiculous but Hannah had grown to love them, hers was watermelon, Indy on mango. She was still surprised every time she got a mouthful of tapioca through her straw, made her feel like a little kid.

Indy wiped her mouth with a napkin, got rid of a smear of chutney. 'I've been thinking about what you said last night. About Brodie.'

Hannah tried to remember. She'd been stressed about Gran. Really, she just wanted this Brodie thing to go away.

'You were pretty harsh,' Indy said.

'What do you mean?'

'When you spoke to him about Jack's grave. I had a chat with him—'

'You talked to him after I did?'

Indy angled her head. 'Babes, I work with him every day, of course I talked to him. He was upset. I mean, you accused him of trying to dig up his son's body.'

Hannah shook her head. 'I don't think he's trying to dig Jack *up*, but there's something going on he needs to address.'

Indy drank from her tea and smacked her lips. 'We need to help him, not vilify him. Did you ever wonder why he came to *you* about this?'

Hannah watched a van head down Whitehouse Loan, and beyond that the putting green, The Golf Tavern, the church spire like a finger pointing to heaven.

'He was asking for help all along,' Hannah said.

Indy nodded. 'You did well introducing him to that professor, getting him talking about his experience. But the stuff with the grave, it's like a different you switches on, the private investigator who needs an answer. Sometimes there isn't an answer, at least not the kind you're looking for.'

Hannah thought about sitting in Rachel Tanaka's class, all those theories of consciousness, how we still don't really know how the mind works.

'Indy, do you really think everything is conscious, like Tanaka said?'

'Of course. My parents weren't practising Hindus, but I was brought up in that culture. People raised with a Western mindset, you can't see outside of it. This whole society relies on empirical, rational "facts". If you can't see something right in front of you, it doesn't exist.'

Indy sipped her tea.

'Your modern physics has taught you to see the world differently,' she said. 'But you're still blinkered, babes. It seems obvious to me and billions of others around the planet that we hear voices, we talk to the dead, our ancestors are all around us. And the things of the world are animate and alive too, they have a point of view and meaning. It's only the reductive Western view that says otherwise.'

Hannah knew all this but she couldn't take the blinkers off.

'You're saying I need to apologise to Brodie,' she said.

Indy didn't say anything, she didn't have to.

❧

She heard the music before she turned the corner. Bursts of jagged rock 'n' roll, big choruses. It got louder as she entered the garden, saw thirty people spread out across the grass, drinking beers and passing joints, from teenagers to folk in their forties, lots of tattoos, strappy tops and T-shirts. All Biffy Clyro fans. The music was coming from a large speaker on wheels in the corner of the garden.

Hannah spotted Brodie at the front door to the house, drinking a beer and chatting to a girl his age. She took a joint back from him and wandered over to the crowd as Hannah arrived. The smell of weed trailed after her.

'I arranged a viewing for Ewan,' Brodie said. 'I didn't expect many to come.'

A group of four fans came out of the front door, fist bumped Brodie as they passed, and another four sauntered inside.

'Second door on the right,' Brodie said, nodding.

'Wow,' Hannah said.

Brodie looked around. 'I guess he was part of something after all.'

Hannah thought about that. We all need to be a part of something.

'Brodie, I owe you an apology,' she said.

He stared at her for a long beat. 'No worries.'

'I shouldn't have said those things to you the other day.'

'Forget about it.'

'I was stupid.'

'It's OK, honestly. I've been focusing on all this.' He waved his hand around the garden. 'Always moving forward, right?'

He smiled at her and she smiled back. She had an idea.

'I'm going to remove the camera from Craigmillar later, do you want to come? Talk to Jack a little bit?'

Brodie grinned. 'Sure.'

47

JENNY

'I'm not going to hospital.'

Thomas's lip was still bleeding, his eye swollen closed. He moved on his bar stool like a man twenty years older, hand to his ribs. Dabbed at his lip with a handkerchief, looked at the blood on the linen.

Jenny had had it with all these old people refusing to do what was best for themselves. Was it pride or a generational thing? 'You might have broken something.'

He cricked his neck and Jenny heard a loud crunch.

'Thomas, stop being such a martyr.'

'I'm fine.'

They were at a window table in The High Dive, view of St Leonard's across the road like it was Mordor, the source of all evil. What the fuck do you do if you're a retired cop who gets beaten up by cops at another cop's funeral? Grab a drink opposite the police station, it seemed.

Jenny had driven the two of them here on Griffiths' suggestion. Low's family were having a wake for him down the road at The Auld Hoose, and she wanted to skip out to chat to them. When Griffiths and others had broken up the beating at Warriston Crem, Jenny half expected her to arrest Webster on the spot, but even she appreciated that might be a little tricky. Again, a cop arresting a cop at a cop's funeral, good luck with that.

Jenny pointed at Thomas's eye. 'I don't just mean being a martyr about your injuries. I'm talking about what happened at the crem.'

Thomas raised a double gin and tonic to his lips and sipped, winced. He wasn't much of a drinker, but Jenny had wanted one and insisted he have one too. Nothing worse than drinking doubles on your own, she knew that from experience.

Thomas shook his head a little as if testing his skull's integrity. 'What do you mean?'

'I was there, I saw you. You didn't *literally* ask for it, but you might as well have. You went there to get a beating, didn't you?'

Thomas looked around the empty bar. The doughy smell of pizza was in the air, a tall barmaid with big curly hair was cleaning glasses. She was wearing a tight Scooby-Doo T-shirt and denim shorts. Jenny was impressed that Thomas hadn't looked at her once.

'No,' he said deadpan.

'Come on,' Jenny said. 'I know when folk are lying.'

Thomas took a deep breath and grimaced. 'I deserved it.'

'What?'

Thomas looked around again, delaying the inevitable. 'The police were right when they arrested me. I was in contact with Low. I emailed him. Eventually phone calls. I talked him into it.'

He swallowed hard and looked at his drink, took a sip.

'Fuck,' Jenny said.

'He was a bad man and a weak man. I exploited that.' The words were coming out faster now, like a confession. 'I knew I couldn't get to Webster. He's the alpha, he's strong. He probably still thinks he didn't do anything wrong. But Benny was soft, I knew that from working with him. He likes to follow, be told what to do. I used that. I knew he'd done terrible things to Billie and Ruby, probably others. I'm sure he did it to be part of Webster's gang, simple peer pressure. But that doesn't matter. He was part of rape, part of murder.'

Jenny had a flashback to watching the girl Ruby being sexually assaulted in the woods near Cramond. By four cops, two still unidentified.

'I don't regret it,' Thomas said.

'You're fucking up the legal case,' Jenny said. 'You must know that.'

Thomas looked at the station across the road. 'I worked for the police for decades. Things only ever got worse. The case against Webster and Low was never going to succeed. I want some kind of justice.'

'You sound like a vigilante.'

Thomas lowered his head, dabbed his lip. 'I'm just tired. Tired of people like them getting away with it.'

Jenny smiled. 'You sound like me.'

Thomas took her in for a long moment. 'What were *you* doing at the funeral?'

'Keeping an eye on Webster. Things have escalated.'

'How do you mean?'

'He pulled a knife on me the other day in broad daylight.'

'What?'

'I told Griffiths,' Jenny said. 'But he's got us over a barrel. And then the whole hit and run yesterday with Mum—'

'What?'

Of course he didn't know, Dorothy had left him in the cemetery.

'On Morningside Road,' Jenny said. 'A car hit her on the pedestrian crossing.'

'Is she OK?'

'She's fine. Got checked out in hospital, nothing broken, no concussion.'

'Do they know it was Webster?'

'Griffiths is apparently on it, someone's checking CCTV.'

Awkward silence as Thomas clenched and unclenched his jaw.

'You should go see her,' Jenny said.

Thomas sipped his gin and shook his head. 'I don't think she would want that.'

'You're wrong.'

Griffiths came in, spotted them and walked over. She looked

out of the window at the cop shop. 'Jesus, keen to get spotted again, are you?'

Jenny raised her chin. 'I presume you've arrested Webster for assault.'

Griffiths stared at her, then Thomas. 'Not unless you want to press charges.'

Thomas looked energised by Griffiths' appearance. 'Have you got anywhere with the car from yesterday?'

Griffiths looked at them both, put together that Jenny had told him. 'Nothing yet. You know what it's like, grunt work takes time.'

Thomas shook his head. He looked like he'd had enough.

'There's something else,' Griffiths said, scratching the back of her neck. 'And you're not going to like it.'

Jenny's stomach knotted, but the look on Thomas's face was resigned.

'What?' Jenny said.

'The drones,' Griffiths said. 'They're gone.'

Thomas touched his forehead.

'What do you mean?' Jenny said.

Griffiths glanced out of the window at the station. 'From the evidence room. Just gone.'

Thomas pressed his lips together.

'Jesus fucking Christ,' Jenny said, and downed the rest of her drink.

48

DOROTHY

She stopped outside the door on Merchiston Place, steadied herself. Popped a couple of codeine out of the blister pack, swallowed them with water. Her headache was down to a dull throb but it never seemed to ease. And walking over here had made her hip stiffen up. She glanced under her skirt waistband, the bruise blossoming over her skin, larger each time she looked. She thought about the blood under the surface, spilled from her thinning veins, nowhere else to go.

She rang the doorbell, waited. The street was in shade, the setting sun blocked by the tenements opposite.

Movement behind the etched glass of the door. The Victorians who built these houses knew how to show off. This was an etching of an elegant horse-drawn coach. If Dorothy squinted, it could've been a funeral carriage.

The door opened and Camilla appeared, looking flustered, hair in a mess, cheeks red.

'Oh,' she said. 'I was just about to head out.'

'To see Oliver in hospital?'

'How did you know that?'

Dorothy glanced behind Camilla, at the staircase and banister, the fresh flowers on a sideboard in the hall. 'Can I come in?'

Camilla thought about it then eventually opened the door wider. 'What is this?'

Dorothy stepped inside, smelling anxious sweat on Camilla as she passed, then the pollen from the lilies in the vase. She stared at herself in the hallway mirror, she looked normal, not as if she'd just been hit by a car.

'Is Veronika in?'

Camilla frowned as she closed the door. 'I thought this was about Oliver.'

She knew nothing. She was Oliver's mother and she knew nothing.

Dorothy glanced through to the kitchen. 'Maybe a cup of tea?'

Camilla looked confused then walked dumbly to the kitchen. She was obviously still in shock over Oliver's attack.

Dorothy followed and watched as Camilla made two mugs of tea with shaking hands. Maybe this was a bad idea. Maybe it had nothing to do with Dorothy. But if someone had information about who beat up Dorothy's nearest and dearest, she would want to know.

Dorothy took the tea and leaned against the kitchen island. Copper cooking pots hung above a turquoise Aga. The kettle and toaster matched them, the whole thing like a twenty-first-century farmhouse.

'I found Yana,' Dorothy said eventually.

'I don't care about that, I only want to know what you know about Oliver.'

Dorothy sipped her tea and looked at Camilla. Maybe she already subconsciously knew.

'They're connected,' Dorothy said. 'It's all connected.'

'How do you mean?' But the look on Camilla's face slowly changed, she was beginning to see. 'What?'

'Yana was at Oliver's flat.'

'Why?'

Dorothy raised her eyebrows.

'Are they ... together?' Camilla said.

Dorothy nodded.

'But she's ... old enough to be...'

She wasn't old enough to be his mother, not quite. But she was so much more grown up, more experienced, had been more exposed to the banal badness of the world.

'I honestly think they're in love,' Dorothy said.

'Ridiculous.' Camilla looked like she'd been slapped in the face. 'He's just a boy. He doesn't know what he's doing.'

'He's old enough.'

Camilla looked around the kitchen. 'I don't understand. Why would she leave her kids to hide round the corner in my son's flat?'

Dorothy didn't want to mention the pregnancy. Bohdan and Marko didn't know anything about that when they beat Oliver up. God only knew what they'd do if they found out.

'The kids knew,' Dorothy said. 'She kept in touch. Oliver took them round there.'

Camilla put her mug down and rubbed her hands against her forehead. 'This is not happening.'

Dorothy watched her stand with her head bowed, body trembling. She breathed in and out, slowly raised her head.

'Those soldiers,' she said under her breath. 'Who knew her husband. They did this, didn't they? They beat up my boy.'

Dorothy nodded.

Camilla shook her head. 'How did they know?'

Dorothy didn't speak. She felt like she'd spent this whole conversation waiting for Camilla to catch up.

'Veronika,' Camilla said.

She looked at the doorway then stuck her chest out and strode out of the room, Dorothy scurrying to catch up, her hip aching.

Camilla went to the door of the adjoining flat and threw it open, slamming it against the wall. She walked to the kitchen and Dorothy spotted the kids in the adjacent living room, Roman on his phone, Olena looking up from a book with fear in her eyes when she saw Camilla and Dorothy.

'Veronika!'

Camilla reached the kitchen and Veronika was there taking something out of the oven, smell of cinnamon in the air.

She froze, then put the tray on the worktop and backed away, oven gloves still on her hands.

Camilla had her cornered. 'You sent those thugs to kill my son.'

Veronika glanced at the doorway and Olena was standing there, mouth open.

Camilla followed her gaze, didn't seem to care. 'Why would you do something like that?'

'I didn't,' Veronika said, dropping the oven gloves and raising her hands. 'I didn't know.'

'I don't believe you.'

Dorothy had to speak. 'Camilla, please.'

She turned on Dorothy. 'My son is in hospital because of her.'

'I didn't know,' Veronika said, cowering. 'I didn't know they would beat him.'

Camilla screamed at the confirmation and lunged at the older woman, slapping her face and grabbing her hair. Dorothy jumped in, tried to separate them. Then she realised Olena was in the mix as well, screaming and trying to grab her gran and drag her away from Camilla's flailing fists.

Dorothy prised Camilla away as Olena dragged her gran to the other side of the kitchen.

'How dare you,' Camilla spat, 'after everything I've done for you. All of you.'

There was something Dorothy still didn't know for sure, but she had an idea.

'Veronika,' she said. 'How did *you* know about Yana and Oliver?'

Veronika was getting her breath back, then glanced at Olena.

Olena pressed her lips together and shook her head. 'It was Roman. Roman told on Mama.'

49

HANNAH

Hannah was driving the hearse, Brodie in the passenger seat staring at the darkness out of the window. They headed along Strathearn Road, waited at the lights, then turned down Kilgraston Road. The high wall to their left hid Grange Cemetery, the only graveyard in the city with catacombs, and Hannah thought of vampire movies. They hardly ever did funerals at Grange anymore, almost full. What would the city do when there was no more space for the dead?

Hannah didn't want a lasting memorial when she was gone, what was the point? A statue or gravestone didn't mean you would be remembered. No one was remembered forever. Once the last person who remembers us is dead, that's it. She didn't see the point of that television show either, where celebrities cried over ancestors they never knew. It should go back hundreds of thousands of years to the first humans, that would be cool. She'd read that humanity was almost extinct at one point. Only about thirteen hundred humans existed for over a hundred thousand years. They'd worked it out from DNA testing. That meant that we were a whisker away from extinction. The planet would be better off without humans, obviously, but all that love and comfort and courage and art and culture and technology would've been blinked out. No telescopes looking at the stars, no holding hands under the moonlight. But also no wars, politics, borders or genocides.

'How's Dorothy?' Brodie said, shaking Hannah from her thoughts.

They were at the lights on Blackford Avenue. In the gloaming to their right, Blackford Hill loomed, a dark outline against the sky.

'She's OK, I think.' Hannah assumed he meant since the hit and run.

Somewhere in this city, some bastard was still driving around knowing full well he'd almost killed Dorothy. If it was Webster, she wanted him to get all that was coming to him. And Mum was right, who else could it be?

'She's honestly one of the strongest people I've ever met,' Brodie said.

'She's also getting older,' Hannah said.

Brodie shifted in his seat. 'Sure, I didn't mean anything.'

Hannah sighed as they hit more traffic outside King's Buildings. 'I know. I didn't mean anything either.'

Awkward silence in the car.

They passed Cameron Toll, its glass façade lit up like a 1980s spaceship. Hannah drove from Lady Road under the rail bridge to Old Dalkeith Road, potholes bumping them continually, traffic stopping and starting.

She wondered about the silence in the hearse. She wanted to talk to Brodie about his son, his grief, the voices, but she didn't know how to start.

They reached Craigmillar Cemetery and realised the gates were locked. They sat in the driveway in the hearse, engine ticking over. Inside the graveyard it was dark.

Brodie checked his watch. 'What time does it normally close?'

'I don't know.'

Brodie pointed. 'We can just head over the wall.'

It was a low, dry-stone dyke, easy to climb.

Hannah wondered at Brodie's eagerness all of a sudden. Was he used to climbing over this wall?

She killed the engine and they got out. Brodie gave her a leg up then clambered after her. She smoothed down her trousers and slung her small backpack over her shoulder. They would be five minutes in and out, get the camera and go.

They passed the waiting room and noticeboard, the silhouettes of the tombstones up the hill like teeth against the skyline. It was less clear down where the babies were buried, against the backdrop of trees.

As they got closer to Jack's grave, Hannah saw the outline of a figure hunched over the grass, moving backward and forward. She took her phone from her pocket, checked the gravecam app. She'd silenced notifications yesterday, after deciding to remove the camera. She had five alerts from the last half hour.

'What the hell?' Brodie said, breaking into a run.

Hannah chased after him.

The stocky figure up ahead had a shovel, was digging a hole in front of the headstone, earth flying into a pile at the side.

'Hey,' Brodie shouted.

The figure didn't turn, just dropped the shovel and knelt, scrabbled on hands and knees, throwing dirt aside. They were like a feral animal following the scent of a kill, frantically scraping at the earth.

'Stop!' Brodie said.

They were only a few yards away now, the shadowy form becoming more solid. For a moment Hannah imagined it was a ghost or one of Brodie's voices made real. But then Brodie reached the figure and grabbed a shoulder and pulled.

It was Amanda Sweet, eyes streaming with tears, snot running from her nose as she threw Brodie off and went back to what she was doing.

Hannah reached the grave and saw that Amanda had dug down as far as the coffin, dirty white wood nestled in the earth, but thankfully she hadn't got as far as opening it.

'Amanda,' Brodie said, grabbing her again and pushing her hard so that she collapsed onto the wet ground. 'What are you doing?'

Amanda lay there crying and staring at her hands. She looked at the hole in the ground, the pile of earth, Brodie and Hannah. She looked utterly lost.

'I just miss him so much,' she said. 'I miss him so much.'

50

JENNY

His body next to hers was comforting, not a feeling she was used to. She'd woken up next to a bunch of guys over the years, her skin usually itching to go, to leave before she was the one left alone. Her ex-husband had really done a number on her. But it felt different with Archie. His presence here felt like an anchor, someone to cling to in a storm.

The morning light through the curtains usually made her pull the covers over her head, but today they felt like an invitation to live. But a large part of her was still wary, waiting to have the rug pulled from under her feet. Maybe she would fuck this up like she had every other relationship, just so she had some control.

She thought about Mum and Thomas. They were in a situation that Jenny was all too used to. Thomas was pushing Dorothy away because he didn't want her to get hurt. Webster was a giant shadow over all their lives. Before all this, Thomas had always been the rational, calm one. Jenny thought about their conversation yesterday. She understood his mindset, wanted to help, but she also knew that, when she was in that state of mind, wild horses couldn't have pulled her to safety.

Archie snuffled in his sleep and Jenny traced a finger from his shoulder to the base of his spine. Her hand was on his bum cheek when he shifted his weight and opened his eyes.

'Hey,' he said.

'Hey.'

'Were you just touching my arse?'

She shrugged. 'What of it?'

'That's sexual assault in the workplace.'

'Good luck taking that to HR.'

Archie ran a finger from Jenny's neck, across her breasts, making her shiver, to her belly.

'I resent being objectified,' Archie said deadpan.

'Hey, don't we all,' she said, and kissed him to shut him up.

It went on longer than she expected but eventually they broke apart. It sounded windy outside, tree branches rustling.

'You think Dorothy is OK?' Archie said.

Jenny and Archie had been out last night at a Mexican restaurant on Teviot Place, and Dorothy was already in bed by the time they came back.

'I honestly don't know.'

Archie propped himself on his shoulder. 'I'm worried about her, I've never seen her like this.'

Jenny knew what he was talking about. 'The kind of shit she gets into, it takes its toll. Physically, obviously, but also emotionally, mentally. I'm surprised she doesn't just stay in bed all day, to be honest. I would.'

Archie sat up. 'Is Griffiths any further forward with the CCTV?'

Jenny shook her head. 'Not that I know of.'

Archie straightened his shoulders, muscles rippling. 'Webster really needs someone to shut him up.'

'Don't even think about it,' she said, stroking his arm. 'Maybe that's what he wants, someone to hurt him so he can do us for assault. Anything like that just clouds things. He's sowing chaos so that the court case gets lost. We can't forget what he did, what Low did.'

Archie shook his head. 'So what, we just sit and take it?'

Jenny had an idea about that but she wasn't about to tell Archie. If she told him, he would be at risk. She was going to do this alone.

A noise came from the pocket of her jeans on the floor, where Archie had dropped them last night. She remembered him touching her gently, then more firmly when she asked. How her body and mind responded.

She took out her phone and frowned. 'Thomas.' She hit answer, put it on speakerphone. 'Thomas, what's up?'

'It was Webster.' Thomas sounded calm down the line.

Jenny looked at Archie. 'What?'

'The car that hit Dorothy,' Thomas said. 'There was CCTV outside Waitrose. They got a partial plate along with the make and model. The car is registered to Benjamin Low.'

Jenny tried to think. 'I mean, that's something, but it's not conclusive.'

'Of course it is,' Thomas said. 'Who else would have access to Low's car?'

'They just have to confiscate the car, check for forensics, right? Prints, DNA, all that.'

Thomas laughed. 'They already found the car, a burnt-out wreck in Telferton industrial estate.'

'I'm sure they can still get something from it.'

'Jenny, I was a police officer for thirty years. I know how things work. This is a dead end.'

'I don't believe that,' Jenny said. 'Griffiths knows what this means to us, she'll—'

'Griffiths doesn't give a shit,' Thomas said. 'Not like us. We have to defend ourselves.'

'Thomas, you need to calm down.'

The line went dead and Jenny stared at Archie, who shook his head.

51

DOROTHY

Her headache was a pulse at the back of her skull and her hip ached to move but grew stiff if she stayed still. She was tired all the way to her bones. She stood with Indy, off to the side of the funeral ceremony. Fabienne De Jong was in the ground in her winding sheet, two dozen mourners, all in bright clothes, which were failing to stave off the sorrow or the cold breeze from the Forth.

The Seafield site was exposed and Dorothy looked at the saplings all around, wondered how they would fare over the years, decades, centuries. There had been more storms in Scotland recently because of climate change, these little babies would struggle if a northerly kept pummelling them without respite.

Dorothy had always found hope in the idea that these trees and this cemetery would long outlast her. But she struggled to feel it right now, as if she'd been infected by Thomas's mindset. Dorothy had seen similar with the spouses of the people they buried, couples who died within days of each other. It happened so often, one partner unable to see the point in continuing when the other was gone.

Dorothy didn't go that way when Jim died. She had Jenny and Hannah to live for, of course. But sometimes you had to just decide that you wanted to live. You wanted to go on because life was worth living.

Fabienne's was another humanist funeral, more of them these days, a bunch of her friends and family taking turns to say something by her graveside, talking directly to her body in the hole. Fabienne was seventy-seven when she was hit by a bus on Milton

Road. A stormy day, poor visibility, the driver devastated by what he'd done.

The fact that it was a road traffic accident made Dorothy think of the hit and run, and she squirmed in her funeral outfit. She pulled at her collar and felt Indy take her hand and squeeze.

'You OK?' Indy said.

'Not really.'

Dorothy felt tears come to her eyes and wondered why. She had plenty to live for, it was Fabienne who was gone. But that's what funerals did to you, they made you think about your own mortality, the deaths of your friends and family. Dorothy never usually minded that but she felt paper thin these days, as if the breeze might carry her away over Arthur's Seat, across Scotland, the Atlantic, the United States, high amongst the clouds, circling the globe forever, part of the storms that battered the planet.

Mourners began throwing dirt into the hole on top of Fabienne's body.

Dorothy expected people to walk away murmuring sadly to each other, heading for the wake. But they all just stood and watched Fabienne being carefully committed to the earth for eternity.

Dorothy was fed up with solving everyone's problems. Where had it got her? Abuse and pain, stress and heartache. And it never ended.

'I have to go,' she said to Indy, squeezing her hand and letting go.

She walked away from the funeral.

❧

She sat outside Söderberg with Yana, looking down Middle Meadow Walk. It was more sheltered here than by the sea, the dappled sunshine through the trees warming Dorothy's face. Yana drank herbal tea, Dorothy on black coffee. They'd talked about

Yana's situation. Dorothy knew from Olena that it was Roman who told Veronika about Oliver. It wasn't the boy's fault, he didn't know what would happen. Dorothy wondered if Veronika really *had* known what would happen when she told Bohdan and Marko.

She spotted Veronika walking up the path, using a stick to take the weight on her left side.

'OK, don't freak out,' Dorothy said, looking behind Yana.

Yana turned and saw her mother-in-law and straightened her shoulders, pushed her chair back. 'Fuck, no.'

Dorothy put a hand on her wrist. 'You have to talk to her, she's the grandmother of your children. You have to live with that.'

'We can manage without her. After what she has done.'

'Just hear her out.'

Yana pressed her tongue against the inside of her top lip, thinking. She sucked her teeth then shook her head. She didn't look behind her, just stared at Dorothy with hard eyes.

Dorothy stood when Veronika reached them, pulled a chair out opposite Yana. The old woman eased herself into it, cleared her throat as she rested her walking stick against the table.

Yana said something fast and low in Ukrainian, spitting the words. Veronika replied in a more defensive tone, hands raised as if Yana was about to strike her. They swapped more words and Dorothy gauged the body language.

'Please,' she said eventually.

Yana looked at Dorothy, then Veronika. 'It is your fault.'

'I did not know what they would do,' Veronika said.

Yana spat on the ground. 'Liar. You told friends of Fedir about the boy I was with. What did you think would happen?'

Veronika narrowed her eyes. 'Exactly, a boy. My Fedir was a *man*. A good Ukrainian man who died for his country, for you. You disgrace him.'

'Am I supposed to stay away from men forever?'

'He is not suitable,' Veronika said. 'He is a baby.'

'Fuck you,' Yana said, and Veronika flinched.

Yana looked down at her own body and touched her stomach. 'I love Oliver. We are going to have a baby.'

Veronika stared then shrank into herself, shuffled in her seat. She spoke again in Ukrainian, a stream of vitriol that Yana accepted with a stoic face.

'This was a mistake,' Veronika said to Dorothy, pushing her seat away from the table.

'Wait,' Dorothy said, though she barely had the energy. She wanted to go and lie down in a dark room for a month, let the world take care of itself. 'None of this matters. You're both connected now forever. You had Fedir and you both loved him, now you have Roman and Olena. You have to accept that you're linked, that's what family is. In the end there's nothing else, not really. Not romance or duty or honour, just people. We need each other to live.'

She wasn't sure if either woman was listening and part of her didn't care. She wasn't talking about them anyway, she was talking about herself.

52

HANNAH

Hannah glanced at Brodie as they stood on the doorstep. 'Ready?'

He nodded.

The door was opened by Phoebe, eyes red and puffy. She didn't look as if she'd slept. She threw herself at Brodie and hugged him hard, gripping his back like she might fall over without the support.

Brodie held her awkwardly at first. He glanced at Hannah with eyebrows raised, then just held her as she sobbed into his shoulder.

'I'm so glad you're here,' she said, eventually extricating herself from him. There was silence for a long moment. 'Come in.'

She walked inside and they followed her to the living room. Amanda was sitting in the armchair, Ray watching her from the window. She was like a nervous bird, he looked like he'd been turned to stone. His eyes followed them as they came in and sat on the sofa.

Phoebe hovered near the door, unable to look at her mum or dad.

No one spoke.

Hannah noticed that Amanda's clothes were clean, hands washed, no dirt under her fingernails.

It felt like they were sitting on a volcano ready to blow.

Amanda cleared her throat and glanced at Brodie and Hannah. 'I told them,' she said.

She had been incoherent last night, almost catatonic. Hannah and Brodie had toyed with the idea of taking her to A&E, but there didn't seem to be anything physically wrong with her and the thought of sitting for hours with her in that bright room was too much. So they brought her home. Brodie let her ride in the passenger seat of the hearse while he sat in the back.

When they'd got to the house they had to ring the bell, Amanda was incapable of finding her keys. They explained a bare minimum to Ray and Phoebe, just handed Amanda over and said they'd be back the next day to talk.

Brodie shifted his weight on the sofa. 'How are you?'

The question seemed to take forever to penetrate Amanda's skull.

Eventually she looked up. 'Thank you.' It sounded like her words were dredged from the bottom of the ocean. 'For last night.'

Phoebe let out a small yelp and put her hand over her mouth.

No one else spoke for a long time.

Hannah looked around the room. Waited.

Amanda pressed her lips tight together. Phoebe stood like a statue.

Ray spoke. 'Maybe I can help.' He glanced at Phoebe. 'We had a big talk last night.'

Phoebe sniffed.

'There was something we never told Phoebe,' Ray said.

Hannah felt herself being drawn towards an abyss.

'When Phoebe was born,' Ray said, 'it was a difficult labour. Thirty hours. They didn't have the medical facilities they have now. Amanda really struggled.' He glanced at his wife, who stayed stony-faced. 'Eventually, Phoebe came out, quiet at first then she screamed, it was so good to hear her voice. So good to meet her.'

Phoebe shook her head.

'But there was another,' Ray said. 'Phoebe had a twin brother. He ... didn't survive.'

Hannah felt a lump in her throat, looked at Phoebe crying, then Amanda, then Brodie. He clearly had no idea about this.

Ray nodded at Amanda. 'Neither of us really remembers what

happened properly. We had Phoebe to look after, that took all of our attention. I think we signed something, they took the boy away, we never saw him again.'

Phoebe's mouth was turned down, tears on her cheeks.

'Phoebe was all we could think about,' Ray said. 'Keeping her alive. We didn't...' He looked at Amanda, who was hunched over. 'We didn't grieve for him. We never mentioned him. To begin with we were in emergency mode with Phoebe, then afterwards it seemed too late. How could we even bring Jack up? It seemed so unfair.'

'Jack?' Brodie said.

Phoebe was sobbing now. 'I didn't know. It was just a stupid coincidence when we named our Jack.'

Amanda nodded. 'We called him Jack. But he never had a funeral, we never said goodbye.'

Ray seemed uncertain what to do with himself. 'When Phoebe told us she was pregnant, we were so happy. But it also brought it all up again. Stuff that had been buried for years.'

Brodie shook his head. 'And the same happened to our Jack.'

Phoebe buried her face in her hands and Brodie got up from the sofa and wrapped his arms around her.

Amanda's head dropped and her body deflated.

Ray watched Phoebe and Brodie hug for a time, then turned to Hannah.

'We've been visiting the wee lad,' he said. 'Just talking to him. It's obvious, I suppose, that we're also talking to *our* Jack.'

Hannah looked at the top of Amanda's head.

'Not just talking to him,' she said.

Amanda raised her face, tears in her eyes. 'I've been drinking. Too much.' She looked around the room. 'I've always had a ... darkness. I would visit their Jack, talk to him. After a while, I thought he was talking to *me*.'

Hannah shared a look with Brodie.

'Nicely to begin with,' Amanda said. 'But that changed. He was desperate. Asking for hugs, wanting to see me. It felt so real.' She looked round the room, crying now. 'I can't believe what I did. What I nearly did. Thank God you were there, Brodie. Thank God you stopped me.'

Ray looked at his wife, face full of sorrow.

'We never got a chance to say goodbye,' he said again under his breath.

Hannah looked around the room. All the broken people, all the grief and sorrow, handled so badly.

'Maybe there's something I can do about that,' she said.

53
JENNY

She sat in the van, parked in the shade of the willow tree, and stared at the house. This was probably insane but she had to do something.

She'd been here for half an hour, humming to herself in the driver's seat as she watched for any movement. Both cars were gone from the driveway which gave her some confidence there was no one home, but who knew? Don Webster was likely at work, but what about Lena and the baby? Maisie seemed young enough that Lena might still be on maternity leave. Maybe mother and daughter were just chilling and bonding in the house.

Jenny remembered when Hannah was that age in a rush of feelings, her stomach lurching. So much good and bad, her life amplified beyond measure. She'd had Craig to help her, of course, and the worst thing was that he'd been a good dad, attentive and caring, sharing the feeds and nappy changes, doing all the domestic stuff so that Jenny could grab a few moments of sleep. It had been such a rush, being a new mother, heady and exhilarating. Like being on a high wire. She could've fallen at any time, Hannah in her arms, the two of them dashed to pieces on the ground below.

But they were still here and Craig was dead.

She'd had enough of waiting, opened the door and got out, grabbed the backpack and shouldered it as she locked the van and didn't look round. This was the kind of street where neighbours had twitching curtains. If you looked round, you were guilty. The secret to doing anything, she'd learned from Craig, was to act as if you were born to it, as if it was your goddamn right.

She walked up the path to Webster's house, pressed the doorbell. No point doing this if someone was in. She stared at the words on the lintel again – *Free Church Manse* – imagined what despicable things had gone on here in the past.

Her stomach was tight as she anticipated the door opening, Don or Lena looking for an explanation. But there was silence, just sparrows in the oak tree to her left.

She waited a few more minutes then walked to the side of the house, looking for a way in. Tried the back door, locked. Looked at the windows above, all old sash and case. A small, frosted glass one on the first floor, slightly open. She looked around the garden, saw a line of bins, went over. Checked inside, the garden waste was fullest.

She dragged it to the back door, climbed onto it from a wooden chair sitting on the patio, then from the bin she clambered onto the roof of the low kitchen extension. She walked carefully across the slate tiles to the edge. The bathroom window was still a few feet away. But there was a drain running down the wall between. She grabbed the drain, hoped it would take her weight, swung herself over the edge, made the small leap with one foot to the ledge of the bathroom window, still holding the drain, which creaked against its brackets but held. She swung her other foot over and stood precariously on the ledge. She bent down and lifted the window open, saw that it was by the sink. She cleared away toothbrushes, toothpaste and a soap dish then crawled inside, sliding over the taps with her bum then onto the floor. She turned and replaced everything where it had been, positioned the window to the same level as before and took a deep breath.

Listened.

Silence.

She left the bathroom and went downstairs. Walked through the rooms, sussing the place out. The living room she'd been in with Lena and Maisie. Through to the dining room then the large kitchen that opened out to a patio at the back. She checked the patio doors, unlocked them, went outside and replaced the brown bin back in the line of bins.

She couldn't leave any trace that she'd been here or it would be pointless.

Back into the dining room. She looked at the shelves, saw an overhanging plant that would provide cover. Unzipped the backpack, took out the first spy camera and secured it in the corner. Switched it on, checked it on her phone. This wasn't her speciality, Hannah normally did the tech stuff, but she wasn't an idiot. She synched the camera to the app, checked the angle of coverage, waved at it and saw herself reflected on her phone screen.

'Check, one, two.'

She downloaded the file, listened back, audio was working.

She moved to the kitchen, placed another camera on a high shelf on top of a pile of cookbooks covered in dust. No one would be snooping up there. Then the living room, a display case full of nick-nacks, artworks and ceramics. Someone had good taste and money, she presumed it was Lena. There was a dark corner behind a Japanese bowl, she placed a camera there. Stepped back into the middle of the room, you couldn't see it unless you were looking for it.

She thought for a moment, then went upstairs, placed a camera in the bedroom, pointing at the bed from on top of a shelf full of bedsheets and towels. Checked it was sending. All good.

She heard the front door open and her stomach dropped to her feet. She stepped out to the upstairs landing, listened. Her heartbeat thudded in her ears. She began to feel dizzy from adrenaline. Strained to hear. Lena making babytalk noises, Maisie gurgling. Waited. Then recognised Webster's low voice.

Jenny was getting notifications on her phone from the app. She checked, the living-room camera, Lena taking Maisie's jacket off, laying her on the play mat, kneeling down, Webster watching the two of them.

The living room faced the front of the house. Jenny tried to remember if she'd locked the patio doors or not.

She crept to the top of the stairs. Her plan had been to go out of the front door, but the doorway to the living room was on the way. She listened to their voices, tried to work out if they were about to leave the room.

She crept downstairs, heart exploding in her chest. Stood at the bottom for a moment then walked quickly with soft feet into the kitchen, touched the patio doors with her flat hand, moved them open as little as possible with a swish, glanced behind her. Webster's voice was suddenly louder as if he was coming towards the kitchen, asking Lena if she wanted a cup of tea, then Jenny squeezed outside, sliding the door closed again with a tiny click just as Webster came into the room still looking behind him. Jenny slid round the corner of the house out of view and stood there breathing heavily for over a minute while she waited, expecting Webster to haul the door open, dash outside, find her there and beat her to death.

But it was just more sparrows chirping, the sound of the sea in the distance.

She walked to the front of the house. Stepped out carefully. Crept to the living-room window, peeked in. Lena and Maisie on the floor, Webster not there.

She turned and ran.

54

DOROTHY

'Goddamn it.' She threw a drumstick across the studio in frustration, watched as it clattered against the wall. Breathed deeply, picked up a spare stick from the kick drum. She'd had this Biffy Clyro song nailed the other day when she showed the rest of the band, but she hadn't written the part down and she was struggling to get back to where she was a few days ago. It felt like everything was a problem, that she was having a hard time keeping control of her life.

She kept losing the place at the offbeat in the fifth bar second time around. It was simple snare and floor-tom hits, but she was always surprised by the eighth note delay that time, and once you'd fallen out of step it was impossible to get back in.

She pressed play and tried again, waited for the muted guitar, counted in her head, tapping a stick on her knee, then into the part, confident, loud, offbeat, on, on, off. They were supposed to play this at Ewan's funeral tomorrow. The rest of the band would probably have it down by now, they didn't have all this other stuff in their lives to deal with. But that was ridiculous, everyone had stuff to deal with.

She'd made it through the intro and the first two verses and choruses, then the middle eight was a mini-version of the intro and she fucked up in the same place, battered the snare drum in anger. She walked away from the kit. When she was in a flow state, it felt like she couldn't tell where the drums started and her limbs ended, but right now it was just a dumb collection of wood and metal and plastic that looked at her accusingly.

She turned and stared out of the window. A bunch of volunteers were planting trees and bushes at the east end of the Links, some rewilding effort she'd read about in the local news. That was the trend now in Edinburgh and she loved it. Eventually, maybe, her granddaughters and great-granddaughters would look out over a Bruntsfield jungle. And in a million years, all this – the castle and churches, the roads and tenements and shops and restaurants and everything else – would be gone. Some unknown creatures roaming the land, the memory of humanity vanished.

Her phone rang on the sofa across the room. She walked over and picked it up. Zara Griffiths.

'Hello, Dorothy.' Griffiths sounded stressed. 'I hope I wasn't interrupting anything.'

Dorothy glanced at the drum kit, beautiful in the dusty evening light. 'Nothing.'

'I was just wondering if Thomas was with you by any chance?'

Dorothy's heart sank. 'Is something wrong?'

Griffiths cleared her throat. 'It's nothing to worry about. I just need to speak to him, but I can't get hold of him.'

'I presume you've tried his house.'

'Just come from there.'

'What's this about?'

Griffiths hesitated and Dorothy watched Schrödinger push the door open, wander over to the thrown drumstick, sniff it then walk away. He didn't like the noise of drums, often came in once she'd finished.

'I need to give him a warning,' Griffiths said eventually.

'What kind of warning?'

'He's retired now,' Griffiths said, with a sigh. 'He needs to stay out of police business.'

'What's he done?' Dorothy thought about the state he'd been in.

'Using old contacts for information,' Griffiths said. 'Officers who should know better.'

'To find out what?'

'I was waiting until we had more to go on, but the car that hit you was Benny Low's. We got a partial plate and traced it, then found it burnt out in an industrial estate.'

Dorothy swallowed. 'So are you arresting Webster?'

'It's not as simple as that.'

'Why not?'

'We already spoke to him,' Griffiths said. 'He's lawyered up. It's a slow process, we need to accumulate evidence. We're working on it.'

'Doing what, exactly?'

'I'm not at liberty to say.'

Dorothy placed a hand on her forehead. 'Forgive me, but that's not good enough.'

'I know it's frustrating,' Griffiths said. 'But trust me, we'll get there.'

Dorothy hung up, didn't want to hear any more.

She checked Find My Phone. She and Thomas had set each other up on the app after everything last year. They'd joked about keeping tabs on each other, but it was serious underneath. But when she checked now, he'd switched it off. She had his last position from a week ago, coincidentally it was outside here in the garden. She remembered being worried about him then. How fast things had moved on.

She called him, straight to voicemail.

'Thomas, it's Dorothy. Please call me back.'

She'd just put the phone away when it rang again.

She pulled it back out. Olena.

'Hello?'

'Please,' Olena said, her voice high-pitched and trembling. 'Mama is in danger.'

She reached the house on Viewforth and ran up the path. The front door of the main house was open, a baseball bat lying on the step. She heard screaming and shouting inside, picked up the bat and weighed it in her hands. She'd swung a few in her childhood, knew how to connect.

She listened in the hall and headed towards the noise, through the adjoining door to the flat. In the kitchen, she was met with chaos. Camilla was unconscious on the floor, Veronika and the two children cowering in the corner. Closer to Dorothy, Bohdan and Marko were standing with their hands out, trying to appease Yana, who was crying and waving a serrated kitchen knife in their direction.

Yana saw Dorothy.

'Call the police,' she screamed.

'They're on their way,' Dorothy said calmly to the men as they turned to her.

The truth was that Dorothy had called Griffiths as soon as Olena put the phone down, but Griffiths hadn't replied. Then she'd called 999 as she drove down the road, but since *she* wasn't the one in trouble and couldn't confirm the details, they refused to send anyone. Said they would do it if they could speak to the woman under threat.

Marko smiled at Dorothy. 'This does not concern you.'

'Yes, it does, she's my friend. Leave her alone.'

'She must pay for what she has done,' Bohdan said.

Dorothy felt the anger in her throat. 'What exactly has she done?'

'Shamed our friend's memory.'

'He's dead,' Dorothy said. 'She's supposed to grieve forever?'

Marko pushed his lower lip out as he stepped towards Dorothy. She raised the bat over her shoulder and he stopped. Dorothy assumed that Camilla had tried to use the bat at the front door. She glanced over at Roman and Olena, both petrified.

'She must show respect,' Bohdan said. 'We are fighting for her.'

'Fuck you both,' Yana spat, her hand with the knife trembling. 'And fuck Fedir.'

Dorothy glanced at Veronika, stony-faced with her arms around the kids.

'That man raped me over and over,' Yana said. 'I know you all were going out and screwing anything that moved. I am not stupid. I was happy when the Russians invaded. I had a chance to get away from him. From men like you.'

Bohdan reached for her. 'You slut.'

She slashed at his hand, blood spurting from his palm like he had stigmata.

Marko used the distraction to lunge at Dorothy. She spotted the movement from the corner of her eye and brought the bat down with all her might, swinging it into Marko's jaw with a crunch. He stood for a moment with a shocked look on his face, then crumpled to the floor.

Bohdan was clutching his hand, blood pouring from a thick gash. He went to Marko, lifted his head from the ground. 'Marko.'

'Go,' Dorothy said, holding the bat over Bohdan's head. 'Go on, fuck off.'

55
HANNAH

Hannah chopped halloumi into cubes and dipped them in shawarma paste, set them aside to fry. Indy was putting together the salad – red cabbage, cucumber, spring onions, chillies, pomegranate seeds, lemon juice and olive oil. Hannah squeezed past her to get flatbreads out of the cupboard. Their kitchen was much smaller than the one in Gran's house, but Hannah liked the intimacy of cooking together, it gave her comfort.

Coming from a Bengali family, Indy had all this in her DNA, a love of long meals, the urge to always be cooking and feeding others. She'd told Hannah once that one of the things she missed the most when her parents died was the simple pleasure of meals together. So Hannah always tried to recreate the pleasure at home, it was time together, a thread connecting them. They'd carried that over to the big house. Hannah and Indy were often over there for meals, Archie too, sometimes Brodie now. Hannah felt a glow at the thought of billions of people all over the world doing the same, sitting down together, sharing what they had, breaking bread in a way that humans had done for thousands of years.

Hannah fried the halloumi and they put everything together on the table with more salad, Greek yoghurt and some lemonade Indy had made from scratch.

They swapped small talk, the cheese squeaking on Hannah's teeth, the spice of the shawarma, the acidity of the salad. She hadn't realised how hungry she was.

'So,' Indy said after a while. 'You're having a memorial tomorrow?'

Hannah nodded and swallowed what was in her mouth. 'At the grave in Craigmillar. For both boys.'

'Both Jacks.'

'Such a weird coincidence.'

Indy gave her a look and Hannah understood it. Indy didn't believe in coincidence, felt there were forces at work all around us. Hannah got that. Her physics studies told her the same thing. But sometimes coincidences just happen. In fact, the world would be a much stranger place if coincidences *never* happened, right? If that person you were thinking of never called, or two people who ended up married had never been at the same theme park twenty years ago on the same day. If nothing weird ever happened, Hannah would freak out.

'Any idea what you're going to say at it?'

Hannah nodded. She'd read something recently, some scientific research, that was perfect. She was about to go into it when she felt her phone buzz in her pocket.

She pulled it out and saw notifications from the spycam app. But she'd removed the one from Jack's grave, switched it off. She tapped through and saw there were a bunch of short videos from a handful of cameras that she thought were back at the house. She clicked the first one and saw a room she didn't recognise, a man and a woman with a baby coming in. She watched them for a few seconds, didn't know who they were until finally the man turned and faced the camera.

Don Webster.

'What is it?' Indy said, holding a stuffed flatbread at her mouth.

Hannah narrowed her eyes. 'I'm not sure, exactly.'

She watched the next clip, from a kitchen camera. Clear as day she saw Mum creeping into the kitchen, then out the patio doors at the back of what Hannah assumed was Don Webster's house.

She closed the app and called Jenny.

Indy raised her eyebrows. 'What?'

'It's Mum, she's up to something.' Hannah listened to the tone until it rang out and went to voicemail.

'Mum,' Hannah said. 'I'm getting notifications from the spycams. From Don Webster's house. What are you up to? Call me.'

Indy put her food down. 'What the hell?'

Hannah handed over her phone, played the first video for Indy. There was audio too, just Webster and his wife chatting to their daughter.

'Watch the next one,' Hannah said.

Indy pressed play, her mouth opening as she saw Jenny sneaking out.

Hannah took the phone back. 'I have it set up that my phone automatically synchs with any of the cameras when they're turned on. I don't even know if Mum's phone is synched to these.'

'Why is she doing this?'

Hannah shrugged. 'Presumably she wants to get some evidence or dirt on Webster. Get footage of him admitting to the murders, or harassing us.'

Indy shook her head. 'But she must've broken into his house, so that stuff couldn't be used in court, right?'

'I assume not,' Hannah said. 'But I suppose it could put pressure on him and his lawyer. Or maybe it's not evidence for court, it's for her own use.'

'For what?'

'If she had something on him, perhaps she could get him to leave us alone.'

Indy's brow creased. 'I don't like any of this. He's a dangerous guy. Why is your mum messing with him?'

Hannah sighed. 'You know what she's like, what she's capable of. She won't care about that. She's just protecting her family. I mean, we're supposed to leave it to the police, and look at where that's got us.'

Hannah's phone buzzed again in her hand. She unlocked it

and opened the app. There was one new file to add to the pile that had been there before, time stamped two minutes ago.

She opened it and watched. It was the kitchen camera again, darker outside than the earlier footage. There was movement outside on the patio, that's what had activated the motion senser. It was gloomy, she couldn't make out what was happening, then the patio door slid open and there was Thomas, looking at the unlocked door as he stepped inside. He was wearing all black and stood listening for a moment. But what drew Hannah's attention was the gun in his hand.

Thomas looked around the room for a long time, then he walked towards the camera, reached up to the shelf it must be sitting on, and lifted it clear. The last thing Hannah saw was Thomas looking into the lens before the camera switched off.

56

DOROTHY

She came here to think. She'd parked the hearse back at the entrance then walked in. The gates to Seafield Memorial Woods weren't locked and she hoped they never would be. This would be like a public park, lighting powered by solar panels for safety, a place for people to come and contemplate life and death, visit their loved ones, get some time to themselves like she was doing now.

She looked around, tried to picture what it would be like in the future. She imagined the saplings as towering trees, their canopies sheltering the deceased. But open spaces too, areas for picnicking and parties, kids playing football or frisbee, teenagers sneaking off into the deeper woods towards the disused railway track for drink, drugs, sex. Why not? It was all part of life. Nothing like that would disrespect the dead. What disrespected the dead was living in a way that denied the connection between people and the planet, the living and the dead.

She breathed in. The wind from the Forth had dropped in the evening gloom but it was still fresh, still letting her know there was a giant body of water out there with its mysteries.

She wouldn't live to see this place mature but she didn't care. She was so tired. She always tried to help, tried to see the other side of an argument, but sometimes it all became too much. It was OK to be exhausted by the bullshit of this world because the way things worked *was* bullshit. We were all trapped in a system where the helpless got dumped on from a great height as the rich got richer. Everyone's freedom and civil rights were eroded, people had to work longer and harder to make ends meet, companies raped the planet and destroyed the land, and it felt utterly powerless trying to stand up against any of that.

In the last few years, Dorothy, Jenny and Hannah had done their bit to stem the tide but it was a drop in the ocean, a tiny moment of respite against an onslaught of crap. It was always so personal for them, husbands and wives, brothers and sisters, mothers and daughters, the dead and the living. Oliver beaten by thugs, Yana fending them off with a knife, Dorothy wielding a baseball bat, for God's sake.

She rubbed at her palms, raw where she'd swung the bat with such force. She'd stood over Marko and felt powerful, and she hated that feeling.

She closed her eyes, breathed.

Stood still for a long time listening to the waves in the distance.

She opened her eyes and knelt, touched the earth where Clover Snowball had been buried in her mushroom suit. She imagined the spores going to work, consuming Clover's toes and eyeballs and nipples and guts and bones, transforming her into new life.

Her phone rang in her pocket and her chest tightened. She didn't need interrupting, not now.

Eventually it rang off. Then started up again.

She left it.

It stopped. Silence. Then it rang again. She took the phone out, saw it was Hannah.

She breathed again, aware of her lungs, maybe taking in spores from the mushrooms, maybe absorbing atoms from other dead bodies, from supernovas that exploded aeons ago.

'Hey,' she said.

'Gran, thank God.'

'What is it?'

'Thomas.'

Dorothy watched a lighthouse blink out in the darkness of the firth, waited for the hammer to fall.

'I haven't spoken to Mum, I've tried getting hold of her, but she's not answering.'

Dorothy frowned. 'What's going on?'

'Mum broke into Don Webster's house and hid spy cameras there. I started getting notifications on my phone. I saw footage of her leaving the house, then more footage of the Websters. And the last video I just watched was Thomas entering the house with a gun and switching the camera off, then all the other cameras went dead too.'

Dorothy closed her eyes and tried to get a handle on it. But there wasn't time, she knew that. 'With a gun?'

'Yes.'

For the last week she'd been worried about Thomas doing something stupid to himself. Now it was clear what he'd intended all along.

'Webster's wife and baby are in the house too,' Hannah said. 'I thought you would know what to do.'

Dorothy was already walking back to the hearse, towards the lights, the roads and traffic and endless life of the city, back to the noise and chaos and tangle of life.

'I'll call Griffiths,' Dorothy said, remembering she'd tried that at Camilla's place and got no reply. 'You call 999, tell them there's an armed intruder and a police officer's life is at stake.'

She reached the hearse, fished in her coat pocket for the keys, pressed the button to unlock the doors.

'What was that?' Hannah said down the line.

'The hearse.'

'You're not going over there.'

'I'm nearby,' Dorothy said, easing into the driver's seat and switching the engine on.

'Do not go over there, he's got a gun.'

'This is Thomas we're talking about.' Dorothy closed the car door and pulled her seatbelt on.

'So what?' Hannah was on the verge of tears. 'Gran, I would

never have called you if I thought you were as irresponsible as Mum.'

'I'm not irresponsible,' Dorothy said. 'But I have to go. I have to try.'

'At least wait for the police. Promise me you'll wait.'

'I need to call Griffiths now and you need to call 999. And try your mum again.'

'Please don't, Gran.'

'I have to go.' She ended the call and sat in the hearse, imagined herself lying down in the back on the way to her own funeral. How sweet the sleep would be.

She called Griffiths, listened to it ring out and go to voicemail.

'Thomas is at Don Webster's house with a gun,' she said flatly, then hung up.

She put the hearse in gear and pulled onto the road, heading west.

57

JENNY

Jenny was nervous. If you were into a guy, the first time you saw where he lived could be a dealbreaker. Was it a shithole, piled high with empty Jack bottles, pizzas boxes and old porn? Or a memorial to his dead mother? Or austere and blank, no internal life?

She looked around Archie's flat and felt a rush of relief. The living room had abstract art on the walls, a bookshelf in one corner. She ran a finger along the spines. She wasn't much of a reader, but there were a lot of women authors and quite a few people of colour. He wasn't one of these sad dudes who only read military history.

In the other corner of the room a desk had been converted into a workbench, woodworking tools hung neatly on a rack on the wall, beautiful smell of sawdust, little sculptures in various stages of completion. A chubby seal, a cheeky-faced monkey, the delicate lines of a heron.

She took her netsuke from her pocket. Looking back, that was the first moment. Subconsciously, that had changed how she thought of him, he had somehow come into focus for her. She rubbed the fox's nose, which was worn smooth. This was her version of worry beads, she got it out for comfort whenever needed.

She went to the window and looked out. They were on the third floor, in his tenement flat on Easter Road. Hibs' ground was five minutes away, and Jenny knew that the Eastern Cemetery was just up the road too, behind Lidl. She sometimes thought she knew too much about this city, the network of death and sadness that interlaced the streets was overwhelming at times. But it also felt like home. It made sense that Archie was a Leith guy. If you knew Archie and you knew Leith, it made perfect sense. Independent, self-assured, unbothered what others thought of him. Cool, but never trying to be. Interested in the world, in people. Just a *good* man.

'Here.' He handed her a gin and tonic, clinked glasses and took a sip.

'Cheers.' She drank.

He waved a hand around the room. 'What do you think?'

'Nice place.'

Archie smiled. 'I mean, it's not like your big house.'

'That's Mum's, really.'

'But you live there.'

'With my mum, how sad.'

'Not at all,' Archie said. 'I think it's great.'

Jenny drank some gin and angled her head. 'Really? A middle-aged woman living with *Mummy*?'

Archie gave her a look and she understood it, she already knew him.

'That's not what it's like,' Archie said. 'You've been out there, you've had a life.'

'Most of which I'd like to forget.'

Archie gave her another look full of kindness. 'What about Hannah?'

'OK,' Jenny said. 'You win, Mr Sensible, I wouldn't be who I am today if I hadn't gone through yadda, yadda, yadda. Now come here.'

She leaned in and kissed him for a long time. She worried she was going to spill her drink on his rug so she pulled away, took their glasses and placed them on the coffee table, then went back in for more. She worried about her breath, there had been a ton of garlic in her food earlier from Pizza Geeks, a place up the road which had some social-enterprise thing, free pizzas for people in need in the local community. Everyone was trying to help others, they always had been, Jenny had just been blind to it for so long.

She was distracted as they kissed, thinking about earlier, Webster's house, the adrenaline rush of almost getting caught. She'd headed straight to Archie, wanted to ride the buzz as long as possible. The plan had been to call Webster, try to engage him in conversation, then get him to confess to some of what he'd done. If that didn't work, then she would go round there and goad him in person to either admit stuff or attack her. She felt sure she could be annoying enough to get him to raise a fist, then it would all be on camera.

But she'd been distracted since catching up with Archie, distracted by the idea of a normal life.

'Come on,' she said, and led him to the bedroom.

They took it slow and she liked it. She'd spent years chasing a quick fuck, her subconscious telling her that she didn't deserve time and consideration. She'd wanted it over, the hit of a junkie.

This was different. He spent a long time kissing her body, going down on her. He *wanted* her and she felt the heat of that, but he knew that delaying it made it stronger.

She eventually couldn't wait any longer and pushed him onto the bed, straddled him and rode him, slow at first, then faster and harder. She was already coming, truth be told, and the look on his face, so focused on her, made her come harder. Then finally his back arched and he came and she felt another wave through her, energy unlike all the stupid, dumb sex she'd had over the years, an affirmation. She mattered and so did he, they were in this together.

She lay there afterwards, sweaty and comfortable with it, running her finger down Archie's bare arm, his chest, stomach.

Archie kissed her and sat up. 'I have to pee.'

She watched his arse as he left, looked around the bedroom. Another bookshelf, bedside table and lamp.

She wondered about Webster, reached over and took her phone from her jeans pocket. Unlocked it.

Dozens of notifications on the app. A ton of missed calls from

Hannah and Mum. Voicemail messages and texts. She flicked through the texts, couldn't work out the sense of them, where they started. Played the last message from Hannah, her throat tensing up and her skin crawling as Archie came back into the room, his cock swinging nonchalantly, and saw her face.

'What's up?' he said, already sensing the nightmare.

The message ended and Jenny waited, trying to hold on to the feeling of safety for a moment before she spoke.

58

HANNAH

Hannah and Indy stood at the corner of Argyle Place and Melville Drive trying to flag down a cab. Indy had ordered an Uber but it had got lost somewhere.

Hannah had called 999 and had a shit conversation with a woman who didn't take her seriously. Maybe because it was night-time and Hannah was young, the woman assumed she was drunk or high. Even when she mentioned Don Webster, the police-call handler remained suspicious. Likewise with Zara Griffiths' name. But she said they would send someone as soon as they could.

Hannah had kept trying Mum on the phone, left messages, got nowhere. She tried Gran again but she was either driving or already in the shit at the house.

'Come on,' Hannah said under her breath.

Indy waved at a taxi but its light went off as it approached. 'Fuck.'

They started walking towards Lothian Road, assuming there would be more taxis there. Finally at Tollcross they flagged a cab and jumped in, gave the address, buckled up as they U-turned and headed across town.

'I feel so helpless,' Hannah said.

Indy took her hand. 'You've done everything you can.'

'You think we're crazy to even go there.'

'No, I don't.' Indy squeezed her hands. 'We need to.'

This surprised Hannah. Indy was always more cautious and protective, the sensible one.

They sat at lights on Lothian Road, then again at Princes Street, tourists wandering across the carriageway gazing at the castle all lit up.

Into the New Town, onto Queen Street then Dundas Street, then a load of brake lights up ahead. They came to a halt in traffic.

'What is it?' she asked the driver.

The crackle of his intercom as he turned his head. 'Dunno, love, not roadworks, I was down here earlier.'

Fuck, come on.

The driver got on the radio to control, tinny voices.

The intercom came on. 'Sounds like an accident, a bad one.'

'Is there another way?' Indy said.

But cars had packed in behind them, and the lane across the road was full of cars waiting at the lights to get onto Queen Street.

'Sorry, looks like we're stuck.'

Hannah shook her head. 'Fuck it, we'll get out here.'

She paid with her phone then leapt out of the taxi, Indy behind her. They started running down the hill towards Webster's place.

59

DOROTHY

The house was dark out front, no sign of life inside. Dorothy parked the hearse and got out, watched the windows, looked up and down the street, listened for sirens. Nothing. She assumed the police were on their way but every second counted.

She walked up the path still listening, looking for signs. Got to the front door, stared at the doorbell. Moved to the window, looked in. Comfy sofas, a large-screen television on the wall over the fireplace. Darkness, no one.

She listened again, could only hear the wind.

She walked to the side of the house, stopped at the corner when she saw a cat disappear into the bushes. Thought about Schrödinger safe at home.

Turned into the back garden, looked in the kitchen through the patio doors. Dark and empty. Walked a little further, saw a light on in the next room. Glanced in quickly then shrank back.

Webster was sitting at a large, oak dining table, hands behind his back. Thomas sat opposite, gun pointed at him.

She walked back to the kitchen, slid open the patio doors as softly as possible, her heart like a bomb in her chest. She stood still for a long moment, waiting for something to give her away. She could hear muffled conversation through the wall.

She left the kitchen and walked to the dining room, stood in the doorway for a long time.

'Thomas.'

He turned, pointed the gun at her instinctively. He seemed serene. It felt like she was looking at the old Thomas before all this, calm and collected, sure of his purpose.

'Dorothy,' he said. 'You shouldn't be here.'

She stood still, blinked a few times. 'You don't get to tell me what I should or shouldn't do.'

'Well,' Webster said with a chuckle. 'Lovers reunited. Is this a Bonnie and Clyde situation?' He turned to Thomas. 'I didn't expect to see your missus here.'

'She's not my missus.'

Webster's hands were handcuffed together through the slats on the back of his dining chair.

'Where are his wife and child?' Dorothy said.

'Thank you,' Webster said. 'Please get them out of here.'

Thomas stared at Webster for a long time, the gun now pointed back at him. Webster was right across the table, point-blank range.

'They're upstairs,' Thomas said, keeping his eyes on Webster. 'Locked in the bathroom. They're safe.'

Webster turned to Dorothy. 'They have nothing to do with this, please get them to safety.'

Thomas laughed, and Dorothy hated the hollow sound of it. 'Nothing to do with this? Just like me and Dorothy, we were nothing to do with the fact you murdered that girl.'

'That's not the same,' Webster said, his voice calm. 'You were going to testify against me, I had to protect myself. Lena and Maisie are completely innocent.'

Dorothy moved into the room and stood at the head of the table. 'Thomas, this is not the way.'

Thomas shook his head. 'It's the only way left to me. To us.'

'Don't bring me into this,' Dorothy said. 'You made it pretty clear the other day there is no "us".'

'Oooh,' Webster said, arching his back in discomfort. 'Trouble in paradise?'

'Shut up,' Thomas said, voice level.

That's what scared Dorothy the most. He wasn't hysterical, screaming and waving the gun around. He was just here to get rid of Webster, to destroy the person who'd ruined his life.

Dorothy pulled out a chair and sat down. With the low overhead light, they might've been conspirators hatching a plot.

'Thomas, whatever has happened over the last year, whatever he's done, this isn't the right thing.'

'You think the justice system will deal with him?'

'We have to let it try.'

Thomas shook his head, mouth turned down. 'He tried to kill you, Dorothy. More than once.'

He meant once on Cramond Island, once with the hit and run. He looked as if he expected her to argue.

'It doesn't matter,' Dorothy said.

'You heard the woman,' Webster said. 'Now let me go.'

Thomas ignored him, kept his eyes on Dorothy.

'It doesn't matter,' she repeated.

That made Thomas angry. 'How can you say that? He has to pay for what he's done.'

Dorothy splayed her hands out on the table. 'And will that make you feel better?'

'Yes.'

'I don't think it will,' she said quietly. 'Not like this. This way, you lose yourself.'

Webster rattled the cuffs against the chair, shifted his weight. 'Just fucking unlock these things.'

Every time Webster spoke, the bubble between Dorothy and Thomas was burst. Webster was so stupid he didn't realise the danger he was in. Because she knew Thomas would do it. Maybe Webster had been in bad situations before and waved them away with his usual arrogance. Maybe he didn't think Thomas was serious, given that he was usually fair-minded and peaceful. Maybe he just thought no one could kill him, that he was immortal. But Dorothy *knew* Thomas, better than he knew himself. And she knew that he'd drawn a line in the sand. There was glorious power in not giving a shit. Dorothy knew that and now Thomas did too.

'Thomas,' she said. 'This is not you.'

He waited a long time to answer. 'It is now.'

He tightened his grip on the gun and pointed it at Webster's head.

'Fuck off,' Webster said, still ignoring reality. 'No way.'

'Goodbye,' Thomas said.

Dorothy held her hands up and stood. 'Wait.'

'What the living fuck?'

This was a voice Dorothy recognised, one she'd known her whole life, one she was deeply in love with, and the sound of it made her shrivel up.

She turned to the doorway, where Jenny was standing with a long kitchen knife in her hand, Archie at her shoulder.

60

JENNY

It was like they were all sitting down to dinner, except Webster was cuffed to the chair and Thomas was about to shoot him. Even worse, Mum looked as if she was about to throw herself between them.

'Mum,' Jenny said. 'I hope you're not about to take a bullet for that cunt.'

Dorothy lowered her hands. 'Jenny, it's all under control.'

Jenny waved the knife around. 'It doesn't look under control. It looks like Thomas was going to put a bullet in this wanker's head, and you were about to get in the way.'

Webster grinned. 'He doesn't have the bottle.'

Jenny felt Archie at her side. Glanced at him, standing motionless with his fists clenched. Ready. She'd never fancied him as much as right now, which was worrying. Something dumb and primal.

She looked at Webster. 'You never know when to shut the fuck up, do you?'

Dorothy shook her head. 'Jenny, you don't need to be here.'

'Are you joking? You think I'm going to leave you with a psycho and a gun-toting maniac?'

'The police are on their way,' Dorothy said, which made Thomas frown.

'Good,' Webster said. 'Who do you think they'll shoot? The serving police officer handcuffed to a chair against his will, or the black, retired cop waving an illegal gun around?'

'Why did you call the police?' Thomas said softly.

'Why do you think?' Dorothy said. 'Thomas, this is over, put the gun down.'

Thomas looked at the gun, still pointing at Webster. He lowered it a little, turned it in his hand as if it was an alien artefact, then shook his head.

'There's no other option,' Thomas said. 'Not now.'

He pointed the gun at himself for a moment and Jenny thought he was about to pull the trigger.

'Wait,' she said.

Dorothy seemed paralysed, likewise Archie. Only Webster was fidgeting in his seat, rolling his shoulders and smiling.

Thomas turned the gun back and pointed it at Webster's head. Across the table was only about a metre away, Jenny assumed the bullet would blow half of Webster's head off.

'Thomas,' she said, pointing with the knife. 'Much as I'd love to see this prick smeared all over the wall, I agree with Mum. There has to be another way.'

She was surprised by the words coming from her mouth, but realised she meant them.

Dorothy put her hands out to Thomas. 'You're not well, please. You're not thinking straight.'

'Too right,' Webster said. The prick really couldn't keep his mouth shut. 'You're going to get put away for a long time. Scaring my wife like this, I'll make sure you never forget what's happened here. I will haunt your every moment for the rest of your life. You'll always have to watch your back.'

Jenny watched Thomas as a sense of calm came over his face.

He squeezed the trigger.

Webster launched himself to his feet and dived to the side, smashing the chair still attached to him against the wall as the gun went off with a deafening explosion. The bullet lodged in the wall behind Webster as he thrashed the chair against the wall again, the back splintering, Webster sliding his arms down and hopping over them so that the handcuffs were in front of him. He launched at Thomas and the gun went off again, this time cracking the window as Webster barrelled into Thomas and knocked the gun from his hand. He pressed the handcuff links against Thomas's throat as they tumbled to the floor, and Archie leapt on top of them and punched Webster in the face, then tried to pull them apart, his big hands yanking on Webster's arms, but Webster lunged backwards and headbutted Archie, whose nose spurted with blood as he fell away. Webster focused his attention on Thomas again, who was scrambling across the floor towards the dropped gun.

Jenny looked at the knife in her hand and thought about what to do, but jumping into all this with a blade was asking to get killed.

Archie wiped blood from his face and swiped at Webster's legs, making him fall on top of Thomas. Webster smashed the side of the handcuffs into Thomas's ear, more blood, Archie trying to pull Webster away, Webster clinging on to Thomas's scalp and yanking as Thomas screamed and swung a punch behind him, but the angle was all wrong, there was no weight behind it. Webster lifted his hands up and over Thomas's head and began strangling him with the handcuffs, Archie pulling Webster's arms, Thomas choking and gagging, swinging his elbow into Webster's temple which made him loosen his grip, then Thomas lifted the handcuffs from his neck and threw Webster's hands out of the way.

Archie took the chance to drag Webster away by his legs. Webster flipped round and threw himself at Archie, he was smaller but strong, pushed Archie onto his back and sat astride him, pressing the handcuff links into his neck. Archie threw fists at Webster but he ducked out of the way, pressing hard, Archie's face going red, legs kicking. Jenny started towards the pair of them, the knife trembling. She couldn't let Webster kill Archie, but there was only one way to stop him. She stood next to them wondering how her mum would cope with watching her commit murder. She raised the knife above her head and looked at the point between Webster's shoulder blades, Archie choking out underneath.

Just as she was about to plunge the knife in, there was another explosion and the back of Webster's head blew apart in a mess of blood and hair and bone and brains spraying up the wall, blood pouring all over Archie underneath. Webster froze for a second then collapsed on top of Archie, who heaved the handcuffs from his neck, gasped in air, rolled Webster's body off of him and looked round.

Jenny still had the knife raised.

She lowered it and looked round, where Thomas was sitting in the corner of the room, the gun still in his hand.

61

HANNAH

Her lungs burned and her feet ached, Indy up ahead of her. They
reached a roundabout at Craighall Road, could see the sea at the
bottom of the street ahead. They turned into Laverockbank Terrace
and saw the flashing lights. Down at the other end of the street,
two police cars were in a driveway next to an ambulance, parked
with its back doors open and facing the house. Lights reflected on
the trees in the garden, the house, the shed alongside. As they got
closer, Hannah spotted the Skelf hearse parked on the street.

'Shit,' Indy said.

Hannah felt sick. 'We're too late.'

They ran to the house, where a uniformed officer was unspool-
ing crime-scene tape.

'We need to get in,' Hannah said. 'My mum and gran are in
there.'

The officer was a young guy, crew-cut hair, eyes glinting in the
pulsing lights. 'Sorry.'

She ducked under the tape, Indy behind her, heard the cop
shout with his reedy voice. She was at the doorway when Griffiths
appeared and grabbed her by the arm.

'No,' she said. 'Crime scene.'

'Where's Mum and Gran?'

'They're OK.'

Griffiths nodded to the bottom of the garden. Dorothy stood
looking shocked, talking to a police officer. A few metres away,
Jenny and Archie were leaning against the corner of the house,
talking to another uniformed officer. Archie was rubbing his
neck, Jenny holding his hand.

'They're giving statements,' Griffiths said. 'You can speak to them in a few minutes.'

'What happened?'

Griffiths shook her head. 'They can tell you, I have to go back inside.'

'Wait,' Indy said, but Griffiths was gone.

Hannah rubbed Indy's arm, and Indy hugged her. Hannah looked at Jenny and Dorothy over her shoulder.

'What do you think?' Indy said as they separated.

Hannah looked inside the house, the hallway full of police.

'Where's Thomas?' she said. 'And Webster?'

Indy nodded down the garden at the others. 'At least they're safe.'

There was noise from inside the house, and Hannah watched the cops make way for two paramedics coming from a room at the back, wheeling a stretcher with a body on it. As they got closer, she saw the body bag. Her heart stuck in her throat.

'Who's that?' she asked a paramedic as they passed.

The paramedics just wheeled the body past, loaded the stretcher into the back of the ambulance. One started doing paperwork on a tablet, the other stowed their gear in the back.

Hannah turned and saw Jenny running towards her. She felt tears in her eyes as they hugged, the smell of sweat and stress coming from her mum as Hannah pressed her face into her shoulder and held on tight.

'You're OK,' Hannah said.

'Everything's OK,' Jenny said.

Indy pointed at the ambulance. 'Who's that?'

'Webster.'

Hannah sniffed. 'What happened?'

Jenny glanced back at Archie, who was still talking to the police.

Dorothy saw them and walked over, breaking into a run, wrapping her arms around Hannah first, then Jenny, then Indy. She stood there, tears in her eyes, as she touched Hannah's cheek.

There was more noise from inside the house, footsteps and voices, and two officers came out followed by Thomas in handcuffs. He stared blankly at Dorothy as he was led to the nearest police car and pushed into the back seat.

62

JENNY

It felt obscene that the sun was in the sky as if nothing had happened last night. But Hannah would say that's exactly because the universe doesn't care. She seemed to find that idea comforting but Jenny wasn't so sure. She'd seen so much, been through so much. She wanted someone or something to care, just for a moment.

Outside the kitchen window, Bruntsfield Links was busy with people on the way to work, school, breakfast somewhere, visiting a friend, taking the baby for a walk, shopping, delivering, opening up The Golf Tavern, where Webster had held a knife to her skin. She touched the scar she'd received from a previous knife to the belly, from another delusional man, and winced at the rubbery feel.

Two dogs were chasing a ball in the park, playing along with their owner. Life was a game, you had to make the most of it because what else was there? Jenny had tried living in a way that didn't create ripples in the cosmos but she'd failed. They all had. The Skelfs were magnets for trouble, for grief and trauma and stress and violence.

She turned back to the room where Dorothy was sitting at the table with a cup of black coffee and a Highland Park in front of her, both untouched. The whisky had been Jenny's idea and it was a bad one, she knew that. But it was all she had.

Hannah was leaning against the worktop chewing a piece of toast. She'd been eating the same mouthful for ages. Indy had gone downstairs to open reception, answer phones, go about the business of being an undertaker. They still had funerals to arrange, they always had death to deal with. And grief, always grief.

Jenny walked to the whiteboards that contained all their cases and funerals. She looked at the schedule for today. The next thing they had was the latest communal funeral for Ewan.

'We should cancel this,' she said, tapping the board with her finger.

Dorothy didn't move for a long time, just watched the steam from her mug. Eventually she turned. 'No. It'll take our minds off things.'

'I don't think that's a good idea.'

'The funeral goes ahead.' Dorothy glanced at Hannah. 'Brodie's done so much work on it. How many people are coming?'

Hannah finally swallowed her toast. 'Maybe as many as fifty.'

'There you go,' Dorothy said.

Jenny stared at her for a long time. 'Mum.'

Silence.

'Mum, it's OK to take time off, you're in shock. We all are.'

Dorothy poured the Highland Park into the coffee, stirred it with her finger, then took several large gulps. She pushed back her chair and came over to the whiteboards. On the PI board was a whole mess about drones, the scored-out names of the Fulton and Conway families, then Webster and Low.

Jenny had flashes of memory, sitting in a hot tub with Marina Conway, visiting her husband in prison. All for nothing. Sometimes being a private investigator just made you feel very stupid.

Dorothy picked up the eraser and wiped it all clean, rubbing too long and hard at each of the names. There were still traces underneath, ghosts of the case.

She tapped the next case, Yana Kovalenko and all the names around her, arrows between them.

'She's sleeping with her landlady's son, Oliver. He was beaten up by two army friends of her dead husband. Her mother-in-law put them up to it. Yana is pregnant with Oliver's baby. It's a goddamn mess.'

She didn't look round as she wiped all the names from that board too, scrubbing as if she was trying to get bloodstains out of floorboards. Jenny remembered doing exactly that here in this room after Craig had attacked her and Dorothy a few years ago. His DNA forever soaked into their home, their lives.

'What the hell?' Jenny said.

'It's been quite something.' Dorothy placed her hand on her hip. 'I thought we were supposed to make a difference. The whole point of what we do here is to help people in need, people at a difficult moment in their lives.'

She waved a hand at the world outside the window. 'I changed the sign outside to *Undertakers* because I thought what we did was an undertaking. We undertake to help these people.'

Jenny took a step forward then stopped when she saw Dorothy's face. 'We *are* helping them.'

'I think we make things worse.'

Hannah pushed away from the worktop. 'You're wrong, Gran.'

Dorothy turned to her. 'Thomas has been charged with murder because of us.'

'No,' Jenny said, trying to contain her anger. 'Not because of us. In spite of us.'

Thomas had already told Griffiths he was pleading guilty. Jenny had gone over this with Dorothy late last night. Thomas wanted to pay. He'd done exactly what he went to Webster's house to do. Premeditated. Jenny had no idea what her mum was supposed to do with that.

'We *do* help,' Hannah said. 'Think of all the funerals, all the bereaved. We've helped each of them cope with saying goodbye to a loved one. And we're doing more, the resomations, natural burials, mushroom suits, human composting, planting trees. Making a better future.'

'It doesn't mean anything,' Dorothy said.

Her voice scared Jenny, she sounded utterly defeated.

'It means everything,' Hannah said. 'What about the communal funerals like today? We're saying goodbye to another human being.'

'He had no one.'

'But now he does.'

Dorothy shook her head, stared out of the window, her eyes wet. Jenny wanted to hug her mum but she felt like there was an invisible forcefield around her.

Eventually Dorothy tapped the whiteboard again, at the final case they still had on the books. 'What about Brodie's boy?'

They'd been so wrapped up in this Webster thing they hadn't kept each other up to date on anything else. Jenny felt ashamed. Brodie was part of the gang now.

Hannah pressed her lips together.

'It's all OK,' she said. 'It was Phoebe's mum, grieving for her grandson and her own stillborn son.' She checked her watch. 'In fact, I have to go. We're having a memorial at Craigmillar in an hour.'

Dorothy looked blankly at her then at Jenny, and Jenny finally pushed past the forcefield and hugged her mum for a long time.

63

HANNAH

Hannah and Indy walked along the central path of Craigmillar Cemetery holding hands. They sometimes still got looks when they did this in the street, all the more reason to do it. The cemetery was bright and quiet, rabbits bobbing amongst the shaggy grass. There was a sense of peace here which Hannah appreciated, she needed it to get her shit together. Everything that had happened, it was all too much. She breathed in the fresh air, imagined she was in the Highlands on a deserted beach, heather-coated mountains watching over her. She gave Indy's hand a squeeze and kissed her on the cheek.

'You don't have to do this,' Indy said. 'Not after everything.'

'Yes I do.'

Up ahead, Brodie was talking to Phoebe, their bodies close. Hannah wondered about that. They'd split up because of what happened with Jack. Maybe there was a second chance. Next to them were Raymond and Amanda Sweet, Amanda's arm linked through her husband's, her head resting on his shoulder. They stared at Jack's grave. They all turned as Hannah and Indy approached.

'Hi, everyone,' Hannah said, a flutter in her stomach. 'Thanks for coming.'

Brodie gave her a look. He'd been at the house earlier, knew what had happened. But Hannah wanted to be here today for this family. And it kept her mind busy, kept her body moving when it felt like that was the hardest thing to do.

She took a piece of paper from her pocket and unfolded it. She'd made a few notes but she preferred to do these things a little off the cuff. Indy kissed her on the cheek and let go of her hand as Hannah stood next to Jack Sweet's grave. The earth had been replaced by the groundskeeper. That had been an awkward conversation, but William just shrugged and got on with it. If you spent your life tending graves, maybe nothing was surprising anymore.

'We're gathered here today to pay our respects to Jack Sweet Junior.' Hannah looked at Brodie and Phoebe, Brodie's hand on Phoebe's back. Then she turned to Amanda and Raymond. 'And his uncle, Jack Sweet Senior.'

She glanced down. There were two teddy bears leaning against Jack's grave.

'Jack Junior was with us all too briefly in 2022, and Jack Senior was similarly with us for a very short time in 2000.'

Amanda and Raymond's son would've been the same age as Hannah if he'd lived. All the infinite possibilities of life, the endless decisions and mistakes and tiny triumphs and everyday annoyances, extinguished before they could ever exist.

Hannah coughed and smiled at Indy's worried look. 'But they are still with us, of course. I'm not particularly religious, but I believe that both boys' spirits live on. I actually have a scientific background, and most people think that is entirely separate from spirituality. But the more I study, the more I realise how similar they are. I've recently been looking into something strange called panpsychism, a theory that suggests everything is alive, consciousness is everywhere, and all we need to do is tap into it.'

She cleared her throat again, looked at her notes. Glanced around the graveyard, saw an elderly woman and two sons at a grave up the slope, flowers in hand.

'I recently read an article in *New Scientist*,' she said. 'Back in the 1990s, researchers found that, in women who had given birth, some cells from their offspring were present in their bodies decades later. They discovered it went the other way too. Cells from the mother are found in their children's bodies, in their blood. This means that, while we're in utero, cells pass between mothers and their children.'

She looked at Phoebe and Amanda. 'So both of you have *your* Jack's cells in your bodies right now. Not just a memory, a real, physical part of them is still alive within you. And that's only the start of it.' Hannah straightened her shoulders, folded away the paper, she didn't need it. 'Scientists also found cells from older siblings in their younger siblings' bodies, presumably passed on by the mother.'

She turned to Phoebe. 'So you are also carrying some of your brother Jack in you right now, swimming in your blood, resting in your bones. If and when you have any more children, they will carry a little of your Jack *and* your brother Jack with them too.' She turned to Amanda. 'Your son is living on in your daughter. And will live on in your grandchildren.'

Part of Hannah hated that this excluded the dads. Their genes were passed on but not their physical cells. But the science didn't lie and she was finding comfort where she could.

'And there's more.' She couldn't help the nerdy excitement creeping into her voice. 'Those cells you both carry, they're not just sitting inside you passively. They have huge effects on your health and even on how you behave. There's evidence that the cells of your child or mother can repair tissue damage and fight disease in *your* body. They make scars heal quicker, fight thyroid disease, tackle heart complaints and pancreas failure. They've been found in every organ in the body, including the brain. Think about that. You have your sons' cells in your brains. And your mothers', and everyone they carried. These cells congregate in the parts of the brain that deal with emotion and behaviour. So your sons are literally affecting the way you think and act. Not just mentally but physically, changing your brain chemistry in the process.'

She paused, felt a shimmer of energy through her body. Jenny's cells were inside her right now, and Dorothy's. All of them in conversation, a choir of voices guarding over her if she was weak or ill, helping her think and behave the way she did.

'So we are never truly alone,' Hannah said, looking around at all of them. 'None of us. We carry all of our people with us. We need to remember that, always.'

Amanda was crying on her husband's shoulder. Phoebe leaned into Brodie. Indy came over and hugged Hannah, and she imagined cells from her wife slipping through her clothing, through her skin, into her blood, her sinews, her bones, her heart. At home inside of her.

64

DOROTHY

She walked around the garden. She felt as if a storm had passed through, knocking down trees and buildings, lifting her into the air. But she was here, placing one foot in front of the other as she listened to the wind in the trees, sparrows chirping, her own footfall.

Schrödinger walked to her from a hedge and she picked him up, stroked him. She wondered what was going through his mind, if he sensed her darkness.

She reached the wind phone. Looked at the white wood already worn, paint flaking in places. She wouldn't patch it up. Life was scratches and flaking, weather damage, slow erosion. She touched her hip, still aching from the car hit. Her knees skinned and sore. She thought about Webster lying in the mortuary, his wife out of her mind with grief. A baby daughter who would grow up without a dad. Thomas in a cell.

She went into the phone box and placed Schrödinger on the shelf where the phone sat. The cat sniffed it and slunk in a tight circle. She picked up the phone.

'Hi, Don,' she said eventually. 'I don't really know you but I think you were a troubled man. I don't know how that happened, but you didn't act like you had love in the world. And yet, your wife and daughter, they love you. Your mother. Maybe others. But you presented a different face to me and my family.'

She swallowed.

'But I'm sorry you're dead. Truly, I am. We should not be allowed to take a life. No one knows what you were carrying, what you had inside you. No one can ever really know someone else, that's the truth. So how can we judge anyone? It's human nature to judge, of course. I do it all the time, the little annoyances, inconveniences. But we must *try* to be better. I used to think we were all connected, but now I wonder about that.'

She was thinking of Thomas of course. But now also Don Webster, Jenny and Hannah, everyone she'd ever met and felt a connection to. Maybe it was all a delusion created by our minds to make us feel less alone.

'Anyway, I hope that, wherever you are, you're at peace.'

It was a platitude but it was all she had left.

She scooped Schrödinger up and left the wind phone, then heard the crunch of footsteps on the driveway. Turned to see Yana holding hands with Olena and Roman, all three of them with backpacks on. Just behind them was Veronika.

Dorothy walked over and hugged Yana, then smiled at the children and Veronika.

'Camilla threw us out,' Yana said. 'Oliver is still in hospital and she's changed the locks on his apartment. We have nowhere to go.'

'I already told you, you're all welcome to stay here as long as you need.'

She'd spoken to Yana after the nightmare at Camilla's house. Camilla had come to just after the men left, took a taxi to A&E. She made it clear she wanted them all gone. Dorothy hadn't hesitated. They had the sofa bed in the studio, a spare bedroom. They could convert one of the downstairs rooms for the kids. It would be good to have kids running around the place, hadn't happened in a long time.

She wondered about Yana and Veronika. And she worried about Roman, his relationships with his mother and sister. He hung his head now and Dorothy's heart went out to him. He was in a strange country, his dad dead, no home, and he'd seen things now that would stay with him forever. Same for Olena, of course, for all of them. What refugees had to live with, all over the world.

Dorothy ushered them all towards the house.

'Make yourself at home,' she said, checking her watch. 'We have a funeral later, it would be great if you all could come.'

❧

She always loved the view from behind the drum kit.

The chapel was packed, all hundred seats filled, the doors to the garden open, another fifty standing outside. There were flags taped to all the walls, dozens of people had brought them. A giant Scottish saltire with *MON THE BIFF* written in thick lettering, flags from France, Belgium, Brazil. A Polish flag with *BIFFY FUCKIN CLYRO* scrawled across it.

It was like a party, people chatting and laughing, catching up. Amongst it all she could see Brodie, Hannah and Indy chatting to two heavily pierced girls by the resomator, Ewan's body already inside, waiting to become dust and liquid, fertiliser and soil, tree and plant roots, flowers and fruits.

At the back of the chapel, Archie and Jenny stood so close their noses were almost touching. Lost in their own world. Dorothy's heart swelled. Next to them, Veronika had a seat by the wall, Olena and Roman chatting to each other alongside.

Dorothy looked at the faces in the crowd, imagined Thomas in the front row smiling at her. Her chest tightened as she thought about him in prison, what he'd done, the darkness in him. But nothing was unfixable, they would find a way through this together.

Some people had come up to the dais to say a few words, what little they knew about Ewan. Conversations at the bar, small talk at festivals. He'd been into the band in the early days when they were slogging around half-empty pubs honing their craft. And he'd been there at giant shows too, the band growing to fill the space, like all music does, really.

Lots of mourners had brought beers and wine, food too. Dorothy smelled weed from outside.

Eventually Brodie pushed through the crowd and came to the dais, banged it for quiet, raised a bottle of lager. 'To Ewan.'

The toast was greeted with cheers and whoops like a gig. Like a celebration, which it was.

He nodded at Indy and she pressed the button on the resomator. Dorothy heard the whoosh of water entering the chamber.

She looked around the tiny stage that The Multiverse were crammed onto. Teenager Zack on bass, his girlfriend Maria on keyboard, middle-aged Will on guitar, Gillian on whatever else. Katy herding the choir, the girls from all corners of the globe, finding joy in this simple thing. Yana standing next to Faisa and Ladan. She didn't know the song but didn't care.

Dorothy stilled herself. She hadn't got this damn song right once yesterday, and she'd been to hell and back since then. Chances were that she would mess it up now, in front of over a hundred of the band's biggest fans.

But if you didn't try something, you never found out. If you didn't scare yourself, what was the point? If you didn't live, you died.

She looked at the band, the crowd, her family and friends.

She nodded and clicked her sticks in time.

'One, two three, four…'

ACKNOWLEDGEMENTS

Huge thanks to Karen Sullivan for her amazing support of me and my writing – the Skelfs books wouldn't exist without it. And thanks to everyone else at Orenda Books for all their hard work and dedication. Thanks to Phil Patterson and all at Marjacq for everything they do for me. I am forever in debt to everyone who has connected with my books over the years, thank you so much. And all my love, as always, to Tricia, Aidan and Amber.